Detective Sergeant Emmanuel Cooper returns in this powerful, atmospheric novel about two communities forced to confront each other after a murder that exposes their secret ties and forbidden desires in apartheid South Africa, by award-winning author Malla Nunn.

disparate and irreconcilable worlds despite the danger that is arising.

Also by Malla Nunn

A Beautiful Place to Die
Let the Dead Lie

A NOVEL

MALLA NUNN

EMILY BESTLER BOOKS
WASHINGTON SQUARE PRESS
NEW YORK LONDON TORONTO SYDNEY NEW DELHI

WASHINGTON SQUARE PRESS
A Division of Simon & Schuster, Inc.
1230 Avenue of the Americas
New York, NY 10020

This book is a work of fiction. Names, characters, places, and incidents either are products of the author's imagination or are used fictitiously. Any resemblance to actual events or locales or persons, living or dead, is entirely coincidental.

First Emily Bestler Books/ Washington Square Press trade paperback edition June 2012

EMILY BESTLER BOOKS / WASHINGTON SQUARE PRESS and colophons are trademarks of Simon & Schuster, Inc.

For information about special discounts for bulk purchases, please contact Simon & Schuster Special Sales at 1-866-506-1949 or business@simonandschuster.com.

The Simon & Schuster Speakers Bureau can bring authors to your live event. For more information or to book an event, contact the Simon & Schuster Speakers Bureau at 1-866-248-3049 or visit our website at www.simonspeakers.com.

Manufactured in the United States of America

10 9 8 7 6 5 4 3 2 1

Library of Congress Cataloging-in-Publication Data

Nunn, Malla.
Blessed are the dead : a novel / by Malla Nunn.
p. cm.
1. Police—South Africa—Fiction. 2. Missing persons—Fiction. 3. Zulu (African people)—Fiction. 4. KwaZulu-Natal Midlands (South Africa)—Fiction. 5. South Africa—History—1909–1961—Fiction. I. Title.
PR9619.4.N86B56 2012
823'.92—dc23 2011044416

ISBN 978-1-4516-1692-7
ISBN 978-1-4516-1695-8 (ebook)

For Mark

ACKNOWLEDGMENTS

Thanks to the ancestors, my parents, my sisters and brother, and my beautiful children, Sisana and Elijah. Also to my husband, Mark—editor, story guide and ruthless destroyer of adjectives—who was brave enough to tell me what wasn't working. My agents, Catherine Drayton of Inkwell Management and Sophie Hamley of the Cameron Creswell Agency, are calm guides in times of doubt. Terence King, military researcher and historian, for fine work on facts and figures. Simon Lapping, Afrikaner Cultural Attaché. My auntie, Lizzie Thomas, for help with Zulu. Eric and Rose Campbell for the cottage and Michael O Klug for his invitation to the Brisbane Writers Festival. A nod to Meg Simmons for asking, "How's Emmanuel going?" and to Burcack Muraben for constantly hounding me for "more Shabalala." Deepest thanks to Judith Curr of Atria books. And to Emily Bestler of the fabulous new imprint, Emily Bestler Books, who helps me find the best version of my story every time.

Thank you all.

BLESSED ARE THE DEAD

PROLOGUE

October 1953

Detective Sergeant Emmanuel Cooper woke to the sound of boots kicking in his bedroom door. He threw the sheets aside and fumbled in the nightstand for his gun. Motionless in the darkness, Webley revolver pointed at the doorway, he listened for whatever would come next. The sound diminished and became more organic. He felt its rhythm. It was not splintering wood that had wrenched him out of sleep. It was his own heart. It slammed against his chest like a prisoner trying to escape its cage of muscle and bone.

He sat back and breathed deeply and detected the faint trace of a flowering jasmine. Three months after he'd officially rejoined the Detective Branch the dreams were back, but now they were more intense than anything he had experienced before.

The familiar vision of his platoon huddled under a pewter sky howling with missiles had been replaced by disjointed images of red flames and black smoke. In these new dreams, he ran through burning debris toward something he could not remember. Hot cinders rained down. The dark-earth smell of blood and the hollow calls of the dying filled the void. He knew the direction he should run but flames blocked his path. The smoke became thicker and it seared his lungs.

He climbed out of bed and crossed the linoleum floor to the open window. A cat stalked an unseen night animal across the empty driveway and slipped into a tangled bougainvillea fat with spring blooms.

"Emmanuel," a sleepy voice said. "Come back to bed."

He glanced at the woman lit by a shaft of streetlight coming in through the curtains. Lana Rose lay naked on the bed, cotton sheets kicked off in the heat, black hair like a ribbon of silk on the pillow.

"Shhh . . ." The sound he made was automatic. "I'll just be a minute."

The cat reappeared with a lizard in its mouth, the lizard's tail twitching.

"Still crazy?" Lana said, and snuggled into the pillow and back to sleep.

Emmanuel said, "Last I checked."

Proof of his craziness was in his bed.

Lana was Colonel van Niekerk's girlfriend, but by week's end the colonel would be married and Lana bound for a new life on her own in Cape Town. That didn't make this night of pure pleasure okay. For a few days longer she was still his boss's mistress and should have been untouchable. She had invited him to her apartment one night earlier in the year and they had fallen into bed and drowned themselves in each other. The next morning, though, Lana went back to van Niekerk and his deep pockets. Afterward, they avoided each other and ignored the memory of how perfectly they fit together. When she called to suggest farewell drinks Emmanuel knew they'd make their final good-bye in bed. Tonight, with her body half wrapped in his sheets, he permitted himself the illusion that he was not alone. At dawn tomorrow, however, Lana would disappear from his life: one more woman he'd failed to hang on to. Wide awake now, he remembered the advice his mother gave him years before.

"Try running away from trouble instead of right to it. Just once, Emmanuel," she'd said after discovering the stolen cigarettes hidden under his bed in their shack in Sophiatown. He was twelve years old and already possessed the terrible knowledge that he would never grow into the good, kind man she dreamed he would become.

The telephone rang on the bedside table and Emmanuel crossed the room. He lifted the receiver to his ear.

"*Ja,*" he said quietly, to avoid waking Lana.

"You're up." Colonel van Niekerk's voice was clear on the line. "Problem sleeping, Cooper?"

"I sleep very well, thank you, Colonel," Emmanuel said. He had no intention of letting the Afrikaner policeman into his head. The less van Niekerk knew about his mental health, the better. Lana rolled onto her back and the bedsprings sighed.

"You have company," the colonel said.

Emmanuel ignored the statement and pressed a finger softly against Lana's mouth. "What can I do for you, sir?" he asked.

There was a pause on the other end, short enough to suggest a gathering of thoughts but long enough for Emmanuel to imagine that the colonel knew just how he'd spent the night and with whom.

"Pack a bag," van Niekerk said. "Enough for a few days. I have a case for you. A murder."

Emmanuel lifted his hand from Lana's mouth and wrote the details of the job in his notebook. A homicide in Roselet, a farming hamlet nestled in the foothills of the Drakensberg Mountains and four hours out of Durban. Whoever had called in the murder left no details of the victim.

"I'll leave early in the morning, Colonel," he said, and hung up. Dirt roads with potholes deep enough to bathe a child, and wandering goats and cows, made the journey to the 'Berg dangerous in the dark. He'd wait for first light to set off.

He checked the bedside clock. Three forty-five on Sunday morning. The colonel knew he couldn't leave for hours, so why call in the middle of the night? Van Niekerk didn't do anything without a reason. What was the reason this time?

"Emmanuel . . ." Lana stretched out against the crumpled sheets with her arms thrown above her head. "Do you have to leave right away?"

"No." He leaned over and pinned her wrists against the mattress, felt the heat of her skin and the lazy drumming of her heart. "Not right away."

1

A ZULU HERD BOY walked quickly up the dirt path, his bony frame bent to meet the steep rise of the mountain. The rhythmic pounding of his bare feet on the rough ground kicked stones loose and raised red dust into the air.

"Higher, ma' baas." The boy was apologetic, afraid of taxing the white policeman in the neat blue suit and the black hat pulled low on his head to block out the light. "We must go higher."

"I'm right behind you," Emmanuel said. "Keep going."

The steady pace was nothing compared to army boot camp or the three years spent in combat, marching between battlefields in Europe during the war. Detective Constable Samuel Shabalala from the Native Detective Branch followed directly behind him and the close rhythm of his breath spurred Emmanuel to keep moving.

"Soon, ma' baas," the boy promised. "Soon."

"I'm still with you," Emmanuel said. The dead were patient. To them, eternity was flexible and time meant nothing.

For police detectives, however, time was everything. The sooner the crime scene was located and sketched in detail, the better chance there was of catching the killer.

The herd boy stopped abruptly and then slipped into the lush grass along the edge of the path.

"There, ma' baas." He pointed a skinny finger to the rise. The path snaked behind a sandstone boulder embedded in the grass. "You must go past the rock and up again."

The boy wanted no part of what lay beyond.

"My thanks," Emmanuel said, and turned to look behind him. He saw the path they had traveled from the floor of the Kamberg Valley and the mountains rising in the distance on the other side. Clouds piled on top of each other behind the peaks. The bronze tops of the mountains, some of them dusted with snow, looked like fortresses for gods. There was nothing like the Drakensberg Mountains anywhere else on earth.

"Where to, Sergeant?" Shabalala asked when he drew even with Emmanuel.

"Around that bend," Emmanuel said. "Our guide has dropped out."

They moved on, slowly skirting the boulder. Three Zulu men dressed in traditional cowhides worn over printed cloth stood shoulder to shoulder across the narrow path to form a roadblock. They held hardwood clubs and assegais, hunting spears with rawhide bindings and sharp blades. Together they made an impi, a fighting unit. The tallest of the men stood in the center.

"Suggestions?" Emmanuel asked Shabalala.

The Zulu men gave no indication that they might move from the middle of the path. Military defeat at the hands of the

British army and Boer commandos had not cowed them. They stood as their ancestors must have a hundred years ago: fearless masters of their own land.

"Should we wait for the local police?" Shabalala asked. Far below and across the emerald stretch of the valley lay the town of Roselet, the closest source of law enforcement backup.

"The station commander might not get the message for hours," Emmanuel said, referring to the handwritten note he'd stuck to the door of the locked police station an hour ago. A small sandstone bungalow adjacent to the station had also been empty. "I don't want to lose any more time."

"Then we must go together. Slowly. Hands open, like this." Shabalala lifted both hands and showed empty palms to the Zulu men. The gesture was simple, universal. It said, *No weapons. No harm intended.*

Emmanuel did the same.

"Now we must wait," Shabalala said. "Do not look away from them, Sergeant."

Sunshine glinted off the fighters' sharpened spearheads. The weapons were not dusty antiques from a grandfather's hut. The men themselves were no relics, either. They were tall and muscular. Emmanuel figured a lifetime of running up these mountains and hunting game had kept them lethal.

"Never crossed my mind," he said.

"Who are you?" the man in the middle demanded in Zulu. He was the eldest of the three.

"*Sawubona, inkosi.* I am Detective Constable Samuel Shabalala from the Native Detective Branch. This is Detective Sergeant Cooper, the boss of detectives in Durban."

"*Yebo, sawubona.*" Emmanuel made the traditional greeting. He let the instant promotion to top boss pass. If Shabalala thought they needed extra status to move ahead, they probably did.

"Cooper. Shabalala. We see you." The elder nodded a greeting but did not smile. "Come. The firstborn child of my father's sister is waiting."

Emmanuel didn't try to work out the connection. Zulus did not have family trees, they had family webs. The men turned and jogged up the slope in formation, weapons held in relaxed hands that were used to the weight.

"You lead," Emmanuel said to Shabalala. The Zulu detective wore the standard Detective Branch uniform, a suit with polished leather shoes and a black fedora, but the hills and untamed veldt had been his childhood playground. He knew this land and its people.

They pushed up the steep gradient for two more minutes. An eerie low-pitched moaning swelled and rolled over the treetops before dropping away again in a wave.

"What's that?" Emmanuel asked but didn't slacken his pace.

"The women." The words were spare, stripped down but full of sorrow just the same. Shabalala had heard the sound before.

The Zulus stopped and pointed their assegais to a rock fig growing out almost horizontally from a craggy ledge. The sound was distinct now: female voices crying out and wailing in the bushes.

"They are waiting," the elder Zulu said.

Emmanuel again let Shabalala take the lead. The tall grass and bush thinned out a few yards off the path and a group of women became visible. They sat in a circle, swaying back and forth. The rock fig branched over them like a sentinel. Emmanuel hesitated. One step closer and the sorrow would engulf him and drag him back to a time and place in his own life he'd rather forget.

"Sergeant," Shabalala prompted softly, and Emmanuel walked on. He'd chosen this life among the wounded and the dead. Dealing with the living was a necessary part of the job.

"She is here, inkosi." One of the women shuffled to the side to make a gap in the circle through which Emmanuel could approach the body. A black girl lay on the sweet spring grass, gazing up at the soft blue sky and the shapes of darting birds in the air. Her head rested on a rolled-up tartan blanket and tiny red and yellow wildflowers were scattered over the ground. Three or four flowers had fallen into her mouth, which was slightly open.

"We need to get closer," Emmanuel said to Shabalala, and the Zulu detective relayed the request in a low voice. The women broke the circle but gathered again under the branches of a paperbark thorn tree nearby. Their wails subsided and were replaced by the muted sound of swallowed tears.

"*Hibo* . . ." Shabalala whispered when they were crouched on either side of the girl. This was not the messy knifing or domestic argument gone too far they'd been expecting when Colonel van Niekerk tapped them on the shoulder for this case.

"Yeah, I know." Emmanuel examined the victim. She was young, maybe seventeen years old, and beautiful. High cheekbones, gracefully arched brows and full lips were features that would have kept into old age. No more. All that was left was a glimpse of what might have been.

"No signs of a struggle," he said. The girl's fingernails

were neatly shaped and unbroken. The skin on her wrists, neck and upper arms was unmarked. "If her eyes were closed I'd say she was sleeping."

"Yes," Shabalala agreed. "But she did not walk here. Someone brought her to this place. Look at her feet, Sergeant."

Emmanuel bent lower to get a better view. Dirt and broken grass stalks were stuck to the rough-skinned heels and slim ankles. "She was dragged here and then laid down."

"I think so," Shabalala said.

Under normal circumstances, with a wooden barricade in place and a few uniformed police on guard, Emmanuel would have pushed aside the neckline of the girl's dress and checked for bruising on the shoulders and under the armpits. Modesty was never a concern of the dead. The presence of the gathered Zulu women stayed his hand and he pulled a notebook and pen from his jacket pocket.

To Shabalala he said, "She wasn't dumped or hidden under branches."

He wrote the letters *R.I.P.* on the first page. Rest in peace. Whoever had dragged the victim to this spot had wanted her to rest in a peaceful place with a rock fig above and a wide valley below.

"And the flowers." Shabalala stood up and surveyed the hillside. Clumps of bright red and yellow broke the stretch of green. "They are growing all around but I do not think the wind blew them to this place."

"It looks like they were deliberately scattered over her," Emmanuel said, picking up a tiny red bloom from the crook of the girl's elbow. He understood this need to mark the fallen. Small gestures made the difference even in the white heat of war: a helmet placed on the chest or a poncho thrown over the face of a dead soldier, the closest thing available to a eulogy or a farewell.

Emmanuel scribbled *loved* on the next clean page. First time that word had come up at a crime scene. There was no doubt the girl had been loved and was loved still. Even now, in death, a circle of grieving women and a group of armed men guarded her.

"How long do you think she's been here?" he asked Shabalala. It couldn't have been more than twelve hours, he imagined. The vultures and wildcats hadn't begun to disassemble her body.

"One day and a half." Shabalala walked the perimeter of the crime scene, examining snapped twigs and flattened grass. "The women's tracks are from this morning but the deep lines from the girl's heels are from before."

Emmanuel stood up and moved to where Shabalala was bent over a crushed leaf. "You sure she's been out in the open all that time?"

"Yes, Sergeant. It is so."

"But she's nearly perfect." He glanced at the girl. Her slender legs were a shoulder width apart, the left knee slightly crooked as if she might sit up at any moment and wave hello. The hem of her white calico dress fluttered against her upper thighs—whether blown by the wind or hitched up by a human hand, it was impossible to tell. A pea-sized mark marred the smooth surface of her left inner thigh. "No animals have disturbed the body. And there are no signs of injury besides that bruise."

"I see this also," Shabalala said, and paused, reluctant to continue. Other detectives burned oxygen throwing out half-formed theories and detailed explanations of the how and the why of a murder, but not Shabalala. He did not speak unless he was sure of the facts. It was a learned caution. Black detectives rarely added spontaneous comments or joined in the competitive banter that buzzed around a dead body. They were junior partners, brought onto a case only if special knowledge of "native situations" was needed.

"Tell me," Emmanuel said. "It doesn't have to make sense."

Bullshit theories spun out of thin air had their uses.

"What I see is strange," Shabalala said.

"Tell me anyway."

The Zulu policeman pointed to scuff marks in the dirt and to a heavy stick lying on the grass. "I think that the animals did not come near because the one who brought the girl to this place kept them away."

"You have to explain," Emmanuel said. The indentations in the dirt meant nothing to him and the stick was clean of blood or other signs of use.

"A man . . ." The Zulu detective hesitated and moved to the right to examine another patch of disturbed earth. "A small man was here. He ran from where the girl is lying to here with the stick. See this, Sergeant?"

The spoor of a wildcat was identifiable even to Emmanuel's untrained eye. "He moved out to defend the body from predators. That means he must have stayed with her."

"*Yebo.* I believe this."

Emmanuel underlined the word *loved* and then added *protected.*

"Was he a human predator and the girl his prey?" he wondered aloud. People often killed the one they loved the most.

Shabalala shook his head, frustrated at not having the full picture. "I cannot say if this man was the one to harm her.

People have come to this place and walked all around. Some of the women scooped the earth with their hands and threw their bodies in the dirt. Many tracks have been lost. A man brought her here and kept the animals away. That is all I see."

"We know a lot more than when we got here," Emmanuel said. "Let's take another look at the body and then we'll talk to the women, see what they can tell us about the victim."

"*Yebo,*" Shabalala agreed, and they walked back to where the girl lay. A yellow grasshopper had landed on the curve of her neck and was busy cleaning its wings and long antennae.

"No visible injuries," Emmanuel said, and waved the grasshopper away. Natural causes couldn't be ruled out yet. "We'll have to turn her over, find what's hidden."

They rolled the body onto its side so the back was visible. A soft gasp came from the women under the paperbark thorn. The girl was theirs and still alive in their minds. To see how easily she slipped from their embrace and into the hands of strangers shocked them.

"There," Emmanuel said. A small hole, the size of a thumbtack head, punctured the white calico dress just above the waist. Spots of blood speckled the fabric. "Could be a bullet entry wound."

"Maybe a knife also." Shabalala pressed his fingertips into the ground where the girl had been lying and checked them. "The soil and grass are damp with blood but not soaked."

"She didn't bleed to death. But this isn't a good time to look at the entry wound." The mourners had edged closer to the crime scene and their anxiety was palpable. "The district surgeon will have answers for us in a few days. Till then we can only guess at what made the wound. Lay her on her back and let's find out who she is."

They rolled the girl's body into its original position and Shabalala pushed the tartan blanket under her head again, as if she might be uncomfortable without the support.

"Do you want to take the questioning?" Emmanuel asked. He spoke Zulu himself, had mixed in with Zulu boys and girls and even been in and out of their homes till the violent events of his adolescence had seen him and his sister banished to a remote cattle farm and then to a whites-only boarding school. This situation was different.

"You must start," Shabalala said. "They will know that the police are serious if a white policeman is in charge."

That made sense. Native policemen and detectives were armed with sticks and given bicycles to ride. They were not allowed to drive police vehicles. The power of the gun and the car and the law itself was in the hands of Europeans. Shabalala knew that. The rural women waiting under the tree knew it also.

"Speak in Zulu," Shabalala suggested in a quiet voice. "And thank them for looking after the girl until we came."

"Will do," Emmanuel said. "If my Zulu isn't up to scratch you'll have to take over."

He approached the mourners. There were six of them, barefoot and dressed in heavy black skirts that fell below the knee. Supple cowhide aprons covered their breasts and each wore a fine black head covering decorated with porcupine quills to signify they were married women; mothers of the clan.

"I'm sorry for your loss," Emmanuel said in Zulu, addressing a woman at the front of the group who was being held up by her elbows to stop her from collapsing onto the ground. She possessed the same beauty as the girl lying on the grass.

Surely the victim's mother or aunt. "Thank you for keeping her safe until we came. We are grateful."

"Amahle Matebula," the woman said. "That is my daughter's name."

Amahle meant "the beautiful one." Emmanuel had run the streets of Sophiatown with a fat Zulu girl of the same name. She was meaner and tougher than most of the street boys and proud of it. Shoplifting was her speciality; she sold the goods for a small profit and a kiss from the boys she favored. He'd used her services sparingly, buying last-minute Christmas gifts from her stolen haul.

"You named your daughter well." Emmanuel introduced himself and Shabalala before retrieving his notebook and pen. "What may I call you?"

"Nomusa."

Mother of grace. Another perfect name. Emmanuel meant "God is with us." He was certain his birth mother had named him in one of those bright, dazzling moods that overtook her every few months, when she shone like a fire.

"Tell me about Amahle," Emmanuel said. "When did you last see her?"

"Friday morning. It was still dark outside. She went to work but did not come home." Nomusa's weight sagged and the women holding her upright couldn't take the strain. They eased her to the ground and propped her up with their hands and shoulders. Emmanuel and Shabalala crouched and waited for the women to settle.

"Where did she work?" Emmanuel asked when Nomusa lifted her head off her chest. Five more minutes and she would not even be able to do that.

"At the farmhouse of Inkosi Reed." A gray-haired woman

to Nomusa's right whispered in her ear and she added, "Little Flint Farm. It is close to here. In the valley."

"What time did Amahle normally leave work?" Other girls, more fortunate ones, would be home from school in the early afternoon, filling exercise books with the vocabulary words of the day.

"Sundown. Amahle knew the paths over the mountains and she never tarried." Nomusa lifted her head high now, spurred on by a sudden flash of anger. "This was told to the white policeman on Saturday morning but he did not come! He did not look for her!"

"You reported her missing to the commander at the Roselet Police Station?" Emmanuel asked.

"*Yebo.* Constable Bagley. That very man," Nomusa said. "He did not care to find my daughter and now the ancestors have taken her."

"Easy, my sister." One of the women placed a hand on Nomusa's shoulder. No good came from criticizing the police.

"What I say is true." Nomusa shrugged off the hand and leaned in closer to Emmanuel. Rage lit her dark eyes. "The white policeman is a liar. He promised to help but sat on his hands. He cares for no one else's daughters but his own."

"Please, sister," another woman said. "What's done is done."

The finality of the woman's words seemed to drain the anger from Nomusa. Her expression softened and she said to Emmanuel, "From the day my daughter was born her eyes were on the horizon and what was beyond it. I should have kept her by my side but she did not like to be watched over. Now she is gone . . ."

Nomusa covered her face with her hands and began to cry. A woman held her and rocked her like a child as she sobbed. Emmanuel put the notebook away and stood up. Pressing for more information would gain him nothing. Nomusa had become unreachable in her grief.

"Find out who discovered the body and see if the women can help us with a list of people to talk to," Emmanuel said to Shabalala. "I'll search the area for a possible murder weapon."

"Yes, Sergeant." Shabalala shuffled closer to the women and waited patiently for the right moment to speak.

Emmanuel walked away. Grief and despair were part of the job. He was used to it. But there were times, like this one, when the ghosts of the dead from his past tried to break through into daylight instead of waiting for night to fall.

He combed the grass, searching for a knife, a spent bullet casing or a sharpened stick—anything that might have caused the injury to Amahle's back. He could do nothing for the war dead. This death on a Natal hillside, however, he could do something about.

2

NOTHING," EMMANUEL SAID to Shabalala when the Zulu detective joined the hunt for a murder weapon ten minutes later. "This area is clean. The only place left to check is that ledge up there."

They climbed a steep grade to a gnarled fig tree with thick white roots that pushed into the face of the basalt. From the ledge, they had a clear view of the majestic spine of the Drakensberg Mountain Range. The air seemed brighter and crisper than in the valley below.

"Wait, Sergeant." Shabalala picked up a half-eaten fig and examined the stalk. He moved to the far side of the rock face and bent low over sprouting tufts of grass.

"The small man was here," he said. "He ate the fruit from the tree and then made a toilet in the sand."

The toilet was a neatly dug hole, filled with dirt and then heaped with a mound of dried fig leaves.

"An African man or a European with bush skills," Emmanuel said, and eyed the wide swath of land running to the feet of the mountains. "Plenty of both kinds of men in a place like the Kamberg Valley."

"A white man without shoes who fights off the wild animals with a stick and also eats fruit from the fig tree?" Shabalala was skeptical. "A man who also makes a toilet like that of a Zulu?"

"You're right. Our most likely suspect is a native man who knew Amahle." Emmanuel peered over the rock ledge to the grassy slope. "If all that's true, the tartan blanket is wrong."

Zulus used carved wooden headrests as pillows.

"The blanket is a mystery. None of the mothers has seen it before. It does not belong to the girl or to anyone at her kraal."

"The person who found the body could have left it." Emmanuel knew that possibility was a long shot. Why leave something expensive under the head of a dead girl? Who would take the time and effort to make a dead girl more comfortable unless there was a deep personal connection to her?

"Who *did* find her?" he asked.

"A man going down to the river for a baptism service found Amahle this morning." Shabalala joined Emmanuel at the rock ledge. "The mothers think this man is still at the river but I do not believe this blanket belongs to him."

"And what about the flowers?" Emmanuel asked.

"Zulus do not bring flowers to the dead. I cannot explain them."

They stood on the lip of the rock and looked down at the crime scene. Spring was all around. It was in the smell of damp earth heated by the late morning sun and in the hum of the bees. It was a perfect day for a beautiful Zulu girl in a calico dress to stretch out in the sun and listen to the rustle of leaves and the sound of birds. Instead, a group of women sat under the branches of a thornbush tree, now mute with sorrow, afraid to let her corpse out of their sight. Nearby, men armed with spears and clubs guarded the crime scene.

"We'll check the blanket for a name or a label once we're clear of the family. We don't want the impi jumping to conclusions and going after the owner," Emmanuel said.

A young man with a dented bicycle wheel tucked into his armpit spilled over the crest of the hill, running fast enough to escape his own shadow. A cloud of brown and orange grasshoppers jumped off the path and a wood dove flew up from the grass. The impi closed ranks but the young man peeled away to the left and dodged past them.

He shouted, "Take up your shields. He is coming."

The impi overlapped the edges of their cowhide shields to form a barrier and looked toward the steep ridge. Emmanuel and Shabalala did the same, impelled by a growing sense of danger.

A lean Zulu man appeared at the apex armed with a short stabbing spear. He surveyed the land and took in the impi defending the pathway. He raised his spear and thumped the wooden handle against his shield to make a bass note like a beating heart. Four more Zulu men appeared on the ridge, each pounding their spears against their shields, until the noise reverberated across the hillside.

"There will be a fight. We must move. Now. Before the two groups clash." Shabalala hit the steep decline at a run, feet sliding on the grade, his arms held out for balance. The drumming grew louder and faster; that human heart now pumped with adrenaline.

Emmanuel matched Shabalala's pace. Zulu military tactics were not his area of expertise, but he figured that the men on the hill would spill down the path with their spears drawn the moment the drumming stopped. He tracked right, aiming for a space between the two groups of Zulu men.

Four harder beats of the spears against rawhide, and then silence. A shout went up and the men on the hill ran fast toward the impi guarding the path. The gap between the two factions closed.

"Sergeant," Shabalala gasped. "The sage bush."

Emmanuel saw it, a clump of scraggly green vegetation that grew on the path a few feet in front of the impi. That was their target, the last point at which he and Shabalala could access the path to form a human buffer between the opposing Zulus.

Footsteps thundered closer, a cloud of dust rising behind the attacking impi. Shabalala and Emmanuel sprinted hard and hit the path just short of the sage bush marker.

"Take the rear impi." Emmanuel pulled out his police ID and unclipped his holster. "I'll take the attackers."

The detectives stood back-to-back, shoulders squared, projecting a confidence that neither of them felt. The advancing impi pressed closer, their spears gleaming in the sun.

"Stop! Police!" Emmanuel held up his ID, a shield of sorts backed by the power of the white government. He reached for the Webley revolver, snug in its leather holster, but thought better of it. He didn't want to escalate the confrontation. "Drop your weapons. Now!"

The leader of the attacking group kept coming, undaunted by Emmanuel's laminated piece of paper. He was tall, with a starkly handsome face built of sharp angles and taut skin.

Keloid scars, silver in the sunlight, spread across his chest and shoulders. The men behind him slowed but did not stop, either.

Emmanuel switched to Zulu.

"Two steps back. Now." He moved to meet the challenge, index finger pointed, his voice loud and dark with menace, just like the training manuals of the South African Police Force instructed. "I will not ask you again."

Shabalala turned and stood at Emmanuel's right shoulder, adding muscle to the police order.

The leader of the new impi stopped and seemed to weigh the risk of pushing the attack. "You speak Zulu very well for a European," he said in English, and allowed his stabbing spear and shield to slip to the ground.

Emmanuel stepped closer.

"Hands up where I can see them," he said. "Your men also."

The four Zulu soldiers held on to their weapons and shields, unwilling to act without a direct order from their commander.

"What will it be?" Emmanuel asked. "Shall we talk or fight? I'm happy either way."

The man smiled. "Only a fool brings spears to fight a policeman with a gun."

He signaled his men to lay down their arms on the grass. They complied.

Emmanuel kicked the spear out of the lean man's reach.

"Name," he said.

"I am Mandla, the great chief Matebula's eldest son."

Mandla. It meant "the strong one."

"Your mother?" Emmanuel asked. Mandla could be

Amahle's full blood brother, so remarkable was their shared physical beauty.

"My mother is La Matenjuwa. First wife of the great chief."

"First son of the first wife," Emmanuel said. Mandla was a chief-in-waiting and Amahle's half brother. "What business do you have here?"

"I come to collect the great chief's daughter." Mandla turned to the impi guarding the pathway. "Her body is the property of the Matebula clan. You have no right to be here."

"You come without honor," the oldest male of the original impi shouted. "You insult the dead and the ancestors with your violence."

Mandla's head snapped back and his lips thinned. "A child belongs to the father, not to the mother. The girl must return with us to her father's kraal as the law says."

"He who fertilizes the egg but has no time for the chicks is no father, even among the Zulu," the elder man replied.

Shabalala sucked in a breath at the accusation and again eased around so he had Emmanuel's back.

"Move off ten paces," Emmanuel ordered both sides of Amahle's family. "Empty palms facing out where I can see them."

The men obeyed, unhappily.

"Listen to me carefully." Emmanuel spoke in a calm voice. "We are the detectives in charge of investigating Amahle's death. She is your sister and your niece, but for the time being she belongs to us. The police. We will say how and where she travels. I know this is difficult for all of you, but it is the way it must be."

He turned to make eye contact with the elder who'd escorted them to the ring of grieving women.

"Is this understood?"

The man took a deep breath, still angry. "It is, ma' baas," he said.

Allowing Amahle to pass into the care of the South African police was worse than giving her back to her father's house, but there was no other choice. The police were stronger than all the valley clans put together.

Emmanuel turned to Mandla and said, "Is this understood?"

Mandla bowed without subservience and replied, "I hear you."

Acquiescing to the detective provided Mandla with a tactical retreat. Emmanuel suspected that Mandla would agree to every request, bend to any threat, but do whatever the hell he pleased as soon as the police drove out of the valley. Beyond the fence lines of the white-owned farms Mandla and his father, the great chief, were the law.

"We cannot leave the girl out on the veldt, even with a guard," Shabalala whispered. It was official procedure to leave murder victims in situ until the mortuary van arrived to pick up the body. "We must take her now while it is still daylight."

"Agreed," Emmanuel said, and motioned to Mandla and his men. "Take up your shields and return to your father's kraal. Place your spears at the base of that boulder until we are gone."

He didn't trust Mandla to walk away without a fight. The great chief's heir was obviously used to being in command, and returning to his father's home without Amahle's body was a blow to his authority.

"As you say." Mandla turned and moved swiftly to the

crest of the hill. He stopped at the top where he'd first appeared and squatted in the grass, flanked by his men, daring the detectives to drive him off.

"We've made an enemy," Shabalala said.

"The first of many," Emmanuel replied.

Amahle was no ordinary Zulu girl. She was the daughter of a chief, loved and fought over. What dangerous emotions had she stirred in both Zulu and European hearts when she was still alive?

3

EMMANUEL EASED THE black police Chevrolet down a dirt track running between the Roselet Police Station and the station commander's house, a small sandstone building with lavender bushes planted on either side of the front steps. The main street was quiet, but he couldn't risk the chance that a pedestrian walking home from church might look in the backseat and discover a dead black girl lying there.

"The station commander and his family are home," he observed. A sparkling police van was parked in front of the stone house. Beyond it, in the shade of a sycamore tree, two glossy-haired girls in blue pinafores crouched beside a small anthill and poked sticks into the entrance, enjoying the insects' panic. They looked up in unison at the sound of the car and ran for the back door, calling, "Pa, come quick!" and "Visitors!"

"We'll take Amahle to the local doctor after we've introduced ourselves here. See what he can tell us about the wound on her back."

"I will explain things to her," Shabalala said, and Emmanuel got out of the car and stood facing away from the Chevrolet. The conversation between Shabalala and Amahle unnerved him, made him think of the millions of war victims left to cross into the realm of the dead alone. He understood the necessity of these conversations for a Zulu worried about unsettled spirits—he just wished the dead would tell Shabalala who killed them.

"She will wait here for us," the Zulu detective said when he emerged from the car. "It is a hard thing to do. Her mother, Nomusa, is calling to her spirit to come home."

"We'll be as quick as we can," Emmanuel said. "But we'll need to determine cause of death."

He and Shabalala knew, however, that if the medical exam proved inconclusive Amahle might have to be transported to the closest morgue for a full autopsy. A long delay could increase the tension they had seen on the hill. It would also give the family ample time to imagine the body of their loved one splayed naked on a cold table with her harvested organs in steel buckets.

"Let's check in with the station commander and get on our way," he said.

The fly-screen door to the sandstone house swung open and the girls who'd been tormenting ants in the backyard ran to the porch railing. They leaned their elbows on the wooden beam and studied the newcomers. Their pale skin, curls and hazel eyes made Emmanuel think of curious elves.

"Look," the older girl yelled over her shoulder. "Like we said. Visitors."

"There." The little sister added a pointing finger. "In the yard."

"Thank you, my lovelies." A solidly built white man in a

green Sunday suit walked out behind the girls and ruffled their hair. In his mid-thirties, he had wide shoulders, cropped red hair and the kind of skin that burned and peeled rather than tanned.

"Can I help you, gentlemen?" he asked, green eyes bright with interest. His accent was County Clare Irish worn thin by decades of living in South Africa.

"Constable Bagley?" Emmanuel paused and gave the station commander time to get used to the sight of two strangers in his garden . . . one of them a six-foot-plus Zulu man dressed in a hand-tailored suit. "I'm Detective Sergeant Emmanuel Cooper from the West Street CID in Durban. And this is Detective Constable Samuel Shabalala of the Native Branch."

"*Yebo, inkosi.*" Shabalala greeted the constable in the traditional way, with his hat off and held to his chest as a sign of respect. Roselet was a white farming town and its citizens would have the traditional expectations of blacks: that they work hard, say little and recognize the order of things.

"Oh . . ." The commander seemed surprised. He bent down and said to the older girl, "Go inside and tell Mum that I've got work but I'll be in just now. Okay, my sweetheart?"

"*Ja,* okay, Daddy."

The girls retreated slowly, clearly fascinated by Shabalala. Their town was populated with the familiar: European parents, European friends, black house servants and a handful of brown and Indian children they were not allowed to speak to or play with. How rare and exciting to see a Zulu man in a suit standing side by side with a white man.

"Constable Desmond Bagley, station commander of the Roselet police." Bagley came down off the veranda and squeezed Emmanuel's hand once, hard. Shabalala got a courteous dip of the head. "You're a long way from home. What brings you all the way out here, Detective?"

"You didn't get the message," Emmanuel said, and looked over at the station entrance. The handwritten note was still pinned to the door. That meant he'd have to tell Bagley, face-to-face, about a murder committed in his own district.

"One of my police boys is normally here to open the station and take messages but both of them are at a baptism service in the valley," Bagley said. "I've just come in from church myself. Has something happened that I should know about?"

"A murder in the Kamberg Valley," Emmanuel said, hoping that Bagley's feeling of inadequacy at being the last to know would fade in time.

"My God . . ." Red tinged the constable's face. "Who?"

"Amahle Matebula," Emmanuel said. "A young Zulu girl."

"Amahle . . ." Bagley frowned and glanced off to the station house. A pulse throbbed visibly in a vein on his forehead. "The name sounds familiar."

"She was reported missing on Saturday morning," Emmanuel said. "By her family."

"Let's see . . ." Bagley dug a pack of Dunhill Cubas from his jacket pocket and punctured the foil top with his fingernail. The telltale vein throbbed harder. "Friday night there was a fight out on the native location, two arrests. Saturday there was a stock theft from Dovecote farm and then a break-in at Dawson's General Store. The boys and I had our hands full."

"Sounds like it." Emmanuel was unimpressed by the rural crime wave gripping Roselet. Bagley was lining up excuses for failing to act on the trifling matter of a missing black girl. "Is Amahle Matebula's disappearance listed in the station occurrence book, Constable?"

"Forgetting" to enter a formal complaint was the easiest way to shelve an inconvenient investigation.

Bagley dug out a cigarette and tapped the cut end against his wrist. "I'm just trying to remember the details."

"Take your time," Emmanuel said, and waited in silence. Sloppy police work, no matter the case, was inexcusable. Bagley would get no help from him in covering up a failure of duty.

"That's right." The constable fumbled a box of matches from his pocket, struck a match and lit up. "A Zulu boy came in on Saturday morning, said this girl Amahle hadn't come home from work on Friday. The details are in the occurrence book."

"What time did the boy come in?" Emmanuel asked. Despite Bagley's efforts to appear nonchalant, the vein on his forehead said otherwise.

"Around seven a.m." He flicked ash into the garden bed and smiled, apologetic. "I'll be honest with you, Sergeant. I didn't think for one minute it was serious. Missing girls normally turn up after a few days."

"Was Amahle known to the police?" Emmanuel asked. Beautiful black girls with a wild streak inevitably showed up in local police records attached to underage drinking offenses or carnal knowledge investigations. "A list of previous offenses would be a good place for us to start looking for suspects."

"Saturday morning was the first time the girl's name appeared on the record," Bagley said. "The Kamberg Valley natives are very traditional and keep to themselves, so that's no surprise."

True. But being off the police offenders list didn't necessarily make Amahle a girl without a history. Only members of the Zulu community would be able to provide a detailed portrait of who she was in life.

"Would the native constables have any idea what might have happened to her?" Emmanuel asked. The black and white communities overlapped in specific work locations: the kitchen, the garden, the farmyard and the nursery. Segregation laws kept them apart in the bar and the bedroom.

"It's like I said." Bagley took a deep draw of nicotine and focused on the note fluttering on the station's front door. "The last two days have been a busy time for us."

Not one phone call was made or one question asked about Amahle Matebula's disappearance. Missing persons were the bane of police work, but Emmanuel had no doubt that things would have been different if Amahle had been blond with blue eyes, freckles and a snub nose. At least Bagley had the grace to look uncomfortable about his negligence.

"I admit I should have looked for her, Sergeant. But you understand how things work . . ."

Emmanuel understood perfectly how things worked. It pained him.

"Inkosi Bagley. Inkosi Bagley . . ." a voice called from the grassy field behind the station. Two black men dressed in the distinctive white robes worn by members of the Zion Native Church ran toward them, sweating and out of breath.

"Constables," Bagley said when the two native policemen stopped short at the sight of Shabalala, now standing with his hands resting on the hood of the Chevrolet. It was an oddly protective gesture considering the passenger in the car was already dead.

"What is it, Shabangu? Spill the news. These men are also police," Bagley said to a gaunt man with a receding hairline; the man's ankle-length robe was splattered with mud and stained with sweat.

"A murder in the valley," Shabangu said to the patch of dirt at Bagley's feet. "Chief Matebula's daughter was found this morning near to Little Flint Farm. Baba Kaleni saw her with his own eyes."

"Where is Kaleni now?" Emmanuel asked Shabangu. "We'd like to talk to him."

"He is at the river baptism, inkosi. You must take the walking track that is four miles past the sign for Little Flint Farm. By the rock that looks like a dog's head."

"Thanks," Emmanuel said, and turned to Bagley. "We need to see the local doctor. If there is one."

There would be no local hospital. Roselet was too small.

"Dr. Daglish lives right here on Greyling Street." Bagley indicated the road running parallel to the station. "What do you need a doctor for?"

"To examine the body." Emmanuel moved to the Chevrolet. "How will we know which house is the doctor's?"

"Take a left onto Greyling. It's the sixth house on the left. There's a yellow fence and a wild pear tree in the front." Bagley crossed the yard while he spoke, drawn to the black Chevrolet by the implication of Emmanuel's words. He peered through the back passenger window at the outline of Amahle's body under the tartan blanket. "It's a beautiful house," he said. "You can't miss it."

Emmanuel paused before getting into the car. "I'll need to use the station telephone when we get back. I have to call Durban."

"Of course, Sergeant. Whatever the boys and I can do to help. Just let me know."

"Much appreciated. We'll scratch around for leads and get you and the native constables on board with the investigation right away."

"When you're ready, you know where to find us." Bagley retreated to the front steps, his cigarette smoked down to the butt. "The station is at your disposal."

Emmanuel imagined a headline across the cover of the monthly police magazine: "City detectives receive a warm welcome and offers of help from the local uniform branch."

The lack of departmental rivalry should have pleased him, but instead he was irritated. Pride and loyalty to your town and your people demanded more than a passive, "When you're ready you know where to find us." Bagley surrendered control of a murder case in his own territory without a struggle. Only a bone-idle policeman did that.

—

Emmanuel reversed the Chevrolet onto Greyling Street. Roselet's main thoroughfare was a wide dirt lane with shops for local white farmers and tourists escaping the humidity in the city. The street also included a farm supply depot, a small café decorated with blue and white gingham curtains and a general store with DAWSON's painted across the window in gold leaf.

"The mother was right," Shabalala said when the police station was out of sight. "The constable did not look for Amahle."

"Not for a second." Emmanuel looked at the houses on the left-hand side. "Weighed up against a break-in at the general store, a missing black girl was easy to ignore. I'm not saying it's right, but you know how it works."

"I understand well the way of things." Shabalala pointed to a yellow fence fronting a huge block of land that dipped away from the road. "This is the place, Sergeant."

"Did you notice anything unusual about Bagley besides that vein on his forehead?" Emmanuel pulled into the driveway and parked.

"Yes. His eyes went to the station house, to the cigarette, to the yard, but never to us."

"He was either ashamed of doing nothing or he was lying about something. Talk to the native constables tomorrow and find out what you can about Bagley. Behind-the-scenes stuff."

"*Yebo*," Shabalala said as they got out of the car.

The scent of roses hung in the air and sunlight shone on the whitewashed walls of the doctor's cottage. The garden was in bloom and alive with bees. A stream meandered along the far edge of the property, and on the other side a green valley stretched to distant mountains wreathed in clouds.

"Second round of introductions," Emmanuel said as they took a narrow stone path to the front door. He rang a gold bell mounted on the front wall and waited. No answer.

"It's Sunday. The doctor might still be at church," he said, and rang again.

Floorboards creaked inside and Emmanuel automatically reached for his ID. He checked that he had the right one. For reasons that he could not explain himself, he still carried the now-redundant small green race identification card stamped with the words "mixed race." To protect his sister's white identity and under pressure from the Security Branch, Emmanuel had opted to secretly accept racial reclassification to "mixed race" and expulsion from the Jo'burg CID. After his reclassification he moved to Durban and got a job at the dockyards and avoided the attention of the police. He might have spent the rest of his life wielding a hammer and hauling freight if not for Colonel van Niekerk, who reinstated him into the Detective Branch as a reward for solving a brutal triple murder. With two new pieces of paper, he became white again and a detective.

Common sense said he should burn the old papers and forget the eight months he'd spent on the wrong side of the color line. But he could not. Maybe the contradictory "European" and "mixed race" papers reflected the tangled path his life had taken so far. He grew up a white kaffir child in Sophiatown, a slum on the outskirts of Jo'burg, became a teenage outcast stranded among the "chosen" Afrikaner people on the veldt, then went to war in Europe and returned with medals for killing people. Now he held a South African police detective's ID card and lived in a schizophrenic society that he felt he'd never fit into.

The door handle turned. Emmanuel held up his ID and smiled. It was the least he could do. He was about to ruin the doctor's perfect Sunday afternoon.

"The police." A tall woman with hazy blue eyes and dark hair cut in a bob held the door ajar with her elbow. She was good-looking in the horse-faced way of English ladies who wore floral print dresses, wide-brimmed hats and cotton gloves. "Has Jim crashed the car again?"

"This isn't about a crash," Emmanuel said, not happy about the possibility that the local doctor was an inveterate speeder with a history of abrupt endings. "We'd like a word with Dr. Daglish, if he's in."

"I'm Dr. Daglish, Detective. Margaret Daglish." She appeared to take no offense at Emmanuel's assumption that the town doctor must be a man. "What can I do for you?"

Emmanuel introduced himself and Shabalala, using the time to recover from his embarrassment. It was provincial and chauvinist to think the words *female* and *doctor* didn't go together. "We have the body of a teenage girl that requires a medical examination to determine time and cause of death. It's urgent."

"Who is it?" Her dark eyebrows lifted.

"A Zulu girl. Amahle Matebula," Emmanuel said, and a flash of some emotion crossed the doctor's face. Anxiety? Fear? And a softer feeling that he couldn't read as well. Regret? "Did you know her?"

"No." Margaret Daglish raised her left hand to show a bandaged wrist. "I'm afraid I can't help you, Detective Cooper. I fell over about a week ago. Manipulating instruments is out of the question. I don't have the strength to carry out a proper examination. Not one that I'd be happy with."

"You're incapable of performing an examination?" Emmanuel said, and held the doctor's gaze. Something more than a sprained wrist was behind this refusal.

"Not a full and proper examination. That would be impossible." Dr. Daglish leaned closer and added in an anxious voice, "You should get another doctor. One from out of this area."

"I see. Where do you suggest we look?"

"Pietermaritzburg or Durban," came the swift reply. "A qualified physician who can stay in Roselet for a few days and then leave after the work is done."

Emmanuel reflected on what Daglish was really saying: Amahle had to be examined by an objective stranger with no local ties who'd sign off on the medical findings and clear town before the shit hit the fan.

"An outside doctor can be arranged," Emmanuel said.

"That's for the best," Daglish said with a strained smile. "I'm happy to assist the visiting doctor with medical supplies."

Dodging the examination was one thing, but Emmanuel wasn't going to let the town doctor walk away from the case altogether. "It will take time for the relief doctor to get here and we need somewhere to keep the body until then. Can you help?"

Margaret Daglish looked at the hearselike Chevrolet surrounded by garden flowers. The color drained from her cheeks and remorse registered in her eyes: a response prompted by the death of a young girl or by her own cowardice in refusing to perform the examination, it was impossible to say.

"There's a basement at the back of the house," she said. "It's dark and cool inside. She will be safe there."

"May we move her in right away?"

"Of course." The doctor blinked hard and pointed to the side of the house. "Follow that path to the rear. The land slopes down to a door that opens directly into the basement. I'll have the room open and ready."

Emmanuel and Shabalala headed for the Chevrolet. *Safe. Loved. Beautiful. Protected.* The words from his notebook played on his mind. Amahle had been blessed, but with every blessing came a shadow. *Envied. Hated. Feared. Harmed.* Those words might also apply to the dead girl.

"The constable did not look for her and now the doctor will not examine her." Shabalala seemed to read Emmanuel's mind. "What is there to fear from a Zulu girl?"

"You think Dr. Daglish is lying about her wrist," Emmanuel said. Outside of the traditional kraals and the native locations, black women had no power and influence. Amahle's name, her existence, should have been of no consequence to a white medical doctor.

"She is hurt. But not so badly."

"I got the same impression." Emmanuel opened the passenger door. "The doctor doesn't want her name on the examination report or the death certificate. Maybe she's afraid of what she'll find."

"There is only one wound on the girl."

"I'm talking about wounds that can't be seen." A dirt-flecked foot fell out from under the tartan blanket and Emmanuel covered it up again. "An old broken bone, long healed. Internal bruising. Rape. Pregnancy. The examination might uncover something no one wants to know."

"The doctor is not responsible for Amahle's bad fortune," Shabalala said. "She has nothing to fear."

"Well, she's scared of something. Or someone." And that someone was most likely a European. Black-on-black violence was expected, accepted. A white killer would bring something new and dangerous into Dr. Daglish's world.

Emmanuel moved aside and Shabalala lifted the girl into his arms with the strength of a river carrying a leaf.

"Let's give her to the doctor and get back to the station. Van Niekerk will be wanting an update." Emmanuel followed the sloping path to the rear of the cottage. "Then we'll find a place to throw our bags down for a couple of days."

The sound of Shabalala's voice behind him whispering to the dead girl slowed Emmanuel's steps. He was not superstitious or religious but an old feeling resurfaced, one born in combat and shared with all front-line soldiers. Time was finite. It was fickle. It ran out. Fate or the God that you didn't believe in could pull the plug and walk away.

During the war, he'd fought for a world where girls grew into women and then to *old* women surrounded by their grandchildren. That Amahle's life should be so easily wasted in peacetime, Emmanuel took as a personal insult.

On the third try the telephone operator found a clear line between the Roselet police station and Colonel van Niekerk's study in Durban.

"What did you find, Cooper?" The Afrikaner colonel skipped the usual formalities. They knew each other too well for small talk.

"A Zulu girl. The daughter of a local chief." Emmanuel sat behind Bagley's neat desk, which faced green fields and distant mountains.

"Fuck!" van Niekerk said. "I was hoping to break you and Shabalala in on a bigger case."

Van Niekerk's disappointment at Amahle's skin color reflected the hard truth: reputations were not built on solving black homicides.

"It's enough that we're out of the city and working a murder case," Emmanuel said.

"Picking up the garbage" was the phrase used by the other white detectives at the West Street CID to describe the jobs Emmanuel was assigned. Four suicides, two drowning victims, three pickpockets, a putrefied old lady dead for four weeks and a serial pantie thief with a penchant for lace . . . that was the grim tally of his cases for the last three months. Shabalala's case list was equally depressing. It was payback for reentering the Detective Branch under the protection of an ambitious Afrikaner colonel who refused to play the role of dumb Boer for the predominantly English police force.

"It's a start," van Niekerk conceded. "Need anything?"

"The local doctor has backed away from the case at a hundred miles an hour. We have to get someone from outside of the area to perform the examination."

"Get the old Jew." Van Niekerk could have been ordering a drink from a bar or demanding a meal be reheated. "He's qualified and he's only a few hours away."

"No," Emmanuel said automatically, and then rephrased the objection. "I'd rather not get Dr. Zweigman involved in police business, Colonel. He has family obligations and a clinic to run."

The Dutch colonel was not used to hearing the word "no" except, perhaps, from his virginal English fiancée. There was a brittle silence before he said, "Finding another doctor won't be a problem, Cooper. I'll make a few calls."

"Much appreciated." Emmanuel's fingers flexed around the telephone cord. A suggestion from van Niekerk was really a de facto order. Giving up without a fight on having "the old Jew" conduct Amahle's medical examination was out of character. Or perhaps the colonel felt the examination of a black girl's corpse was not worth fighting over.

"Who called the case in, Colonel?" Emmanuel asked, curious.

"It was an anonymous tip-off from a local woman. A European. The constable on duty figured the victim was white as well."

"I understand." Emmanuel saw the bigger picture. The out-of-town murder of a European, as van Niekerk had assumed, provided the perfect opportunity to get the names Cooper and Shabalala back on the board at the European and Native Detective Branch. Van Niekerk had, with characteristic patience, waited for the right moment to move them up the ladder to a more powerful position.

And Emmanuel had repaid that loyalty by sleeping with Lana Rose. An excusable error for a hormonal teenage boy but not for a grown man able to weigh up the risks and consequences. Running, still running toward trouble. Nonetheless, he wasn't sure he'd take back the night with Lana, even if he could.

"Everything okay, Cooper?" Van Niekerk spoke over the soft whirr of a ceiling fan. Durban was humid this time of year, the air thick enough to carve into ribbons.

"All fine at this end, sir," Emmanuel said. "We'll interview the girl's family and friends and report any news tomorrow afternoon."

"Make it late. I have a tailor's fitting in the morning, a final meeting with the minister and a wedding rehearsal dinner to get through." No joy there, just lists of duties to be endured till the wedding night reward.

"No problem, Colonel." Emmanuel dropped the heavy Bakelite handle onto the cradle and pushed the phone back onto the grooves marked on the table surface. He noticed that Bagley had a specific place for each pen and notepad.

White clouds bloomed on the horizon, backlit by shafts of early afternoon sunlight. A white woman had reported the murder. One of the European-owned farms in the Kamberg was the most likely source of the call. Why the tip-off was directed to the Durban Detective Branch when Constable Desmond Bagley of the Roselet police lived less than fifty miles from the crime scene was a mystery.

FORTY OR SO members of the local Zion Christian Church, known as Zionis, gathered by a wide river. They clapped and swayed in rhythm on the sandy bank as they sang "Come, Holy Spirit, Dove Divine." In the middle of the river, a girl in a white robe with green trim rose up from the water, newly baptized, to shouts of "Amen" and "Hallelujah." A second group of Zionis clustered around a wood fire with their hands held out to the flames while water dripped from their gowns and pooled at their feet.

"How do we find him?" Emmanuel asked.

"The mothers sitting with Amahle said that Baba Kaleni is the head of the True Israelites congregation," Shabalala said. "I do not recognize any of the markings on the robes, so we will have to ask."

Looking around as they walked along the compact dirt path, Emmanuel noticed half a dozen different robes, some trimmed in black, others in moss-green. A group of women in pale blue robes with navy blue collars sat on rocks by the river, sharing an orange. Two men with leopard-skin trim stacked Bibles into a wheelbarrow to be transported back to church.

"Different congregations wear different robes," Emmanuel said, and wondered why that distinction had never been clear to him before. Perhaps he'd never looked closely enough.

"*Yebo,* Sergeant. My church wears green robes with a white cross."

Shabalala was full of surprises. The Zion Church mixed Christian and traditional African beliefs. Men like Shabalala, who operated in the white world, generally did not admit to an association with a church that allowed polygamy and practiced animal sacrifice.

"I thought you were Anglican," Emmanuel said. He remembered the Zulu detective standing outside a red-roofed church in the town of Jacob's Rest.

Shabalala closed in on the group huddled around the fire. "I belong also to the Anglican Church," he said.

"Laying a bet both ways." Emmanuel couldn't resist the chance to get under the Zulu detective's skin. "That's cheating, my man."

"God in His infinite wisdom understands all and forgives all, Sergeant," Shabalala answered with a smile. "That is what makes Him great."

"And here I took you for an Old Testament guy." Since returning from the war, Emmanuel had kept almost completely to himself except for his odd three-way friendship with Shabalala and Zweigman, the Jewish doctor. He'd met them both a year ago during an investigation into the murder of a corrupt Afrikaner police captain. Together they'd faced violence and almost certain death and remained close after the case was shelved and forgotten.

Just for a moment, while they walked and worked by the river, Emmanuel allowed himself the illusion that he and Shabalala were two ordinary cops with no barriers of place or race between them.

"Now I see that you're strictly New Testament," he continued. "With a God that lets you slip out the back door of the church and run barefoot across the veldt like a heathen. I'm not sure I trust you anymore, Constable."

"Two churches are better than none," Shabalala said.

Emmanuel laughed at the deadpan comment, and the sound disturbed the sudden quiet. The recently baptized Zionis huddled silently around the fire like a flock of white-feathered birds banding together before a storm. One day, Emmanuel supposed, he'd get used to the hunched shoulders and the averted gaze of nonwhites about to be questioned by the police, but today it still made him uncomfortable.

He caught the attention of a man who looked up from the flames.

"Baba Kaleni," Emmanuel said. "Where is he?"

"Ah . . ." The man squeezed water from the sleeve of his damp gown, playing for time. "Ah . . ."

"I am Kaleni." The words came from the far right of the fire. A Zulu man shrugged on a dry robe with the help of a young girl. His beard was dazzling white but his age was impossible to tell. His sagging right shoulder and arthritic fingers indicated long years lived under harsh conditions but his clear brown eyes and smooth round face gave the impression of a child.

"You are the police," Baba Kaleni said, and smiled a greeting.

"That's right." Emmanuel introduced them both and

puzzled over Kaleni's beaming expression. Back in the city, only gangsters, prostitutes and simpletons smiled at the police.

Kaleni pointed to a rock protruding from the veldt over a hundred yards away. "That is a quiet place to sit and to talk."

They turned from the riverbank and the shivering band of True Israelites bunched around the flames. The men and women drying their robes had all perfected the subtle African art of looking away while listening in.

"After you," Emmanuel said.

"*Yebo, inkosi.*" Baba Kaleni started out across the grasslands with slow deliberation, the muscles of his right shoulder slumped. The young girl who'd helped him into his robe ran up and held out a tattered Bible, as if it were a shield and the old man poised to enter a mighty conflict.

"*Ngiyabonga,* Sisana. You are a fine child." Kaleni patted the girl's braided hair and gripped the Good Book awkwardly in his left hand. "Go now. All is well."

The girl returned to the embrace of the True Israelites and inserted herself between two large women. Kaleni struck out again toward the rock without glancing back.

"I will walk with you," Shabalala said, and fell in by the preacher's side. Emmanuel held back and let the two Zulu men go ahead. The gap had to be wide enough for Kaleni to be certain that a European detective was not overhearing the conversation. White cop/black cop was the homegrown South African version of the good cop/bad cop routine used by police across the globe, and was just as effective.

Occasional Zulu words carried to him on the breeze during the walk over the flat terrain. Emmanuel caught "water," "bread" and "blood" but didn't try to make connections. Shabalala would report on the conversation later. A few feet ahead the flat rock split the red earth to make a natural platform.

"Please, sit." Baba Kaleni motioned to the rock in the same way a prosperous farmer might offer a seat in his kitchen to a guest.

Shabalala climbed on first and found a spot to the rear of the warm stone. He squatted down with his broad hands resting on the curve of his knees and his fedora pulled low on his forehead. It was a signal for Emmanuel to lead the conversation.

"Take the shade," Emmanuel said to Kaleni in Zulu. "I have protection from the sun."

The old man squeezed into the shadow cast by a paperbark thorn tree and rested his right arm on his lap. The river now looked like a thin silver ribbon on the horizon, the church members gathered on its distant banks smudges of white, blue and green.

"Tell me everything you remember about this morning. From before finding Amahle to what you did afterwards," Emmanuel continued in Zulu.

"It happened like this. I awoke before the sun and dressed. It was dark in the hut but my wife is very neat and my church hat, my robes and my Bible were placed just so. My wife has always been like my right hand and a true helper."

"A blessing . . ." Shabalala mumbled before the preacher set off again, describing in minute detail the chill of the water in the wash bucket in the hut and the texture of the breakfast porridge, eaten cold and without milk.

Emmanuel breathed in the scent of dirt and crushed grass and waited for Kaleni's recollections to reach the crime scene.

"After many miles of walking my legs grew tired and I

stopped to rest. That is when I came away from the path." Kaleni traced a finger over a tear in the Bible's worn cover. "And that is when I saw her. The daughter of the chief."

"Saw her where?"

"Under the fig tree. I . . ." He shook his head, embarrassed. "I thought maybe the chief's daughter was sleeping. Even though the dew was wet on the leaves and the dawn just breaking."

"Did you see anyone else in the area?" Emmanuel hoped his patience would be rewarded with a name or a physical description of the man who'd guarded Amahle's body.

There was a pause, a mere pulse of a heartbeat, before Baba Kaleni said, "I saw no one, inkosi."

"You absolutely sure?"

"The chief's daughter was alone." The tear on the Bible cover widened under the rub of the old man's fingertips. "Of this I am certain."

"So it was just you and her on the hill?" Emmanuel leaned closer and established eye contact. This was the first pressure point in an interview. Letting a witness know he wasn't fooling anyone, certainly not a city detective who had heard some of the most accomplished liars in the world doing some of their best work. The eye contact also contained a hint of a threat. It was a ploy but worth a try.

"The chief's daughter was alone," Kaleni said again. "Of this I am certain."

"All right." Emmanuel let it go. The old man had his story and he was sticking to it. "Describe the place where Amahle was lying."

"Under the fig tree with flowers all around. There was a red blanket rolled up and placed under her head."

"Did you put it there?" Emmanuel had checked the tartan blanket after leaving the crime scene. It was pure wool and made by Papworth's Fine Fabrics in Cape Town. There was no name on it to identify the owner.

"No." A glimmer of a smile curved the older man's lips. "But that I owned such a blanket. It would keep me warm in winter. My wife also."

Emmanuel dug his pen and notebook from his jacket pocket. "After you found her?" he prompted.

"I went to the kraal of Chief Matebula. He was asleep and would not be disturbed. I reported the news to Nomusa, the girl's mother."

"Why didn't you go to a farm where there was a telephone?"

Kaleni looked away to a bank of clouds massing on the horizon. "It was dawn, inkosi. I did not wish to disturb the farmers or the night watchmen who guard their homes."

Nor would he want to rouse their dogs. There was no curfew in the countryside, but a black man wandering before dawn wouldn't be welcome in any house wealthy enough to own a telephone. A stupid question, Emmanuel realized. He tapped his pen to the page, bothered by a wrinkle in the timeline.

"Was it dark when you reached the Matebula kraal?" he asked.

"No. The sun was on the crest of the mountains and the birds were awake."

Colonel van Niekerk had assigned the case to him at three forty-five a.m., well before Kaleni had brought Nomusa the bad news. The woman who'd called in the anonymous tip-off must have known about Amahle's murder prior to the discovery of her body; a woman who might be connected to the small man whose prints littered the crime scene. Emmanuel scribbled the mismatched times into his notebook and continued the interview.

"Who do you think killed Amahle?" Patience hadn't paid off and subtlety wasn't for policemen with a blank list of suspects.

"The chief's daughter was much loved," Kaleni said. "By everyone."

That pause again. A space of three seconds filled with hidden meaning that eluded Emmanuel. Was Amahle loved from afar or loved in a more physical way?

"Did you know her?" Emmanuel asked.

"Not well. She was not a member of my church."

A black bird with yellow markings flew into the branches of the paperbark tree and whistled four long notes in rotation. Baba Kaleni tilted his head and looked at the bird with joy.

"Cut yourself shaving?" Emmanuel said, and pointed to drops of fresh blood leaking from a small wound in the preacher's throat.

The old man shrugged his good shoulder and said, "My eyes are weak and the mountain way is steep. I stumbled and fell onto rocks."

There were no scrapes or bruises on his hands and those "weak" eyes had not a half hour ago picked out a distant slab of basalt protruding from the veldt.

"Sharp rocks," Emmanuel said.

"Sharp as the tip of a spear, inkosi," said Baba Kaleni.

Shabalala glanced up from the shade of his fedora and Emmanuel understood: *The old man was telling them exactly what had happened.* A real spear had pierced his throat, not stones.

"Did you get hurt anyplace else in the fall?"

"*Yebo.*" Baba Kaleni touched gentle fingers to his sagging right shoulder. "Another rock hit me here. It was round and hard as a knobkerrie."

Mandla's impi were armed with spears and hardwood clubs called knobkerries and they were one step ahead of the official police investigation, questioning witnesses and demanding answers with weapons.

"This is bad, Sergeant," Shabalala said. "Mandla must be stopped before he harms others and frightens them away from talking to us."

Emmanuel agreed. Mandla and his impi had to be stopped. "Where is the Matebula kraal?" he asked the preacher.

"The kraal is one hour past the river." Kaleni pointed to a mountain covered with trees and a rock outcrop at the top. "It can be seen from that place."

Zulu time was set to a different clock than the one Emmanuel operated by. The trip would only take an hour if he and Shabalala ran to the kraal; in their suits and leather shoes that wouldn't be easy.

"Any way to get to the kraal by car?" Emmanuel asked, even though he could see only small walking tracks traversing the hills and knew that the access road to the white-owned farms was eaten away by potholes.

"No," Kaleni said. "You must go there on your own two feet."

There was no option but to go up the mountain. At a steady pace, Emmanuel hoped the trip to and from the Zulu compound would be completed in full daylight.

"You'll get us there and back to the car again, Shabalala?" Emmanuel removed his tie and shoved it into his pants pocket, then freed the top three buttons of his shirt.

"I will find the way, Sergeant." The Zulu detective shrugged off his jacket and tied it around his waist. They were going to set a blistering pace to try to close the gap on Mandla's impi.

"If you have anything to add to your statement, now's the time, Baba." Emmanuel expected nothing new from the preacher and his mind was already on the hard miles ahead. Chief Matebula and his son had to be brought into line or more people could get hurt.

"There is but one thing more, inkosi."

"Yeah?" Impatient to get going, Emmanuel turned to Baba Kaleni. The preacher's hand moved in a blur, his palm slamming hard against Emmanuel's chest. The physical contact literally took his breath away. He lifted his own hand to defend himself and push back.

"Wait, Sergeant," Shabalala said. "He means no harm."

The heat from Kaleni's hand burned deep into the skin. Emmanuel had never felt palms so charged. His heartbeat slowed and amplified to a boom. Time lagged. Baba Kaleni leaned closer and Emmanuel could smell river mud and grass.

"Where are the two boys and the girl that you promised to give to your mother?" the preacher asked. "They are ghosts, still waiting to be born. You are also a ghost. You float in the land of the dead."

Emmanuel tried to speak but couldn't. Pressure built in his head and his ears rang just as they had when a concussion wave from an exploding shell had knocked him off his feet outside a French village during the war. He blinked. He was twelve years old again, sitting in the kitchen in Sophiatown: The wind rattled the corrugated iron walls and rain lashed the grimy windows. From outside, he heard the squeal of children splashing in the mud and footsteps running to the front door. Then came his mother, hurrying into the room humming a tune, with her silky hair tousled by the rain and a bag of groceries in her arms.

"You're early," Emmanuel said. She normally came home after dark, when candles lit up the windows and the bars opened their doors. "And you've been drinking."

"Three glasses of sherry isn't a crime, Emmanuel." She put the grocery bag on the kitchen table, sat down on a rickety chair and kicked off her shoes.

Emmanuel made her a cup of rooibos tea, black with three sugars. She smiled and stared at him over the lip of the cup. He looked to the door. His father would be home soon, seriously drunk and angry with the kaffirs, the coloureds, the Indians and the rich English bosses. He'd be angry most of all with this rain-washed woman, happy and beautiful in a shack with dirt floors and a leaking roof.

"Come here, Emmanuel." His mother grabbed his hand and pinned it to the kitchen table. "Let me read your fortune."

"I don't want you to." He already knew the future. A fight, broken cups and plates they could not afford to replace, a black eye for her and a cut lip for him.

"Keep still." She traced each individual line on his palm with the tip of her index finger and said, "You'll have three children: two strong boys and a girl with the heart of a lion. Your sons will favor you but the girl will be different, more like her mother. Life won't be easy but you'll have a home and a happy family."

Emmanuel tried to jerk his hand away but she hung on, tightening her grip. Her hair retained the scent of cooking spices and cigarettes and the peppermint candies kept in a jar at the front of the Cape Trader General Store, where she worked.

"Promise me, Emmanuel." She was deadly serious now. "Promise me you'll try to make this fortune come true."

"I promise," he'd said, and looked away from the fierceness of her love, the unspoken hope that one day he would leave the heaving slum of Sophiatown and build a life without violence or fear.

Three hard taps of Baba Kaleni's fingers against Emmanuel's chest brought him back to the wide reaches of the Kamberg Valley. He sucked in a mouthful of air, trying to break the preacher's spell.

"Listen, my son." The old man hadn't finished ripping out Emmanuel's internal wiring. "Pleasure is easy to find between the legs of a woman but happiness is built over time and with much effort, like a hut. The woman who shares this hut with you will help carry your burdens, and you, hers. Keep your body from strange beds and the night will reward you with stars bright enough to guide your way. In the name of the Father and the Son. Amen."

"Amen." Shabalala mumbled the word but kept his face turned to the horizon. Physical pleasure and strange beds were not matters he'd ever discuss with the detective sergeant.

"Stay well," Baba said, and moved away.

"*Hamba khale,* Baba," Shabalala called the traditional farewell. Emmanuel remained silent, wavering between shock and embarrassment at the revelation of private events.

"And you stay well, my son," Kaleni said, and trundled back to the True Israelites. A gospel hymn drifted across the grassed hillside and Emmanuel glanced at his partner, trying to assess the effect on him of Kaleni's words. Shabalala continued to study the drifting clouds with a blank expression. The preacher's message had disturbed the easy camaraderie they'd shared earlier.

"If you've got something to say, then say it." Emmanuel took off his jacket and tied the sleeves tight around his waist with angry movements.

"The old one means no harm, Sergeant," Shabalala said. "The spirits of the ancestors send messages through him and he must speak these out loud."

"Well, the spirits have no idea what they're talking about." He could count on one hand—no, less—the number of strange beds he'd crawled out of in the last year. There was Janice, the divorced hairdresser from London Styles Salon with the freckled nose and dimpled chin. And Lana Rose. Two women were hardly a tide of flesh.

Davida Ellis, the coloured girl he'd broken the law to have over twelve months ago, stayed alive only in his dreams. He'd met Davida in Jacob's Rest, the isolated rural hamlet where Shabalala and Dr. Daniel Zweigman had both once lived. His investigation into the murder of Captain Willem Pretorius exposed the Afrikaner policeman's secret double life and put Davida in danger. When she'd come to his room in the middle of the night, open, vulnerable and to find comfort, he forgot his professional obligation to protect the weak. He could still remember the way she tasted and the feeling of her legs wrapped around him. Sleeping with Davida was a mistake, an error in judgment. Yet he couldn't shake the notion that if the Security Branch had not dragged them from bed they might have stayed in each other's arms forever.

"If you say the spirits are wrong, then it is so." Shabalala motioned to the path. "Ready, Sergeant?"

"You lead. I'll keep up." Emmanuel vowed to keep up even if it meant coughing up a lung.

"To the river," Shabalala said, and hit the downward-sloping terrain at a sprint. Emmanuel followed him, crushing the red earth underfoot. The sun was hot on his shoulders, the breeze cool on his face. He pushed hard to a place of pure physical sensation. Five minutes more and the world would break down to sweat, breath and aching muscle. It would hurt, but in the temple of his body he was safe and strong.

Baba Kaleni's words echoed in Emmanuel's head. The promise he'd made to his mother was a wound that had scabbed over, healed and vanished. Yet with one thump on his chest the past had come roaring back as vivid as if it were right here, right now.

The grueling mountain climb brought his mind back to the case. Mandla's men would need to bend to the law or be broken. Together with Shabalala, he'd find Amahle's killer and bring him to justice. There was so much still undone in his life, but the job of detective he did well.

5

TWO MANGY BROWN dogs with fur hanging over their bones and an old man smoking a corncob pipe flanked the gateway to the Matebula family kraal. Behind the old man, a stick fence made of dried thorn branches surrounded a collection of thatched beehive-shaped huts.

At the sight of two city men sweating and panting on the threshold, the old man struggled to get to his feet.

"Sit," Emmanuel said. "Is Chief Matebula home?" The dogs raised their heads and growled but then went back to sleep in their sun patch.

"*Yebo, inkosi.*" Smoke escaped from the man's mouth when he spoke. "But the great one cannot be disturbed."

"He'll make an exception for us." Emmanuel stepped onto the dirt path leading to the interior. Ahead was the heart of the family kraal, a dusty cattle yard with a huge stinkwood tree at the center. The path split to either side of the enclosure.

"This way, Sergeant." Shabalala indicated the right-hand path. "The chief's hut is always at the back of the cattle byre."

They moved past squat beehive huts with grass mats rolled

down over entryways. A clutch of brown chickens scratched for food in the dirt and a swarm of flies settled on the rim of an uncovered cooking pot. The only human sound was that of voices whispering behind the hut walls. There was no sign of Mandla or his men. It was as if the whole kraal were holding its breath and waiting.

"Everyone's under house arrest," Emmanuel said quietly. "I wonder if the chief is afraid of a riot."

The crash of splintering wood and a male voice raging in Zulu came from the northeast corner of the compound. The dozing dogs awoke and barked at the sky.

Emmanuel and Shabalala passed a large hut with dried buffalo horns at the entrance and proceeded to a wide yard with an umdoni tree at its center. Nomusa crouched on a woven grass mat, her head bowed in supplication. A young girl huddled against Nomusa, her skinny arms circling the woman's waist. Items of clothing and a small cardboard box with the lid ripped off were flung across the wide yard.

As the detectives approached, a giant Zulu man snapped a tree branch across his knee and raised the limb high enough to cast a shadow over Nomusa and the shivering girl.

"Drop that," Emmanuel said in Zulu, and crossed the dirt circle in four paces, raising dust. The man turned, surprised. He was easily six-foot-three and had been handsome once but carried a ring of fat on his belly and under his chin. The onset of middle age had thinned his hair and evidence of too much good living could be seen in his bloated face and red-rimmed eyes.

"I am the great chief . . ." the man said, blood still running hot. "No one, not even a white man, tells me what to do in my own kraal."

"We're the police, which means we can," Emmanuel said. He disliked the chief on sight. "Now drop the stick."

Shabalala took up position at Nomusa's right shoulder, ready to deflect an attack. The chief threw the limb against the perimeter wall, rattling the thorn branches and startling a thrush into flight. Nomusa and the child remained hunched over in the face of Matebula's wrath.

"Have you found out who killed my child?" the chief demanded. "There is a debt owing for her life and it will be paid."

"Who do you think is to blame for your daughter's death?" Emmanuel stepped around Matebula's bulk and caught a whiff of sour maize beer and dagga smoke. He checked on Nomusa and the girl, who looked about eleven years old and wore the short beaded skirt of an unmarried female.

"The mother is to blame for Amahle." Matebula pointed at Nomusa. "She let my child roam across the valley and sent her to work in the house of the white farmer instead of keeping her in the kraal."

"I was thinking of a person who might actually have killed Amahle. A boyfriend or maybe an old enemy." Emmanuel reached out to lift Nomusa to her feet before he caught the quick movement of Shabalala's hand. A short, sharp wave that said, *Do not touch the woman, Sergeant.*

He dropped his arm.

"My daughter was good," Nomusa whispered. She kept her face turned away to hide a swollen eye and a cut on her left cheek. "Amahle had no boyfriends. No enemies."

"Lies." Chief Matebula grabbed the cardboard box and upended it. A toothbrush, a lipstick, some candy-pink nail polish and two lead pencils scattered across the mat. "Explain these things! Where did they come from when all your daughter's pay was meant to come to me, her father?"

"Shut up and sit down." Emmanuel had had enough of Matebula's big mouth. "There. Up against the fence."

"A chief does not sit on the floor." Matebula shouted an order in Zulu to someone hidden inside the largest hut and stood with his hands folded across his bare chest.

Emmanuel permitted him the small victory. There were more immediate concerns than the maintenance of Matebula's ego. He crouched at the edge of the mat and tried to make eye contact with Nomusa. She shut him out, looking up and beyond the fence line to the mountains wrapped in clouds. Traditional Zulu women, especially those married to an arrogant chief, did not speak to outsiders without their husband's permission.

"Sergeant." Shabalala nodded toward the narrow passage connecting the circular yard with the rest of the kraal. Another signal.

"Go," Emmanuel said. "Take Nomusa and the child to their hut and come back when they're settled."

"Just so." The Zulu detective picked up the vanity items scattered on the mat and repacked them in the cardboard box. Emmanuel wondered if these little luxuries had been given to or bought by Amahle or if she had stolen them from her employers at Little Flint Farm. Beyond her startling physical beauty, he knew nothing about her life or her personality. What unknown event might have placed her in harm's way?

"Let go, Mama." The girl broke free of Nomusa's hold and scooped up the four cotton dresses and a blue hand-knitted sweater from the grass mat where they'd been thrown. She clutched them tightly, a fierce little creature with wide brown eyes flecked with gold, black cornrowed hair and a smooth oval face that would one day match her murdered sister's beauty. A double-stranded necklace of blue and silver beads and a row of glass bracelets indicated her superior social status in a valley devoid of manufactured items.

"Come." Shabalala shepherded Nomusa and her daughter toward the passage. They crossed paths with a lushly proportioned female who came out of the great hut carrying a carved wooden stool and a rolled cowhide. The newcomer's ocher-stained hair was brushed high into a stiff crown and adorned with shells and porcupine quills.

"My fifth wife," Matebula said as the woman sidled barefoot across the dirt circle, her hips swaying widely enough to knock a child to the ground. Amahle's little sister clutched the dresses tighter and narrowed her eyes like a cat ready to unleash its claws. Nomusa cast the woman a cold glance. Matebula's wives were rivals, not friends.

"Great chief . . ." The fifth wife unrolled the black and white cowhide in the shade of the umdoni tree and placed the stool at the very center. A dried leaf fluttered onto the hide and she flicked it away.

"Tell me, policeman from the city . . ." The chief settled onto the stool, feet apart, chest thrust out like a pigeon. "How will you compensate for the loss of my daughter?"

"The police and the courts will exact a payment for the crime," Emmanuel said. "Whoever killed her will be found and punished."

Matebula grunted. "These courts are far away in Pietermaritzburg and Durban. They cannot know the depth of my loss."

The chief's words did not contain a shred of genuine emotion. He was talking about money. A beautiful daughter of marriageable age had been killed before lobola, a bride-price, could be paid.

The fifth wife cooed in agreement from where she'd sunk down on her knees at the chief's feet. She simmered for her husband. She was still young enough to enjoy her favored status and did not yet understand that another nubile girl would, in time, replace her. Matebula clamped a hand on his knee and massaged the flesh under his palm.

"How much was Amahle worth?" Emmanuel asked, curious to gauge the depth of Matebula's callousness.

"Chief Mashanini from Umkomazi offered twenty cows. Not ordinary ones. A fat herd with long horns and speckled skins."

"Did you accept his offer?"

"Of course, yes. Amahle was getting old and the price for her was fair." The chief pursed his lips. "Now I will get nothing." His wife made a sympathetic sound and shook her head.

The mixture of self-pity and greed fascinated Emmanuel. Matebula's world ended at his fingertips.

"Amahle was happy to marry and move to Umkomazi?" he asked. Not far from this kraal missionaries taught girls to read and write and do sums, preparing their souls for heaven and their minds for life in the twentieth century. Marriage was no longer the only option for a Zulu girl.

"Happy?" Matebula grappled with the word, trying to find its relevance. "She was satisfied to do her duty to me."

Maybe, Emmanuel thought. Marrying to escape was common in every racial group: indeed, he'd often suspected his own ex-wife Angela had chosen him as the quickest way to break free of her overbearing father and her defeated mother.

Life as a detective's wife was not the peaceful refuge Angela was looking for. They divorced when it became clear to them both that their marriage was a way station, not a sanctuary. Amahle might have decided that life under the chief's rule was worth ditching.

Shabalala returned, silently stepping up to Emmanuel's left.

"Your daughter had no admirers? No one she fought with?" Emmanuel asked.

The chief heaved a sigh, bored by the question. "Amahle spent much time with the white people on their farm but here at the kraal she was modest and silent," he said.

The fifth wife leaned back, her shoulder almost touching Matebula's thigh, and whispered softly in Zulu.

"There was one such man." The chief followed his wife's prompt. "Philani Dlamini. He is a garden boy at the farm where my daughter worked. He told many people that he was betrothed to Amahle."

"Was he?" Emmanuel wrote the name on a blank page. The first and only suspect in the investigation so far.

"Never." The word was dismissive. "This man has a herd of five cows and he is not a chief."

"Where does Philani live?" Emmanuel asked.

Another urgent whisper came from the fifth wife, who kept her eyes cast down to the cowhide, the model of a good Zulu wife.

"Near the farm of the Afrikaner." The chief pointed over the thorn fence to a mountain flecked with orange aloe blooms. Shabalala marked the direction and the travel distance at a glance. "But Dlamini is not there. His mother has not seen him for two days."

"How do you know that?" Emmanuel asked.

A small bump of the shoulder against the chief's thigh acted as a warning from the fifth wife to take care. Matebula shrugged and kept quiet.

"Where is Mandla?" Emmanuel asked. "We'd like to speak with him and his impi."

Matebula sat up higher on the stool. "My son does not have an impi. Everything in this kraal belongs to me."

"Excuse us, great chief." Shabalala stepped forward with his shoulders dipped to decrease his size and presence. "We wish only to warn your son and your men that searching for Amahle's killer is a job for the police and the police only."

"Why should my impi withdraw when the police stay in the town and never set foot on this land?" Matebula asked.

"Because," Emmanuel said, "if the impi continue to threaten witnesses, the chief of police will send more policemen to this valley, enough to trample the cornfields and outnumber the rocks."

"The truth is spoken," Shabalala said to emphasize the point. Black-against-black violence rarely caught the eye of the authorities but if the trouble spilled over to white-owned farms, Matebula could expect his world, and his authority, to come under threat.

"I will talk to my men when they return," Matebula said grudgingly.

After you've rolled your fifth wife, had a nap and smoked another marijuana cigarette, thought Emmanuel. It was time to move on with the information they had obtained. He pocketed his notebook, happy for the one name in it.

"Stay well, great chief," Shabalala said, taking up the burden of good manners when Emmanuel turned to leave. A flock of tiny red birds flew overhead and settled in the branches of the umdoni tree above the chief. The crimson flash caught Emmanuel's eye and he glanced back over his shoulder.

The fifth wife remained nestled close to the chief's thigh, but her gaze was no longer on the dried cowhide but on the two detectives leaving the yard. She looked away but not fast enough to hide the calculating expression on her striking face. Not so naïve, then, and probably brighter than her husband by fifty watts. Yet Matebula would go to his grave believing that she was soft and yielding and born to please.

As they walked through the kraal Emmanuel asked Shabalala, "What do you think of the great chief?"

"Unworthy of the title."

"Can he rein Mandla in?"

"No chance."

"Thought not." Emmanuel paused outside a hut and noticed Nomusa and her daughter seated in its front yard. They were hunched over a bowl of brown lentils, picking stones and other impurities from the dried food with their fingers.

Nomusa lifted her head like an impala testing the air for the scent of a predator and saw Emmanuel and Shabalala standing at the boundary of her home.

"Go," she said to them and shuffled her child back into the hut. "Please, go from this place."

Emmanuel moved to a small break in the stick fence. He wasn't happy leaving Nomusa here, battered and grieving. A palm touched his shoulder.

"Sergeant," Shabalala said. "You must not walk past the fence. Things will go worse for the chief's wife if you do. This is not her family kraal. It belongs to her husband and his clan."

Shabalala was right. Long after Amahle's murder was written up in a case file and handed to a judge in robes and a wig, Nomusa would still be here, living in the shadow of the great chief.

Emmanuel turned and walked away. He remembered his own mother, injured and hiding in the dark. He cut off the memory. He hadn't been able to save her, either.

—

Five minutes out from the Matebula kraal, with Shabalala scouting the way across a rocky field covered in mountain aloes, Emmanuel sensed they were being followed. A small shape darted from boulder to boulder and slipped behind clumps of sagebrush in an attempt to stay undetected.

"It is the little sister," Shabalala said without turning around. "She has been with us since we left the chief's kraal."

"Let's sit down and rest for a minute," Emmanuel said. "Give her a chance to catch up and talk."

Even with Shabalala as the only witness, Nomusa had added nothing to what she'd said in the yard of Matebula's hut. Amahle was a good girl. She was loved. She had no boyfriends and no enemies. The cardboard box with the lipstick had come as a surprise to her mother.

Shabalala stopped at a grass area between two large boulders. They sat down and waited. A breeze lifted the scent of wet rocks from the valley floor. Emmanuel took off his hat and set it down, letting the air cool him.

Stones skittered down the rock behind the detectives and a girl's voice said, "Do not go to the Dlamini kraal. Philani is not there."

Emmanuel turned slowly and saw Amahle's little sister crouched in the rocky field like a sprite.

"What is your name?" he asked.

She shook her head, refusing the information: smart move for a child.

"How do you know the gardener is not home?" he asked.

"His mother came to the chief yesterday morning and said her son did not come home from work at Little Flint Farm on Friday night. He is missing."

Shabalala picked up a stone from the grass and examined it closely. "Could it be that Philani's mother is not telling the truth to protect her son?"

"My brother and the impi went to the mother's kraal." The girl twisted her glass bracelets one way and then the other around her wrist: a nervous habit. "They did not find Philani even after breaking the hut apart and scattering the goats and chickens."

"Amahle knew Philani Dlamini?" Emmanuel nudged the conversation back to the dead girl. That Mandla was a major problem for the investigation he already knew.

"They worked for Baas Reed at Little Flint Farm. Philani tended the garden and Amahle tended the white women in the big house."

Shabalala smiled encouragement. "Philani and Amahle were friends."

The little sister stopped twisting the bracelets and said, "Philani followed her up the mountains and down again and she did not chase him away."

Walking together over mountains was love in a child's mind. Emmanuel thought she might be right. He took his notebook and pen from his jacket and scribbled the word *flowers* next to Philani's name. Ordinary Zulus did not bring flowers to the dead but a Zulu man employed by white farmers as a gardener might have adopted the European habit.

"Tell me about this chief from Umkomazi," Shabalala said. Emmanuel had filled him in on the bride-price and the chief's bitter disappointment. "He is rich and handsome, I'm sure."

"He is fat and slow and smells of cow dung," she said flatly. "The great chief agreed to the marriage because he is greedy and not fit to work in the gold mines in Jo'burg. Amahle had no love for him."

"Huh . . ." Shabalala was impressed by the blunt assessment. At around eleven years old she could already tell the chaff from the wheat and silver from tin. His own wife, too, told things as she saw them. "Perhaps there was another for whom Amahle had love but that she kept hidden from the chief and from your mother?"

The girl looked away and began to spin the bracelets around her slim wrist, faster and faster. Emmanuel took his cue from Shabalala and focused on the stones peppering the field. They might each have been sitting alone in the grass and listening to the chirp of crickets.

"There was one other," the girl said. "A man with a strange name."

"Mmm . . ." Shabalala breathed out, keeping the conversation going without asking a direct question.

"Mr. Insurance Policy," the little sister said in English.

Black Africans adopted names from a rich array of sources. Emmanuel knew a juvenile delinquent called Justice, a housemaid named Radio and a shoeshine boy with the evocative moniker Midnight Express Train. Every name was linked to a real story, an actual event that had shaped their lives. Where had an Insurance Policy sprung from in an isolated valley connected by a network of dirt paths? This bastion of shimmering cliffs and meandering rivers was surely one of the few places on earth that traveling insurance salesmen had not penetrated.

"Did you ever meet this Mr. Insurance Policy?" he asked.

"No." The girl shook her head. "Amahle mentioned him one time. Never again."

"Was it in the winter or now in the springtime that she spoke of him?" Emmanuel asked. In the country, the seasons told the time. At the turn of each season, the men working in the gold mines of Jo'burg returned home to plow the fields or hand out modern marvels like aluminium cooking pots, lengths of brightly printed cotton and cash.

"It was on the day the Afrikaner farmer burned the edges of the field by the river. I remember that my sister came home after dark and our mother was angry with her."

Farmers lit firebreaks in winter. The memory of stinging smoke and black ash embedded in his skin and hair for weeks was still vivid in Emmanuel's mind. Tilling the fields and harvesting crops for six years alongside his adopted father had destroyed any romantic notion he might ever have had of living off the land.

"I understand," Shabalala said. "Your sister was with this Mr. Insurance Policy and paid no attention to the sun going down. That is why she came home late."

"No, inkosi." The girl's lips pursed to a perfect rosebud.

"Amahle was left behind in the town by accident and it took many hours to find and return her to the kraal. It was on that night when she couldn't fall asleep that she whispered his name and said, 'He is the one that I have waited for . . .'"

Emmanuel leaned a fraction closer to the girl and initiated eye contact. "Tell me everything that Amahle said about this man, little sister."

"Amahle did not speak of men often. She said they were like stepping-stones to be skipped over lightly until you reached the other side."

It was a deeply cynical point of view for a teenage girl, and one that might have led to her early death. Emmanuel knew that some men viewed being "skipped over" by a young beauty as a motive for murder.

"Did your sister say what waited for her on the other side of the river?" Shabalala asked.

"Life," the girl said.

Twigs snapped and stones rolled loose from the approach path as a calf stopped to nibble grass. The sound startled the girl, who was up and flying across the field before the word "wait" left Emmanuel's mouth. He stood and watched her weave between the orange mountain aloes like a little springbok, the outline of her body soon absorbed into the landscape. Fleet as she was, she'd never be able to outrun the future. In three or four years she'd likely be married off in exchange for a herd of long-horned cattle.

"I can catch her, but . . ." Shabalala cleared his throat, uncomfortable with having to explain his lack of action.

"Let her be." Emmanuel adjusted the rim of his hat. "She risked a lot by leaving the kraal without her parents' permission. I don't want her punished for helping us."

He did not want her punished, either, for having the heart of a lion—just like the girl his mother had requested.

—

They swung by the Dlamini kraal and found a ransacked hut and two white-haired goats nibbling corn spilled from a broken clay jar. Chickens roamed the yard and a skinny cat dozed in the afternoon sun. Philani Dlamini and his mother were long gone.

Emmanuel reread his notes out loud. "The mother told Chief Matebula that Philani didn't come home from work on Friday. That's the same night Amahle went missing. It can't be a coincidence."

"We must find the gardener before Mandla and the impi," Shabalala said. "They think this man is guilty of murder and they will punish him."

"What if he pays a fine of twenty cows?"

"It is too late for an exchange of cattle, Sergeant," Shabalala said. "Only blood washes blood."

"Great," Emmanuel muttered. Was there one country, just one on earth, that did not demand blood for blood? Before striking out for the path leading down to the river he paused to study the terrain. A deep valley cut through a string of towering mountains covered in alpine grass and native forest. The sky stretched in endless blue over Mandla's vast backyard.

Two detectives looking for one gardener in all that landscape and they were getting tired. Emmanuel hoped Philani was getting tired, too.

6

EMMANUEL DRESSED AT dawn in a shaft of pale yellow light. Clouds the color of India ink broke the crests of the far mountains. Birds sang from the branches of the jacaranda trees in the hotel garden, too late to wake him.

He left his jacket hanging in the stained pine wardrobe with mothballs piled in the corners and took the stairs to a side exit. A night watchman in a long overcoat and gum boots shone his torch across the garden and the patio. Emmanuel slowed and let the beam find him. He raised his hand in greeting and got a "Morning, ma' baas" from the watchman.

He thought of Shabalala, billeted for the night and for the remainder of the investigation five kilometers north of town in the black location. He had probably already left the back room of the cement-block dwelling with one window and an outdoor toilet and would be making his way to Roselet. By black location standards the local shop owner's house where Shabalala was staying was deluxe, but it was many rungs below Roselet's "Europeans Only" guesthouse and eight-room faux-Tudor hotel.

Shabalala did not complain. He thanked Emmanuel for the lift when dropped off at the house late yesterday afternoon and declined a pickup for this morning. How many words and thoughts were sealed in the Zulu policeman's mouth because all that was required in the presence of a majority of whites was a "Yes, ma' baas," "No, ma' baas" and a "Thank you, ma' baas"?

A gravel path cut through the formal garden to the rear of the hotel and led on to a smaller pathway signposted SCENIC WAY. This curled around the outer edges of town and ended at the mouth of Greyling Street. "For guests who enjoy a brisk walk after breakfast or before lunch," the rotund receptionist had explained over a map of the hotel grounds and an exhaustive list of "things to do while in Roselet." Investigating the murder of a Zulu girl was not one of the recommended activities.

The Reed family were not home when he and Shabalala had called by Little Flint Farm late the day before. The essential facts of the investigation—time of death, last known sighting of the victim alive, suspects and motive—were still unconfirmed. But other worries, less obvious than the puzzle of the murder, had awakened him in the pitch-black of his hotel room.

Clumps of sugarbush protea on either side of the path glittered with dew and the air was chilly. Goose bumps prickled Emmanuel's skin and the knot of heat at the center of his chest slowly dissipated. It felt good to be cold; to wake from the tangle of images that surfaced only briefly and then disappeared into a void without knitting together into a fluid dream.

Eight years out of his infantry uniform and he'd learned, in an incomplete way, to defeat the dead that visited him in his dreams. Wake up, switch on the light, breathe deep and name the place where your body lay wrapped in a patchwork quilt: Roselet. At the foot of the Drakensberg Mountains. South Africa.

Last night was different. No firestorms or missiles or swollen rivers washing the dead out to sea broke his sleep. Instead, he remembered Sophiatown. The family shack with the corrugated iron roof held down by stones. His sister, Olivia, playing in the dirt street with Indira, the Indian shopkeeper's daughter, the smoke from winter fires blanketing the sky above them. And his parents, sitting in the doorway of their crumbling home laughing at a joke he'd not heard. They were relaxed and beautiful, even in the dusty township light.

Emmanuel walked on. He had unwittingly unlocked a forgotten memory of his mother and father happy and in love.

The heat in his chest was in the exact spot where Baba Kaleni had laid his hands. The old man had smashed a hole in him and now ghosts and secrets were climbing out from the inside. The past bled into the present. He remembered his difficult adolescence. For six months after a staunch, God-loving Afrikaner family had adopted him and his sister he'd tried to be good. No fighting with the boys who called him unclean and his dead mother a whore, no talking back to the brutal teachers at the Fountain of Light Boarding School, no questioning the superiority of whites over blacks despite knowing English and Afrikaners who were thicker than mud.

It was exhausting work. After six months cracks began to appear. By then he'd learned to exact revenge in cunning and insidious ways.

Not now. Emmanuel stopped the past from breaching the

walls punched in by Baba Kaleni. The damage was done, the cuts and bruises healed. All that mattered was now.

The stars dimmed and a few hundred yards ahead the outline of houses became more distinct. Emmanuel skirted the edges of Roselet. Wide gardens and wood fences enclosed pretty cottages and a silver stream marked the border between the town and the countryside. He recognized the thatched roof and whitewashed walls of Dr. Daglish's home.

He walked past two more lots and the clustered buildings of the police station appeared. Yellow light shone from the yard.

Curious about the source of the glow, Emmanuel jumped the water. He moved along the back wall of the station house, careful of twigs and loose stones, and edged around the corner.

Constable Bagley sat on the rear steps of the station commander's house, smoking a cigarette by the light of a paraffin lantern. He huddled against the cold, red hair spiked out at odd angles, the chilled mist of his breath mingling with exhaled tobacco smoke. If he'd slept at all the night before, it didn't show. Spent butts littered the ground.

A smudge of movement at the back window caught Emmanuel's attention. He squinted and made out the figure of a woman in a white nightdress standing behind the glass. Bagley had no idea she was there, watching his nocturnal struggles tip over into day.

Emmanuel heard a footstep and turned to check the field sloping down to the stream. Shabangu, the older of the two Roselet native policemen, hesitated on the path to the station, also caught by surprise. He quickly stepped aside to give the visiting city detective right-of-way, then remained perfectly still, face turned away, eyes to the ground. Questioning the actions of a white man caught spying at dawn was unwise. Playing the silent and obedient native was the safest option.

Emmanuel slipped past the Zulu policeman and continued in the direction of Greyling Street. He hit the top of the main street and followed the line of unlit shops and country cottages. The next twenty-four hours were critical to the investigation. He and Shabalala had to generate a list of suspects before the trail went cold.

Empty parking lot, empty yard and empty station. The rustle of the giant sycamore tree provided the only movement at the Roselet police command.

"So much for 'Anything we can do to help,'" Emmanuel said, looking around the unmanned station. The room was unchanged from yesterday afternoon but for the position of the telephone on the station commander's desk. At some point Bagley had made or received a phone call.

"There could have been an emergency, Sergeant." Shabalala stopped to examine a map of the world hanging from a nail in the wall. The pink stain of the British Empire spread over several continents.

"What kind of incident takes three grown men to bring it under control, Detective? A multiple cow theft or a cat stuck up a jacaranda tree?"

"Maybe it is both," Shabalala said, deadpan, and Emmanuel smiled.

He walked to the window and contemplated the wide grasslands and the steep mountain peaks.

"It's odd, don't you think . . . a station commander stepping back from a murder in his own district? We're not the Security Branch. We didn't demand control over the investigation."

"Strange, yes." Shabalala circled around to the window and gazed out. "Maybe the commander does not care about the death of a Zulu girl."

"A murder is a murder. Solving a homicide is the closest we come to being heroes. You'd have to be lazy or stupid to give up the chance."

"Then we are alone," Shabalala said.

"As always." Emmanuel checked his watch. Eight-fifteen. "We'll let the doctor know her substitute is on the way and then head back out to the Reeds' farm."

"Just so, Sergeant."

With hat brims tilted low to block out the sun, they stepped out into the dirt yard. Bagley's daughters peered through the back window, their noses flattened to the glass as they studied Emmanuel and Shabalala. The older girl rapped her knuckles against the wood frame, demanding attention. Shabalala lifted his hat in greeting. The girls squealed with delight and the hand of an unseen person yanked them away from the window.

"Dr. Daglish?" Emmanuel knocked on the front door of the cottage a third time, harder, and got no response. "It's the police. Open up."

Shabalala peered through the window and into the front room. The curtains were open to let in daylight and a small reading lamp shone on the mantel. A paperback novel lay facedown on an oak side table.

"Someone is home," the Zulu detective said. "But there is no movement inside."

"Around the back. The doc might have skipped town and the lights are just a bluff." Emmanuel skirted the hydrangea bushes and walked quickly. He shouldn't have let the doctor off so easily yesterday afternoon. With a little more pushing Daglish might have agreed to conduct the examination right away. Now she could be anywhere in the province of Natal.

They took the path to the rear of the house and to the root cellar where Amahle's body lay on a retired examination bed. The door to the basement room was ajar, held open by an old typewriter with rusted keys. The clinical scrape of surgical steel broke through the music of birds and insects hidden in the dense garden foliage.

"Doctor . . ." Conducting an impromptu autopsy on a body she was too scared to examine twenty-four hours ago was beyond the realm of the possible. "Doctor?"

"One minute, Detective Cooper." Daglish soon appeared in the cellar doorway, her dark hair held in a fine net. She was gloved and gowned and ready for surgery. "This cellar is like a bomb shelter and sound bounces right off the walls. I didn't hear you coming."

"What are you doing?" Emmanuel asked.

"Assisting the police surgeon," Daglish said. "A car dropped him off at the front fifteen minutes ago. I didn't expect him to get here so fast."

"Neither did I." Roselet was four hours' drive from Durban, putting the doctor's departure at around four o'clock that morning. "Constable Shabalala and I will say our hellos and head out to the valley."

"Come in." Daglish retreated into the root cellar, pulling

off her gloves. The wrist bandage was gone. A bruise darkened her skin but otherwise it seemed she'd staged a remarkable overnight recovery.

Emmanuel and Shabalala ducked under the low eaves. The air in the dugout room was chilly, the gloom lifted by the glow of two naked bulbs dangling from the ceiling. Glass jars of yellow and pink fruit added a block of color to the bare walls.

"Jesus Christ." Emmanuel was caught by surprise. "You."

A man, on first impression a mix of mad wizard and wise professor, pressed inquisitive fingers into the back of Amahle's skull, seeking out what secrets lay below the skin. Gold-rimmed glasses resting on the tip of his nose defied the laws of gravity.

"You're thinking of another Jew, crucified two thousand years ago by the Romans," Dr. Daniel Zweigman replied. "As you can see, I am alive and well."

"Colonel van Niekerk said . . ." Emmanuel didn't bother with the rest of the sentence. He should have known better than to believe the crafty Dutchman's promise to find another doctor. It had been given all too easily. The colonel wanted the old Jew on the case and the colonel always got what he wanted.

"Yebo, sawubona." Shabalala greeted the German physician with a fingertip touched to the brim of his hat and a smile. Amahle was in the best hands. In a private moment, when the room was empty, he'd tell the girl to let this good and kind man uncover things that she kept hidden from others.

"Shabalala." Zweigman thumbed the glasses higher onto the bridge of his nose. "Your wife sends her best. My wife also."

The lack of a personal greeting from the wives to him didn't worry Emmanuel. He was the unpredictable single man who dragged their husbands from their safe, domestic worlds into the embrace of a violent and often dangerous one. While Lilliana and Lizzie liked him personally, he knew it would be just fine with them if they never heard from him again.

"Did van Niekerk strong-arm you?" Emmanuel asked. He didn't want his friends to be pressed into service as part of the Dutch policeman's private militia.

"Colonel van Niekerk is too cultivated to issue threats," Zweigman said. "He bribed me."

"The colonel doesn't have anything you want," Emmanuel pointed out. After spending three years in the Buchenwald concentration camp, Zweigman cared nothing for money, social status or appearance.

"True, but Lilliana wishes to start another tailoring business, like the one she ran in Jacob's Rest. The colonel placed an advance order for ten dresses for his bride, to be made when they return from honeymoon. Money to be put aside for Dimitri's schooling."

Dimitri, a white-blond Russian baby boy, was born at the Zweigmans' medical clinic during a counterintelligence operation gone wrong. His father had been an ailing Russian general captured by the South African secret police, and his mother, Natalya, was a young, beautiful actress. Two weeks after giving birth, Natalya discarded Dimitri. A child would slow her down in her quest to find a new man, drink champagne and see the rest of the world beyond Moscow. The Zweigmans believed Dimitri's abandonment at the clinic was an act of God. Their own three children had been killed in the German death camps and the orphaned Russian boy gave them a miraculous opportunity to love like that again. Dimitri was now their adopted son. For those with the patience of stone, the German couple had a list of the baby's outstanding qualities memorized and ready to be repeated ad nauseam.

"How did van Niekerk know Lilliana's plans?" Emmanuel asked.

"The usual way. Via a direct line to the devil," Zweigman replied drily. "It hardly matters, Detective Cooper. My wife is happy and I am here. With Dr. Daglish's help the postmortem examination to determine time and cause of death will be complete by lunch."

"Anything interesting so far?" Emmanuel asked. The puncture wound on Amahle's back and the small amount of blood at the crime scene made determining the murder weapon difficult.

"The injury to the girl's spinal cord is highly unusual. I've never seen one like it before." Zweigman bent close to Amahle, who was propped on her side and covered by a white sheet, like a child sleeping through a hot night. He touched the base of her skull tenderly. "There's also a red-purple color stretching from the wound all the way up to her hairline. Fascinating."

"Yes, indeed." Daglish joined Zweigman and they examined the affected skin with the same intensity that Emmanuel imagined lit the faces of stamp collectors and pornography enthusiasts when they encountered something new and rare.

"A few more hours," Zweigman said, still puzzling over the mystery presented by the wound, "and we'll have some answers and some educated guesses for you, Detective."

"What next, Dr. Zweigman?" Margaret Daglish's right hand hovered above a line of steel instruments arranged on a fresh bath towel that had been draped over a sideboard.

"Cotton wool and the small scalpel, please. Let's see what's causing this skin discoloration." Zweigman glanced up from the examination bed and appeared surprised to find Emmanuel and Shabalala still in the room.

"We will see you both at noon," he said, and resumed probing the flesh at the base of Amahle's neck, his attention wholly absorbed in the task, a strange and subtle joy lighting his face. Emmanuel imagined that running a medical clinic in the Valley of a Thousand Hills was tiring, the days filled with whooping cough, smallpox vaccinations and broken limbs. Every operation was vital to the health of the isolated rural community and few of them challenged a man of Zweigman's intellectual caliber.

"We'll be at Little Flint Farm, if anything comes up. You have the telephone number, Dr. Daglish?"

"Yes, of course. I'll call when the examination is done."

Emmanuel moved to the cellar door and hesitated, remembering something.

"Does anyone in town sell insurance, Dr. Daglish?"

She looked up and frowned. "Not as a permanent job. A salesman from Sun Life drops in once a year. Usually in early January. We pay our premiums every month at the post office. Why?"

"Just curious." Emmanuel left the root cellar before the sheet could be peeled back to reveal Amahle lying naked and vulnerable under the harsh electric light. He and Shabalala walked to the car. Neither of them wanted to imagine the scalpel blade slicing into the dead girl's skin, exposing the secrets hidden in her blood and muscle.

"The little sister said the Afrikaner farmer was burning his field on the day Amahle met Mr. Insurance Policy." Emmanuel dug out the car keys. "It can't have been the real insurance salesman if he only comes to town once a year, in January."

"Summertime." Shabalala spoke across the hood. "When the fields are planted and there is no burning."

"Exactly." Emmanuel opened the door, slid behind the wheel and cranked the engine. "Ask around about a Mr. Insurance Policy when we get to Little Flint Farm but don't spend a lot of time on it. This mystery man might have no connection to the murder. What we really need is a list of Amahle's friends and enemies and the name of the last person to see her alive. Any ideas on where the gardener Philani might have disappeared to would also help."

That was the job. Ask questions, cross-check the information and follow the leads till they led you somewhere or disappeared into the sand. Conducting a criminal investigation provided calm, purpose and direction for dealing with the chaos in the aftermath of a murder.

Without the law and the promise of justice for the victims, Zweigman was just a charnel-house sawbones and he and Shabalala mere undertakers.

7

EMMANUEL PULLED INTO the driveway of a beautiful sandstone building with a wraparound porch dotted with wicker lounge chairs. He cut the engine and looked over the rural scene through the dusty windscreen. Rows of bright yellow roses in the formal garden and the circular drive made of white river stone clearly stated, *Servants, police and Jewish tinkers enter via the rear door.*

A middle-aged Zulu maid in a green housecoat and blue sandshoes worn without socks rushed from the front door to the top of the stairs. She glanced at the car, then back over her shoulder, like an anxious actor who'd stumbled onto the stage before the other players were ready to take their places.

"Quick work," Shabalala said. "She could not have come from the kitchen or the back of the house."

Emmanuel pocketed the keys. "She must be the maid in charge of greeting visitors before their car doors are open."

They got out of the Chevrolet and a scruffy dog of undetermined breed bypassed the maid and trotted toward them. It was rheumy-eyed and broad as a tailor's table, and there was no bark and little bite left in the old hound.

"This one is not so bad." Shabalala scratched the mutt behind the ears with rough fingers, instantly disproving the old belief that all black Africans were afraid of dogs. Although fear of German shepherds specially trained to attack native men on sight seemed perfectly reasonable to Emmanuel.

They crunched across river stones and stopped at the bottom step. The distant lowing of cattle and the shouts of workmen came from the rear of the property.

"Good morning." Emmanuel nodded at the maid. "We are here to speak with the Reed family. Are they home?"

The maid waved a hand to a circle of wicker chairs on the porch. "Please come and sit. I will fetch the baas for you."

"It would be better if we talked to all the Reeds, not just the one," Emmanuel said, and made the shaded porch in four steps. "Is the madam inside?"

"The big madam is resting. The little madam is swimming." The maid attempted a smile, gave up and pointed to the outdoor lounge chairs again. "Please sit and I will get the baas for you."

"Fine. We'll wait here." Emmanuel crossed the polished hardwood floor and sank into a chair with three fat cushions. The maid had a set of instructions to follow and she would not stray from the script. Shabalala gained the top step with the panting dog at his heel. The maid twisted agile fingers together, flummoxed by the sight of a Zulu dressed in a big baas suit. Workers returning home from the underground mines of Johannesburg insisted that there were black men such as this in the city but she'd never seen one before.

"Umm . . ." Her glance flickered to the lounge chairs, off-limits to natives. Next came a check of the front entry, also off-limits. The stairs, too, had to be kept free of loafing gardeners and lazy delivery boys.

"Go, please." Shabalala put the maid out of her misery and leaned against the porch railing, relaxed and easy. "I must wait here with my baas, Sergeant Cooper."

That power arrangement the maid understood: one person to give orders and another to follow them to the letter. She retreated into the house and the slap of running feet echoed in the interior. A rear door opened and then shut. Emmanuel stood up.

"I don't like being corralled," he said, and began circling the porch to the back of the farmhouse. "Let's look around for ourselves."

"But the woman said—"

"Don't worry." Emmanuel understood Shabalala's anxiety. If Reed's orders were ignored the maid would be the one in trouble. Life was difficult enough for housemaids and garden boys without the police adding extra weight to their shoulders. "I'll make sure the boss knows she did her job and I'm the one to blame. All right?"

Shabalala gave a self-conscious nod and they continued along the wide stone and hardwood porch. Formal gardens flanked the house, planted with rows of white roses, pink madonna lilies and flowering lavender bushes. Untamed bushes and wild grass pressed against the perimeter fence.

"Not bad," Emmanuel said when the Reeds' panoramic landholding came into full view. Green fields sloped to the shores of a silver lake, and beyond that a sandstone escarpment shimmered gold and red in the morning light. A lone swimmer, the little madam, moved through the water with languid overarm strokes. The rear porch was a perfect place to stand with a drink in hand and wonder what the poor people were doing.

"This man Reed is a white chief," Shabalala said.

"Definitely." Emmanuel walked down the rear stairs to a kitchen garden planted with rows of lettuce, tomato and spinach. "Let's hope he's more helpful than Matebula was."

Two garden boys in blue overalls and tatty cotton hats pulled weeds from between the crops and talked in low voices. The crunch of footsteps disturbed them and they glanced up. Seeing the two government men, they resumed work with extra vigor.

"I'll take English, you take Zulu," Emmanuel said quietly to Shabalala before peering over the hip-high fence enclosing the garden. He addressed the elder of the "boys," a dark-skinned man with a fractured cheekbone that gave his face a jagged, uneven appearance. "Where is Mr. Reed?"

"There, ma' baas." The gardener straightened up and indicated a narrow lane leading to a far-off cattle yard shrouded in dust. The housemaid was almost there, running at a steady pace. "At the dipping station."

Emmanuel touched a finger to his hat in thanks and took the concrete path. An almost physical quiet settled over the gardeners and he slowed till Shabalala and the old dog caught up. "Hear that?" he said.

"*Yebo.* They know we are here about Amahle and they are holding their breath."

"The way superstitious people do when a funeral hearse passes by or they see a cripple in a wheelchair." Emmanuel glanced over his shoulder. Sure enough, the "boys" had stopped weeding and stood immobile amid the turned rows of earth, like statues sculpted especially for African gardens.

"I will come back and try to find out why they are so scared," Shabalala said.

The path turned to gravel and then to dirt halfway to the cattle yards. Beyond the yards was the dipping station. A line of black farmworkers clustered along the side of a deep trench filled with chemical wash. The cattle were prodded with sticks through the sluice gates and into the bath till they emerged on the other side, dripping and immune from tick fever.

"That will be the Reeds," Emmanuel said. "Looks like father and son."

Two white men sheltered under the branches of a monkey apple tree, counting the dipped cattle before entering the numbers into individual notebooks. The younger Reed looked up when the maid arrived with her news. He cocked his head to the left, listening, and then dismissed the servant with a flick of his finger. She wheeled full circle and hit the homeward path. Both Reed men followed.

"Back to the house," Emmanuel said. "The dipping station isn't the right place to conduct an interview."

Sharp whistles and shouts reverberated across the yards and reached all the way to the servants' quarters and the back veranda. The noise and dust were good reasons for having the meeting on the porch. Maybe the Reeds were not trying to corral the police after all. Emmanuel tried to be more generous; rich and landed did not necessarily mean arrogant and controlling.

"You're the detectives from Durban," the younger Reed said when he and his father rounded the corner and found Emmanuel and Shabalala standing on the front porch.

"Detective Sergeant Cooper and Detective Constable Shabalala from West Street CID," Emmanuel said, wondering how the young farmer guessed they were from Durban and not from Pietermaritzburg, the closest major town to the Drakensberg foothills.

"I'm Thomas Reed and this is my father, Ian Reed."

A quick glance confirmed that father and son were real farmers, with dust on their skin and dirt under their fingernails. With an enormous piece of fertile land underfoot and a sprawling house high on a hill, the Reed men were highly enough placed in the world to not give a damn about appearances.

"Welcome. Welcome." Reed senior squeezed his fingers around Emmanuel's outstretched hand, a half smile playing on his lips. He was in his early seventies, with bushy gray brows and a vague expression in his hazel eyes, as if he'd forgotten some important fact and was trying to retrieve it.

"You've met Tubby, my eldest." Ian Reed held on to Emmanuel's hand. "He drives the car now. I sit in the back."

"Nobody calls me Tubby anymore, Dad. It's Thomas." Young Reed touched his father on the shoulder. "Go sit down and add up the numbers on your list before we dip the next batch of cattle. There's still a lot of work to be done."

"Of course, yes." Ian Reed released his death grip on Emmanuel's fingers and squinted down at the grubby notebook in his hand. Scribbled numbers, some half formed, bled off the sides of the paper. "Sunup to sundown, a farmer's work is never done."

"That's right, Dad. Sit over there and finish your calculations." Thomas physically turned the old man around and pointed to a wicker chair facing the driveway. "I'll come just now, okay?"

Ian Reed wandered off, gripping the notebook like a life preserver keeping him afloat in a vast and boundless ocean.

"Five minutes," Reed said. "We have work to do."

Thomas Reed was dressed in khaki but the smooth English accent and the dismissive manner were sure markers of a South African king of the veldt. Under the dust and sweat Emmanuel smelled a posh public school education and elevated social connections.

"Just a few questions," he said. "How long did Amahle Matebula work for your family?"

Thomas shrugged. "Hard to say. She was in and around the farm from the time she was a kid."

"There were no problems with her that you know of?" Emmanuel fished out his notebook, eager to fill in the half-empty pages. "No fights or bad blood between her and the other staff, for example?"

Thomas motioned to the vast acres merging with the gentle hills. "We don't have a lot of trouble on Little Flint, Detective. Our boys get a new set of clothing and a new pair of sandshoes at Christmas. At Easter they get double provisions of sugar and flour. The housemaids, also."

"Good to know." Emmanuel glanced at his blank page. Thomas's response aggravated him. A young girl was dead and they could be discussing farming equipment for all the emotion he showed. "So, Amahle Matebula was a regular house servant who didn't stand out in any way."

"We employ fifteen, maybe twenty natives on Little Flint." Thomas worked a fingernail over a seam of dirt on his thumb. "From my end, none of the servants are remarkable so long as they do their jobs right."

That was country-fresh bullshit. Amahle was exquisite. Any man with a pulse would have noticed her crossing the yard or hanging up the laundry. Then again, Thomas Reed might be one of those rare white men so caught up in the differences between the races that they showed no interest in black or brown girls. Emmanuel didn't trust those men.

"Any idea who killed Amahle?" he asked.

"None whatsoever," Thomas said, and offered nothing more.

Shabalala moved back a pace and fixed his eyes on the peaked horizon. Frustration made his face appear carved from stone. If Amahle had been white, the farmer would be crying over himself at the loss of one so special.

"Constable . . ." Emmanuel sensed the tension in Shabalala. Standing by while Thomas shrugged off questions took effort, but there had to be a reason for his evasiveness and for his not once referring to Amahle by her name. "Get statements from the gardeners and from the housemaids. Find out who was the last person to see Amahle on Friday night. Same goes for Philani Dlamini."

Thomas Reed frowned, the ingrained dirt on his thumb suddenly less important. "Philani's not here. He didn't show up for work on Saturday and again today."

"Is that unusual?" Emmanuel asked.

"Very," Thomas said. "He's one of my best boys. He turns up rain or shine."

"See if Amahle and Philani left the farm together," Emmanuel said to Shabalala.

"I will ask, Sergeant." The Zulu detective walked to the rear of the big house, his steps slowed to allow the old dog to keep up.

Emmanuel looked at Reed. "Did any of the workmen take a fancy to Amahle and have to be warned off?"

"I have no interest in the love life of kaffir girls." The younger Reed turned to the circle of wicker chairs, ending the interview. "Come, Dad. It's time to dip the next batch."

His father got up and walked out to meet him, the notebook now scrunched to scrap paper in his fist.

"Is she coming back?" Ian Reed whispered to his son.

"Who?" Thomas frowned.

"The one you were just talking about. The chief's daughter."

Thomas steered the old man away from Emmanuel. "Back to work now, Dad," he said. "We'll talk about it later."

"If he comes home from school and she's not here, there'll be trouble," Ian Reed muttered. "Your mother won't like it. Not one bit. Not after last time."

"Quiet, now, Pa." Thomas gently prodded his father around the corner. Emmanuel lost the remainder of the conversation. No matter. He'd heard enough to know that Amahle Matebula was more than just a housemaid. He waited for Thomas's response to the revealing comments.

"My father isn't all there," Thomas said when he reappeared solo from the rear of the house. "He mixes things up in his mind, gets his wires crossed. You can't take anything he says seriously."

Especially when it concerns a dead black girl, Emmanuel figured. While old man Reed was clearly losing the thread, there was enough substance in his words to have drained the color from Thomas's suntanned face.

"One more thing." Emmanuel ignored the tight lips and

the tense shoulders encased in khaki. "I'd like to speak to your mother if she's available."

"Not today," Thomas said. "She suffers from migraine headaches and needs bed rest. Feel free to telephone tomorrow morning. She might be better by then."

Thomas Reed was so cool, it was almost as if he'd practiced his responses and knew them by heart. Every question was answered but nothing of value was revealed. The old man's ramblings were the only spontaneous moment in the entire interview.

"Thanks for your time, Mr. Reed. I know you have work to do." Emmanuel cut the young farmer loose. He'd find another way into the family sanctum. "I'll wait here till Constable Shabalala has finished collecting statements."

Young Reed hesitated, weighing up the risks of leaving a policeman loose on the property. "Farms are dangerous," he said. "Don't wander off the paths or into the fields, Detective Cooper. For your own safety."

"I won't." Emmanuel returned Thomas's hard stare. Lying without blinking was a skill he'd mastered at boarding school. "I'm a city man born and bred."

Reed accepted the assurance and strode to the rear steps. The second component to being a successful liar was patience. Emmanuel gave the self-possessed farmer a full five-minute head start before tailing him. Thomas was under the shade of the monkey apple tree by the time Emmanuel had circled the porch. Movement caught his attention and he stood for a moment and watched. A rangy Zulu man crossed the dusty yard with the loping stride of a hunter. He stopped a foot or so in front of the young white baas and held out his empty hands in apology. Thomas moved closer, index finger pointed, body tight as a fist. The cool farmer was gone, replaced by a furious big baas giving orders. The Zulu man set off again, heading for the hills. It looked like he'd been sent back on the trail of something or someone.

"Excuse me." Emmanuel stopped a dark-skinned maid with a wicker basket of dirty laundry balanced on her head. She, too, wore a pair of blue sandshoes without socks. Reed wasn't blowing smoke about the generous handouts to the help. "Can you point the way to the lake?"

"There, inkosi." The woman's voice was quiet, her face turned to indicate a path flanked by white posts. "That way leads to the lake."

"Thanks." Emmanuel let her go without further questions and set off. The Little Flint garden boys and Shabalala stood talking in the kitchen garden. Shabalala ignored Emmanuel completely, a cue to all the servants that the European detective was no friend. Zulu, Pondo, English and Afrikaners alike believed that members of their own tribe were more trustworthy than outsiders. That bone-deep belief might work in Shabalala's favor and get the gardeners talking.

Good luck, Emmanuel thought. Up till this point, at least, straight answers about Amahle were in short supply no matter who you asked.

A wooden jetty jutted out from a small boathouse and straddled the silver water. Reflections of sky and mountain rippled in the wake of the woman plying the lake with powerful strokes. Emmanuel reached the shore moments before the "little madam" emerged, exhausted and panting from her swim.

She moved to the boathouse, dried her hands on a towel and then dug a packet of cigarettes and matches from behind a fishing box. Emmanuel watched her light up and draw deep, savoring the tobacco with an almost postcoital enjoyment.

"It's rude to stare," she said, and exhaled.

"Just giving you time to enjoy your cigarette." He walked across the wooden planks. "It looked like you needed it."

"Does my brother know you're talking to me?"

"No." For some reason he suspected that fact might work in his favor.

"Didn't think so." She held out the crumpled packet. "Want one?"

"Not right now."

"I thought all police detectives smoked."

"Most but not all." He presented his ID card, knowing she'd barely glance at it. Girls with blue blood and family money, even those with plain faces and sturdy limbs, divided the world into two groups: people who counted and those who did not. Detectives were servants in suits—useful but still not equal.

"I'm Ella." She flicked ash onto the lake, drawing a fish to the surface. "You're here about the murder."

"That's right," he said. "Amahle's death must have been a shock."

Ella shrugged and droplets of moisture ran down her bare arms. "If it was going to happen to any of the house girls, it was going to happen to her."

"Why's that?" Emmanuel kept his tone casual, almost uninterested. In Ella Reed's world Amahle was a marginal entity, a housemaid who'd come to a bad end. All madams, big or little, kept mental lists of their servants' shortcomings. He was happy to hear every one of Ella's gripes.

"For starters, she had everything. A job in a nice house, food to eat and all the native men fighting over her." Ella pulled off her swimming cap and shook free a coil of lank brown hair. "Other girls would have been happy. Not her."

"A complainer," Emmanuel prompted.

"*Ja,*" Ella said. "She was always making escape plans. The Kamberg Valley wasn't good enough. Or big enough."

"Fancy that." Emmanuel caught the resentment in Ella's voice. Holding down a job in a European house was supposed to be the apex of a native girl's dreams. Steady employment, leftover food, hand-me-down clothes . . . to want for more was greedy. He looked across the shimmering water to the sandstone escarpment and said, "What place could be better than this?"

"Exactly." Ella ground her cigarette butt against the jetty railing. "I went to Durban Girls' High and I said to her, 'Cities are dirty and dangerous. Not like here in the valley, where things are clean and peaceful.'"

"She didn't listen," Emmanuel said, thinking of the corpses he'd seen strewn across the French and German countryside: some with flowers growing through their rib cages, others with their eye sockets emptied by crows.

"No. She wanted a house. A car. A business in one of the black townships. Like she could ever have those things." Ella returned the butt to the packet and carefully stashed the cigarettes and matches behind the fishing box: smoking was a secret pleasure. "She just didn't see."

And that, Emmanuel figured, was the beauty of dreams. The impossible was just one sleep away. "Empty talk," he said. That was what most dreams came to, his own included. Where was the life too large to be lived in provincial South Africa, the wife he loved with fierce devotion and the children he treated with kindness because he wasn't his own father but a better man? They were vanished wishes, long gone. Baba Kaleni had picked up the echo of a life unlived.

"She tried to take off." Ella blotted water from her sturdy arms and legs with the towel. She stretched out her tanned limbs. The presence of a strange male barely registered. A blue mark tinged with purple bruised the skin of her inner thigh. The shape was too circular, too bite-sized to be accidental. "Got all the way to the bus stop in town," Ella continued. "That's what I heard."

Emmanuel reached into his pocket, fingers automatically closing on the case notebook. Finally, a new fact to fill in the pages. Amahle Matebula was a runaway, a dreamer.

"When was this?" He left the notebook where it was, realizing that taking notes would remind Ella of the difference between harmless gossip and an official police interview. He needed her to keep talking.

"Winter sometime." She wrapped the towel around her body and tucked the loose end under her armpits to make a strapless dress. "I was away at university. I heard through the other servants."

"Are you finished for the year?" Emmanuel asked. Most universities ran classes till the Christmas break. Ella should still be in Pietermaritzburg or Durban.

"Got the week off. Asthma attack. Mountain air and exercise help."

Plus the cigarettes to strengthen your weak lungs? thought Emmanuel.

Ella pushed her feet into a pair of leather sandals and took the path to the big house. White butterflies rose from a bush and scattered in the air like confetti. She brushed them aside and kept walking.

"Any idea what Amahle was running from?" Emmanuel asked, following.

"God knows." Ella plucked a blade of grass and chewed on the sweet end. "Probably the wedding. If that's what you'd call an exchange of cows."

"I heard she wasn't keen on the arrangement. Did she have an eye on anyone here at work? Philani the gardener, for example."

"No way. He's a common laborer. She was the chief's daughter." Ella spoke of them as two different species, barely able to communicate, let alone reproduce. "She might have led him on but it was nothing."

"Led him on how?"

"Not like that." Her nose wrinkled in distaste. "She let him do errands for her. Pick up, fetch and carry. That sort of thing."

"She had Philani on a string," Emmanuel said.

"Of course. Men are easy that way." Ella slowed her pace when the big house came into view. "Amahle was no different from a white girl. She was having a little fun before she got married."

Philani wanted more from the relationship. According to Chief Matebula he'd even told people that he and Amahle were betrothed. That must have been wishful thinking verging on delusion. Thwarted love was a strong motive for murder.

Emmanuel said, "What time did she leave on Friday, do you know?"

"I went for a walk before she left." Ella frowned, trying to retrieve the memory. "Knock-off time is normally just around six but my mother always let Amahle go home early on pay-day."

"I see." Emmanuel memorized the time. "Amahle was paid in cash?" That wasn't always the rule. Some farmers doled out bars of soap or tins of sardines in lieu of actual money. Others provided small stipends boosted by food rations and gifts.

"Of course. She spent some of it in town."

Emmanuel noted this with surprise. Until now, robbery had not even crossed his mind as a motive for the murder. The crime scene indicated something more premeditated than a smash-and-grab.

"Tell me about Friday," he said. "All that you can remember."

The big house was closer now, the sunlight reflecting off the windows. Fortunately, Ella was ambling and in no hurry to get indoors.

"Friday we went into town for a dress fitting at Mrs. Anderson's house. My mother gave Amahle half an hour to walk around while Mrs. Anderson took up the hems. Next we went to Dawson's to collect our hats for the county fair. Amahle came along to carry the boxes to the car." Ella stopped at the top of the lake path. "After that we came home and had lunch."

"What made you think Amahle spent her pay in town?" Emmanuel asked.

"When she came back to the fitting room, loose change was clanking in her pocket. It made a racket."

"Any idea what she bought?"

"No, but she was smiling when she got back to Mrs. Anderson's, so it must have been something good."

"Was she carrying anything?" Emmanuel persisted.

"No," Ella said. "Nothing."

That didn't prove much. A pair of earrings or a necklace could easily fit into a pocket. Nothing like that was found at the crime scene or on Amahle's body in the prelude to Zweigman's examination. He and Shabalala would have to comb all the shops in Roselet to find out what Amahle had spent her money on. It was hard to think of an item bought for a servant's wages that was worth killing for.

"After lunch . . ." Emmanuel prompted.

"Like I said." Ella wound a new strand of grass around her index finger and tugged at the roots. "I went for a walk and got home after dark."

"Part of your health program," Emmanuel said. Four hours in the wooded hills was more of a hike than a walk.

"*Ja.*" She tore the grass from the red soil. "Doctor's orders."

The fresh air and exercise were obviously working. Ella's lungs were clear of congestion and her tanned body was strong. She was convalescing beautifully.

"Do you walk alone?" Emmanuel asked. The love bite on her inner thigh was not self-inflicted, and, while its origin had no bearing on the case, he was curious. The isolated valley and scattered farms brought back memories of the long twilight hours he'd spent seeking out and then ticking off the extensive inventory of sins the predikant of the Dutch Reformed Church preached against during Sunday service. Maria, the preacher's eldest daughter, topped the list of most repeated transgressions.

"Thomas runs the farm and my mother spends all her time

in the garden or the house, so I go out by myself." Ella stripped green from the blade and tiny flakes clung to the front of her towel. "All the natives know I'm a Reed. I never have any trouble."

Of course not. Harming the daughter of a white chief was an informal declaration of war against every European settler in South Africa. Swift punishment would arrive at the hands of the police or a coalition of local white farmers with guns and rope.

"Madam . . . little madam." The older maid who'd appeared on the front porch to greet the Chevrolet hurried across the lawn. "The big madam is up. She asks for you."

"Tell her I'm on the way." Ella's shoulders tensed and she stepped over the trimmed grass edge separating the formal gardens from the bush. A white-pebbled path led directly to the rear of the farmhouse.

"Come and meet Mother," she said.

Emmanuel had seen students on their way to the principal's office for a "six of the best" who looked more relaxed.

"Ella?" a voice called from the left side of the porch. "Where are you?"

"Coming." Ella climbed the stairs, then trudged on with joyless steps, trailing sand across the mahogany floorboards. Dirt from the lake path muddied the soles of her leather sandals and darkened her heels.

Emmanuel hesitated on the top step. If Mrs. Reed was still in a dressing gown the interview was off. The family lawyer—and there'd likely be more than one—would later have Mrs. Reed's words deemed inadmissible in court if there was the slightest suggestion she was pressured into talking.

He followed Ella around the corner to a stretch of sun-dappled porch. An elegant white woman sat on a wicker couch drowning in scatter cushions. She held a silk pillow on her lap like a cat and stroked the fabric. Unlike the rest of the Reeds, who were lanky-framed, with brown skin and hazel eyes, this woman was petite, with black hair and skin pale as milk.

"Where have you been?" Her bright blue eyes narrowed. "Running in the hills like a native again?"

The locked-jaw accent evoked green playing fields and robust schoolgirls lolling in the shade of ancient yew trees: a mythical England that hadn't existed for a hundred years, if at all.

"Swimming." Ella leaned a hip against the railing and motioned Emmanuel closer. "This is Detective Cooper. He's come about Amahle."

"A terrible thing," Mrs. Reed said. "Right here in the valley. Not five miles from the house. I can't sleep at night thinking about it."

The big madam wore an immaculate jade-green dress. Her hair touched her shoulders with the casual perfection of a movie star. Her appearance was probably not her own handiwork but that of unseen hands that washed and ironed her clothes, heated her curling irons and drew her bath. She smelled of dried roses and cinnamon.

"Do you have any idea who might have harmed Amahle, Mrs. Reed?" Emmanuel figured a few questions couldn't hurt. If cracks began to appear in the madam's façade he'd back off.

"Nobody I know would be that wasteful. The other natives cook and clean but Amahle was the only one I trusted with the flower arrangements and setting a proper tea service for guests. She was an impeccable housekeeper."

The porch railing creaked as Ella shifted her weight: she

was still damp from the lake swim, with tousled brown hair and dirty feet, and *impeccable* was not a word that could be used to describe her.

"How much did Amahle get paid on Friday?" Emmanuel asked. Robbery was an unlikely motive for the murder, but the thought kept niggling.

"Two pounds. She got more than the other servants. She did extra projects around the house." Mrs. Reed lifted the cushion from her lap and held it out. "This is her work. See if you can find one dropped stitch or a loose thread." A delicate branch of orange blossoms was embroidered onto the silk fabric, the stamens sewn in with clear glass beads.

"Don't waste your time, Detective," Ella said with an edge of bitterness. "Everything is perfect."

Emmanuel imagined a drawer in Ella's room stuffed with unfinished arts-and-crafts projects: pillowcases with mismatched seams, unraveling scarfs, hessian dolls with one eye and no hair. Children invariably failed their parents. To fail in comparison to a servant must burn.

"That's right." Big madam tucked the cushion back onto her lap. "There's nothing sloppy or ungainly about the design or execution."

Heavy steps hit the rear stairs and eased the tension between mother and daughter. Thomas Reed in a hurry, Emmanuel guessed. He checked over his shoulder. Yes.

"What are you doing here?" Thomas demanded. "I said my mother was sick and couldn't be questioned. Your native has done taking statements from the servants and you're still here, badgering a sick woman."

"If Detective Constable Shabalala is finished, I'll be on my way." Emmanuel started walking toward the stairs.

"Listen here, Cooper . . ." Thomas began the lecture. Emmanuel stopped listening. He was a servant of the South African Police Force and one master was enough.

He cleared the corner of the house. Shabalala stood at the foot of the steps, with the old guard dog still tagging along. Emmanuel held up his hand, giving the signal to wait, and strained to hear the scene he'd left behind.

"You did this." That was Thomas, sounding like a vindictive headmaster. "You allowed that man to question our mother out of spite."

"I didn't *allow* anything. He's a policeman and I'm just a girl," Ella said. "Why didn't you stop him just now when he walked off without listening to you?"

"Children . . . please," Mrs. Reed said.

The children talked over their mother's interjection. "The sooner you're married and off Little Flint, the better," Thomas said.

"I plan on being a spinster," Ella replied, more adept at the family game of tit for tat than her brother.

"Good. Because I don't know a man who'd have you." Thomas's footsteps creaked on the hardwood floor. He was heading back to the cattle yard.

Emmanuel closed the distance to the rear steps and took them two at a time on the way down. Another lesson from boarding school and perhaps the most valuable one was: Don't get caught.

"Quick and steady to the car," he said to Shabalala. "We'll talk on the way."

The sun was higher in the sky, the clouds darker than when they'd arrived an hour ago. A thunderstorm was building.

"Get anything, Detective?" Emmanuel asked.

"Yes, Sergeant. There is no Mr. Insurance Policy here. The kitchen maids and the garden boys have never heard this name." Shabalala produced his notebook and scanned the pages. "Also, Philani the gardener did not leave with Amahle on Friday night but fifteen minutes after her. It was customary for them to walk home together but the madam said Philani must finish weeding the flower beds."

"Amahle left when?"

"At six o'clock. Philani at six-fifteen."

"You got the gardeners to talk," Emmanuel said. "What did you use, threats or charm?"

"Neither, Sergeant. The young gardener is also a Shabalala. He told me everything. The gardener with the broken face said not one word."

"And the housemaids?"

Shabalala grinned. "For them I used charm."

"So the National Party government is right." Emmanuel kept a straight face. "A black man in a suit is a danger to the community. What else did the maids tell you?"

"That Philani was angry that he was left behind. He ran after the chief's daughter and tried to catch her."

"Maybe he did," Emmanuel said.

8

EMMANUEL SLOWED THE Chevrolet to thirty and shifted down to third. The dirt road connecting Little Flint to Roselet was a rough strip of corrugated bumps and loose sand. Tall kaffir weeds whipped against the car doors. He checked the western sky and saw black thunderheads swollen with rain. Dark specks circled in a clockwise direction, against the gathering tempest.

"Vultures?" Shabalala said, and leaned out of the open passenger window to get a better look.

Emmanuel pulled over and parked in a patch of dried mud.

"Could be anything," he said, and got out. "How far off, do you think?"

Shabalala studied the terrain. The land sloped down from the road to a trench and then climbed steeply again to a hill covered in thick native forest. The vultures circled the peak, riding the air current, patient as undertakers at a funeral.

"Half an hour," Shabalala said. "A quick climb."

Worth the detour, Emmanuel figured. He shrugged off his jacket, loosened his tie and rolled up his sleeves. Reviewing the information gathered at Little Flint could wait another hour without any damage being done to the investigation. Shabalala laid his folded jacket on the passenger seat and wound up the window. He unbuttoned the top two buttons of his shirt and eyed the rise.

"You enjoy this," Emmanuel said. Shabalala was a Zulu sphinx but Emmanuel was learning to see beyond the mask. "Climbing mountains, running across the fields and breaking a sweat."

"Sitting at a desk and writing notes, that is no life for a man, Sergeant." Shabalala shrugged an apology for maligning the job of detective. "But my wife, she likes the pay and the nice suit and the hat."

"Then you're stuck," Emmanuel said with a grin, and dropped the car keys into his pants pocket. The clouds edged closer, casting blue shadows over the grasslands.

"Yes, stuck," Shabalala agreed, but his tone said, *Happily so.* He set out across the narrow dirt road and down the slope. At the bottom was a ditch overgrown with prehistoric-looking ferns and moss-covered stones.

Emmanuel followed close. "Happily stuck" also described his relationship with the Detective Branch, for now. Three months of hard graft he could take. But if this murder case hit a wall and he slipped back into a series of thankless investigations broken up by troubling dreams and the occasional night with a woman, the future looked grim. Unlike him, Shabalala and Zweigman had wives and children to hold them steady through rising and falling tides of fortune.

Emmanuel used two stepping-stones to cross the stream at the bottom of the trench, setting off a chorus of frogs. Saplings with lichen-covered trunks gave way to stands of Natal mahogany, wild fig and marula trees. They climbed higher on an overgrown walking trail for twenty minutes, then Shabalala slowed and tilted his head to the wind.

The odor filtering from the woods was familiar to Emmanuel. Blood, spilled stomach contents and urine: butchered animals and humans smelled very much the same. Seven vultures rode the air current, their black shapes now almost indistinguishable against the rain-swollen clouds overhead.

"Dried blood and flesh," Shabalala whispered. "Behind that rock." A raised stone outcrop surrounded by bush blocked a view of the kill.

"Slow and steady." Emmanuel crept through ankle-deep leaf litter and climbed onto a flat sandstone ledge wide enough to lay a blanket and a picnic basket on. Vultures rose up from their meal, their black and brown wings blocking the sky.

Emmanuel leaned forward with his hands on his knees, fighting the urge to vomit. The flies, the overwhelming stench, the odd twist of limbs were all too familiar.

"*Inkosi Yami.* My God." Shabalala stumbled back. He made it to the rock edge and threw up over the side, his body convulsing.

"Get it all out." Emmanuel moved a little closer to Shabalala but not too close. Leaving well enough alone and letting a person know he was *not* alone was a fine balance. "You'll be sick for a while longer and then again, just when you think your stomach is empty."

A vulture descended from a tree limb and hopped across the sandstone ledge, eager to continue feeding. Emmanuel chased it off and stood awhile to steady his nerves. He pulled a handkerchief from his pocket and pressed it to his nose and mouth to block out the smell.

A black man of small build lay on his right side with his arms and legs twisted in opposite directions. He wore a pair of faded blue overalls: the uniform of the South African laborer. The heel of his right foot was rough and cracked from walking barefoot across the mountains, while his left foot still wore a blue sandshoe. Broad, calloused hands confirmed that the man did hard physical work. A deep cut sliced his stomach open to expose lengths of bloated intestine.

"One of us has got to take up smoking," Emmanuel said when Shabalala joined him, looking drawn and washed out.

"First thing, Sergeant." The Zulu man acknowledged the joke with a wan smile and pressed his handkerchief to his face. He studied the corpse and said, "Philani?"

"That's my guess. He's wearing the blue sandshoes given to Little Flint workers at Christmas. And there are grass stains on the knees of the overalls. We'll still need to get a formal ID from someone who knew him."

The vultures had been at work on the man's face and body, breaking him down to mere flesh and bone. Emmanuel leaned closer and said, "That cut across the stomach is deliberate."

"*Yebo.* From the blade of a knife or a spear." Shabalala circled the body, reading hidden signs. "Made after he was already dead."

"Mutilation," Emmanuel said.

"No, Sergeant. A kindness. We Zulu believe the soul lives here in the intestines." He pointed to the wound. "If the stomach is not cut, the soul will be trapped in the body and fester. It is a tradition from the old days."

Emmanuel absorbed that fact and said, "So a Zulu did this."

"More than one. Four men were here, around the body and on this ledge. Maybe five hours ago."

"Mandla and his men." It all added up. The motive was simple: revenge for Amahle's death. "They tracked down the gardener and killed him. Blood washes blood, like you said."

Blue cloud shadows darkened the ledge and lightning forked across the sky. The wind picked up. Leaves and dust blew across the ground. Rain would come soon.

"Four men. One cut across the stomach made postmortem." Emmanuel puzzled over the sequence of events. "What actually killed him?"

Shabalala followed some tracks to a curve of basalt jutting from the hillside to form a natural shelter. Rising wind blew a pile of burnt twigs and ash against the back wall of the sanctuary: the remains of a night fire. Scraggy tree branches were thrown in a pile a few feet away.

Emmanuel skirted the ledge and approached the shelter, sure that this was where Philani the gardener had hidden away after disappearing on Friday night. He hadn't run far enough.

"This is where he lay covered in the branches." Shabalala crouched close to the spent fire. "This is the place he died. Lying on his back."

A few tablespoonfuls of dried blood stained the rock. Very similar to the discreet pool found under Amahle's body.

"Let's check his lower back for injuries." Emmanuel returned to the corpse. Deep lacerations made by tearing beaks crisscrossed the man's spine and shoulders. There might be a small puncture wound on the skin somewhere but finding it would take a detailed examination: yet another job for Dr. Daniel Zweigman.

"Died over there. Placed out here in the open for the vultures to devour," Emmanuel said. "Make sense of that for me, Detective."

"I can think of only one reason for the four Zulu men to uncover the body and bring it onto the rock. They wanted this man to be found."

Thunder rolled and the birds in the trees raised a chorus. Lizards and ants scurried into cracks and crevices. The rain came down, first in fat lazy drops and then in a lashing torrent. Shabalala and Emmanuel raced to the shelter and crouched under the rock like cavemen. They stayed quiet for a long while, content to watch the power of the storm on the landscape. Tridents of lightning sliced the sky, illuminating the treetops and the far valley.

Emmanuel shook raindrops from the brim of his hat and said, "You're right, Shabalala. The only logical reason for leaving the body out like bait was because the men wanted to draw attention to the location of the murder. The question is, why?"

Shabalala pointed to brush marks raked across the loose sand in the shelter. "Whoever killed the man wiped their tracks from the scene. They did not want to be found but the men did not try to hide what they had done with the body."

"Like pointing a finger and saying, *Come and see what's happened but we're not responsible.*"

"*Yebo,*" Shabalala agreed. "That is what I think."

"The motive for attracting attention could be selfish. Someone got to Philani before Mandla and his soldiers and they want the guilty party found and punished. They've got no leads of their own so they've handed the job over to us," Emmanuel said. "Do you think the Durban Detective Branch called Mandla and told him that hopeless cases are our speciality?"

Shabalala laughed softly. It was the best self-defense for a detective surrounded by vultures and decomposing human remains.

The rain continued to lash the hillside. Thunder boomed and spectacular rods of lightning forked across the mountaintops. From the damp ground rose the scent of Africa after the rains: a mix of dust, crushed leaves and clean rivers cutting through open veldt. What Emmanuel's mother had described as "the smell of heaven in the morning."

Within minutes the storm dissipated and the lightning faded. Birdsong filled the silent woods and the world was fresher, greener than before the rains.

"We need to find the nearest farmhouse and phone the murder in to Roselet." Emmanuel stood up and brushed creases from his trouser legs. "If Bagley's available we'll request backup to get the body off the mountain and to Zweigman for examination."

A big if. Instinct told Emmanuel that Constable Bagley and his native police were still out in the countryside and would be for hours yet. There was no way that he and Shabalala could transport the corpse over rough terrain without help.

"There will not be much of him left in one or two hours." Shabalala motioned to a string of vultures gathered in the branches of a yellowwood tree. They'd fly away if chased and come back just as quickly. Time was their ally. All they had to do was wait.

"Christ above . . ." Emmanuel knew what had to be done and so did Shabalala, who took a jagged breath to calm his nerves. "I'll sketch the scene for reference and then we'll move him back under the shelter."

Shabalala gathered the discarded branches and pulled them across the ledge. He laid them next to the corpse to make a bush stretcher and waited. Emmanuel finished drawing the crime scene and then scribbled the victim's approximate height and weight in the margin. At around five-foot-three and between nine and ten stone, the victim was a compact man. Next, Emmanuel added details of the rock shelter, the raked-over footprints and the deliberate exposure of the body, then tucked the writing pad away.

"One moment, please, Sergeant." Shabalala turned away from the smell and the flies. His broad shoulders hunched and flexed and his breath was labored.

"There's no hurry." Emmanuel took the lead. Working quickly and with grim determination, he rolled the man onto the branches and settled his arms across his distended stomach. War was the best training ground for dealing with the dead: malnourished children, pretty girls in tattered dresses and soldiers barely old enough to shave, Emmanuel had seen and buried them all.

"I am ready," Shabalala said, and turned back to the corpse without being sick.

"Take the right branch, I'll take the left." Emmanuel grabbed the thickest limb of the makeshift stretcher and prepared to haul. "Straight to the shelter on the count of three."

"*Yebo.*" The Zulu detective grabbed a branch and helped drag the body to the spur of rock.

"In the hollow," Emmanuel said, and they laid the body in the sandy indentation with the blood spill. Philani's next journey would be much longer: all the way down the hillside, into a mortuary van or car and into town. It might be the only time the diminutive Zulu had had the luxury of traveling in a motor vehicle. "Let's cover him and find the nearest telephone."

They collected fallen branches from the damp undergrowth and re-covered the body. Shabalala found two heavy logs and weighed the branches down to make it harder for the wildcats and jackals to uncover it.

"We can see all the farmhouses from up there, Sergeant. At the top."

"Not all the white-owned farms have telephones," Emmanuel said on the slippery climb to the summit. "But the nearest European house will do as a starting point."

They gained the rise in under five minutes and scanned the valley for whitewashed walls and the glitter of corrugated iron roofs. Smoke from cooking fires rose from kraals and from two European dwellings connected to the main road by narrow access lanes.

"Little Flint Farm." Shabalala gestured to a sprawl of buildings miles away from their vantage point and then pointed to a smaller homestead, much closer. "That house is the nearest."

Glimpses of mud-brick walls and a silver roof showed through the dripping trunks of the wild pomegranate trees. Emmanuel led the way along a grass path that brought them to a dirt yard and a homestead. Geese bathed in the mud puddles and a rooster crowed in the world made bright by the rain.

"It doesn't look promising," Emmanuel said. "No electricity wires. No generator. And I'm betting no book in the house but the Bible."

His adopted father was a staunch Afrikaner who viewed modern conveniences as works of the devil. The mean little homestead and the scrappy yard he stood in now triggered memories of days on the sun-blasted veldt and of his stepfather and mother praying through endless cycles of drought, flood and bush fire.

"On the back veranda," Shabalala said. "There is a person."

They crossed the sodden ground to the patched-together house. The bathing geese scattered from the puddle, honking loudly. Emmanuel reluctantly stepped across the threshold of a porch at the rear of the house.

A young, tanned white woman with thick black hair held in a single braid bent over the carcass of a gutted springbok. The tip of her bone-handled hunting knife flicked under the animal's skin with expert precision. Flies swarmed over the pile of intestines thrown to the side of her worktable.

"Who are you?" She stopped working and looked at Emmanuel across the veranda. Her pale green eyes showed mild interest and no fear. A sighted .22 rifle lay within reach of her bloodied hands.

"Police." Emmanuel took shallow breaths. The smell of death brought back the memory of the man they'd left concealed under branches.

"Is it illegal to hunt for buck now?" She spoke with a guttural accent. A backwater Afrikaner.

"No." A clean hole was bored into the animal's bloody temple; a single shot had brought the buck down. "Your name?"

"Karin Paulus," she said. "You?"

"Detective Sergeant Cooper from West Street Detective Branch in Durban, and that's Detective Constable Shabalala. Do you have a telephone I can use?"

Karin was probably only in her early twenties but she looked older and harder than that. If she had grown up in the ritzy suburb of Berea, surrounded by flowers and servants, she might have been beautiful.

"Nearest phone is at the English farm." Karin went back to work. Her strong hands swiftly stripped away the hide before she inserted the blade into the joints to quarter the carcass. Sweat glistened on her top lip. "Quickest thing is to send Cyrus, our runner, with a message and one of the English can ring through for you."

"Don't worry about it. Our car is only half an hour away."

"That won't help you," she said.

"Why not?"

"The. Rain." She put equal emphasis on both words, as though giving condescending instructions to a native. "It will take an hour, maybe two, for the creek between here and the main road to go down. Cyrus can make it to and from the English in an hour."

"I see." They were trapped in this Afrikaner Eden for a few hours longer. Emmanuel retrieved his writing pad and pen. "Where are we exactly?"

"Covenant Farm." The butchered carcass was piled on one side of the table and the bloody knife was cleaned with a piece of cloth. "My great-great-grandfather settled this land over a hundred years ago, before the war with the British, but the newer people in the valley might not know where we are. I can draw a map."

Karin's words contained both pride and resentment. The Paulus family must have wrestled this fertile valley from the Zulus and tilled its soil with only oxen and a plow. Now the English, with their telephones and tractors, owned most of it and the blood and sweat of the Boer pioneers were forgotten.

"Would the Roselet station commander know the way?" Emmanuel asked. He didn't recall a signpost for Covenant Farm or a track splitting off from the main road.

"Could be." Karin sheathed the knife and stuffed one hindquarter of the carcass into a hessian sack. "He came out when the thieving started from the house and the barn. That was four years ago. No sign of him since."

English law was another bitter pill to swallow—for a long time crimes against Afrikaner families were a lower priority for the mostly English Natal police. As a result, resentment of the British was common among the Afrikaners but Emmanuel remembered that Nomusa and Chief Matebula had also complained about Bagley's absence from the valley. This professional neglect might be the reason the anonymous caller had contacted the Durban police rather than the local constable.

He tore a clean page from his notebook and placed it on the corner of the butcher table along with the pen. "A map would be good," he said.

Karin drew a rudimentary map, picked it up by one corner and gave it to Emmanuel. Then she lifted the full hessian bag and shoved it in Shabalala's direction, saying in perfect Zulu, "Boy, take this meat to the hut behind the big barn and give it to the workmen. Tell them it's springbok for the evening pot. Go. Quick."

Shabalala grabbed the heavy sack, speechless. Karin crossed the stoep with a crunch of boots and said over her shoulder in English, "I'll get Cyrus."

Emmanuel and Shabalala remained rooted to the spot,

stunned by the command and by the faultless Zulu used to issue it. Karin did not speak the "kitchen kaffir" used by whites to give basic orders to their servants. Her inflection and pronunciation were perfect. With eyes closed she'd be mistaken for a native.

"Hiya . . ." Shabalala made a sound of grudging admiration. "I will go, Sergeant. The workmen will be waiting for their food."

He held the dripping sack away from his suit and made for the stoep. A native policeman was still subservient to a white woman.

"While you're there, ask around about Mr. Insurance Policy and see if the workers have anything to say, good or bad, about Amahle. Someone wanted her dead."

"*Yebo.*" Shabalala set out across the muddy yard, keeping to the grassy edge to save his leather shoes from the mud.

Emmanuel moved away from the bloody table. Impala and springbok were the staple food of his teenage years because his adopted parents couldn't afford anything else. Even now the memory of eating the gamy meat roasted, dried, fried and stewed made his stomach turn.

He stepped into the yard, which was ringed by lush green fields and hazy mountains. It was easy to see why the early Boer settlers believed that God Himself had ceded this land to them. The rise and fall of the terrain and the crystal-clear air were divine.

Karin appeared from behind a low milking shed, a loose-limbed Zulu boy trailing two steps behind her. Emmanuel folded the hand-drawn map into a second piece of paper with a simple message written on the page: *Immediate help needed. Covenant Farm.* On the outside he wrote Ella Reed's name along with instructions to call the Roselet police station with the message and to verbally describe the map if necessary.

"This is Cyrus, our runner." Karin motioned the boy forward. "He knows the quickest way to the English farm."

"Baas." Cyrus bowed his head in greeting and withdrew from his pocket a stick with a split top. "I will return within the hour."

"My thanks." Emmanuel gave the runner the message, which he slotted into the split at the top of the stick for safekeeping. "If Miss Ella Reed, the little madam, is not at home you must give this message to the young baas Thomas Reed."

"I understand." Cyrus wheeled in a half circle and hit the muddy yard at a run. Within a minute he'd disappeared into the stand of wild pomegranate trees and was gone.

"You know Ella?" Karin asked, and returned to the butcher's table. She lifted a bucket of salt from the floor, balanced it on a corner and wiped the wood surface down with a dry cloth.

"Not really," Emmanuel said. "I interviewed her and her brother this morning."

"About the chief's daughter?" Karin unrolled the buck skin and pegged it to the table. She scraped the blunt edge of her knife over the underside of the fresh skin, removing fat.

"You heard about Amahle?" Emmanuel asked by way of a prompt. If he had to stand by and watch a hide being dressed, he'd make the minutes count.

"Of course." Karin kept scraping. The muscles on her arms and shoulders were strong from physical labor. There was no trace of the pampered white madam about her. "The whole valley is talking about that girl."

The statement was resentful and intrigued Emmanuel. He decided to persist with this blunt Afrikaner female.

"Do you have much contact with the Matebulas?" he asked.

"The Matebula kraal is on our land but it's Pa who collects the rents." Karin flicked fat onto the pile of innards slopped on the floor. "I could do the job easy but the chief won't allow it. He only does business with men."

"Not much of a chief," Emmanuel said.

"A full stomach and a new wife to stick his piel into every five years, that's all Matebula cares about." Karen grabbed a fistful of rock salt and sprinkled it over the hide. "He takes everything for himself. The children from the kraal come to trade for bread and meat from the farm store—they get sick of eating ground corn and nothing else."

"Did Amahle ever trade with you?" The lipstick, toothbrush and pencils in Amahle's cardboard box must have come from somewhere.

"She didn't have to trade," Karin said. "The Reeds spoil their servants. Amahle especially."

"How do you know Amahle was spoiled?" Emmanuel asked.

"It was obvious." The statement was sharp. "They gave her special food and dresses and even let her wear earrings. She was their pet."

Emmanuel understood the pet system, knew it well. Afrikaner, English and native boarding schools all practiced this colonial institution. The simplest and sweetest version saw the pet following his or her owner, weighed down with books, eager to run and fetch on command. The more complicated version was darker: a relationship of intrusive fingers and tongues perpetuated under the weight of silence. Despite the privileges, being a "pet" could break a person into pieces.

"Pretty girls always get more of everything," Emmanuel said, hoping to provoke Karin into revealing more.

"That's the way of things." Karin worked the coarse salt into the buck's skin. "The English made a big mistake with that one. She forgot she was a kaffir and treated everyone like they were the servants."

Karin called them "the English" with barely concealed contempt. Little Flint and Covenant were adjacent to each other but the only thing the English and Afrikaner families had in common was they were white.

"You included?"

The Afrikaner woman glanced up at him across the hide, suddenly aware that an answer to the question might reveal more about her than about Amahle. She continued salting and said, "Pa knows the Matebula family better than I do, Detective. He'll be able to answer all your questions."

Nice try, Emmanuel thought, but too late to cover her antagonism toward the dead Zulu girl. Karin was jealous of a black maid.

"Tea?" The question was accompanied by a tight smile before she rapped a salt-encrusted knuckle on the back door of the homestead. "Come." She opened the door and disappeared into the house without waiting for an answer.

Emmanuel hesitated for a moment, then ducked under the low entry and stepped into a scrappy kitchen.

"Take a seat over there." Karin pointed to an oak table at the center of the room. A Zulu maid, no taller than a ten-year-old child but well past her fiftieth year, stood aside while Karin reached into an upper cupboard and removed what must have been the good china. She handed the porcelain to the miniature servant, who wiped the inside of the cups with her apron.

Emmanuel's eyes gradually adjusted to the dim light. He looked around. Thrift and invention characterized the Paulus kitchen. A long wooden counter was inset with an iron bucket to make a rudimentary sink. Old flour sacks covered the dirt floor, a poor man's carpet.

The maid set two cups on the oak table and then waited for the madam to retrieve the teapot painted with yellow roses and green leaves. Emmanuel leaned forward, curious to see what was in the bowl placed at the center of the table. A pyramid of fresh honeycomb dripped through cheesecloth into the wide bowl. This was how his adopted Afrikaner mother had strained the honey that he'd collected from the wild bees when he was fifteen.

"Sugar or honey?" Karin asked.

"One sugar, thank you." He resisted the urge to run out of the house, away from the smell of blood and wild honey and the faint trace of wet dog mixed with mud. The odor was familiar and repugnant. It was the smell of his adolescence, of hard winters and scorching summers on the veldt, of narrow boarding-school hallways and fistfights. But it was also the smell of praying girls who turned their backs on him in public and then came creeping through the tall grass to the abandoned shed with its bed of stolen blankets and contraband cigarettes.

The maid lifted an iron kettle from a wood-burning stove and poured boiling water into the teapot. Emmanuel returned to the present time. The kitchen was stifling but he decided against removing his tie. He took off his hat.

"You were born and bred here?" he said. The scarred walls and wooden table looked like they'd been there since just after the Voortrekkers came over the hill.

"*Ja,* of course. Except for boarding school in Pietermaritzburg, the farm is it."

"You don't mind being all the way out here by yourself?"

"I have my pa." Karin sat down and signaled the maid to pour the tea. "And I know how to make my own fun."

Where and with whom? Emmanuel wondered.

"Cooper. That's an English name." Karin's tone was accusatory.

"Afrikaner mother, English father." Emmanuel switched the facts around, kept the family lineage simple to put off further digging. He left the possibility that he might be part Cape Malay unsaid. "You?"

"Pure Dutch. My people came over the mountains on the tail end of the Great Trek. Their wagon is in a museum in Pretoria."

The Paulus family were one of God's chosen few, then. It didn't change their fortunes. God had still only given them a basic education, no running water and no cash in the bank. They had plenty of bullets for their guns, though.

Emmanuel brushed off the reference to the Great Trek, the holy Afrikaner caravan traversing southern Africa in search of land to establish a racially pure, slave-owning society. It meant less than nothing to him.

"So it's just you and your father . . ." That would be unusual. Old Dutch families bred in the tens and the dozens.

"My ma died having me, so Pa keeps me close." Karin traced her fingertips over her arms. The maid poured tea, careful not to clank the spout against the rim of the good cups.

"Where's your pa?" Emmanuel asked. The water in the creek would not recede for another hour and he wasn't sure he'd last the next ten minutes in the stuffy room.

"Down by the river, filling water barrels for the week." Karin's brown fingers curled around the pale teacup. "You and the kaffir policeman found something on the mountain. What was it?"

"You're very sure." Emmanuel sipped his tea. It was sweet and dark, with a bitterness that caught in his throat.

"Two and two makes four," she said. "The vultures were on the crest of the mountain this morning and then you come asking for a telephone. Something is up there."

"Why didn't you go and check?" Emmanuel asked.

"Lammergeiers circling a kill are common as dirt out here. I'd run myself thin going to every sighting." She leaned back and gulped a mouthful of tea. "I could track your path back up the mountain easy and find out what you won't tell me."

"So you could." Karin was a hunter and tracker who had spent her life in these mountains. She'd find the shelter and the body in half an hour. "But you're too clever to interfere with official police business."

Karin shrugged and turned to the maid, now perched on a stool in the corner closest to the woodstove. "Do you think Mandla found the gardener from the English farm?" she asked in Zulu.

The maid rubbed the soles of her bare feet against the sacks on the floor and then answered in a quiet voice, "It might be so. The chief's son and his men came down from the mountain just after dawn this morning. They did not stop to pass the time but went straight to the river and cleaned their spears with sand."

"The spears were used." Karin glanced at Emmanuel with bright eyes and continued in Zulu. "I think this *umlungu* policeman found the gardener."

"If that is so, I will get the word to his mother." The maid sat in the dim corner with her hands folded on her lap. Her business would have to wait until knock-off time when the sun fell below the mountains.

"What did she say?" Emmanuel asked. It was an effort to keep a blank expression and pretend he had no idea what was going on, and more difficult still to ignore Karin calling him an *umlungu*, a derogatory term for a white man.

Karin pointed to the straining bowl. "I asked where she got the honey from and she said from out in the woods, just behind the barn. It's good. You should try it."

Emmanuel dipped his index finger into the bowl and tasted it. Playing the clueless city detective had advantages. The clandestine conversation confirmed that Shabalala was right about when Mandla and the impi had discovered the body. Cleaning their spears in full view of Covenant Farm proved they had nothing to hide.

"Delicious," Emmanuel said, and Karin smiled, enjoying the ruse. Toying with an out-of-town policeman might be one of the ways that she made her own fun out here in the sticks. Three distant whistles and the faint snap of a whip broke the quiet in the kitchen.

Karin drained her cup and stood up. "That's Pa and the boys. They're getting ready to load the water barrels. Come to the river, I'll introduce you."

Emmanuel was glad to get out of the hot kitchen and onto

the stoep. The springbok entrails on the floor were gone, removed by a faceless servant. A filthy cat lapped at the blood puddle left behind.

"Forgot my hat," he said, and ducked back into the house. The maid hadn't moved from the corner. He moved closer and caught her attention.

"Do you know where the gardener's mother stays?" he asked in Zulu.

The maid looked up, surprised at his fluid command of the language. She hesitated, then said, "The mother is staying at the other side of the English farm. At the Mashanini kraal."

Emmanuel held her gaze and saw that the cornea of the woman's eye was frosted over at the center. Blindness was a few years away but inevitable. "When the time is right I will go and collect her and tell her what has happened to her son. Will you let me do this?"

There was a pause before she answered, "*Yebo, inkosi.*"

"I thank you." He collected his hat and moved outside. That the maid should not mention their conversation to Karin did not need saying. He had promised to go directly to a frightened Zulu woman and explain things face-to-face. That gesture had earned the maid's silence.

9

WE'LL STOP ON the way and pick up your kaffir," Karin said when Emmanuel joined her at the side of the house. "He needs to be introduced. Pa doesn't like strangers roaming the property."

The Boer farmer might not be so different from Thomas Reed after all. The sun was high in the bright sky and the muddy ground steamed with heat. Karin cut straight through the mud in her heavy boots and stopped at a large wooden barn. Emmanuel picked his way across the yard, stepping from one clump of damp grass to another. Karin watched him, amused.

"The workmen's hut is back there," she said. "Careful of the wet ground, Detective."

"Thanks." Emmanuel took the insult on the chin.

"Sergeant." Shabalala broke away from a cluster of Zulu workmen leaning on their shovels and drinking tea from tin mugs. A half-dug irrigation ditch ended a few feet away from them.

Emmanuel waited by the barn. Any trust Shabalala had built with the workers would be compromised by the intrusion of a white man.

"Time to meet the boss," he said to Shabalala. "We'll talk afterwards."

They caught up with Karin on a wide, uncultivated field cut by deep wagon tracks. A wrought-iron fence circled a crop of white headstones eroded to stubs. The Paulus family graveyard, Emmanuel supposed.

Shabalala hesitated on the lip of a steep drop to the river and whispered, "Look there, Sergeant."

An ox wagon was drawn up on the near bank of a fast-flowing river. Two black laborers lifted a five-gallon water drum onto the flat wagon bed while a pack of dogs splashed in the water. A white man wearing torn overalls and worn boots cracked a whip over a team of oxen straining at the yoke. The man's face was tanned and his high cheekbones and a wide forehead suggested an infusion of Hottentot blood: a true Afrikaner. Pure Dutch my arse, Emmanuel thought.

"My pa." Karin pointed to the whip hand. "And the dogs."

"Six of them," Shabalala added quietly. A pack of African boerboels with massive jaws and sleek brown coats lurched up the bank, barking and snarling.

"Stay close and don't move," Karin said. "They look tough but they're gentle. Honest."

One bite and you'd lose a hand. Easy. Paws found purchase on the rise and spit flew from their mouths. Emmanuel and Shabalala stood motionless and waited for father or daughter to stop the dogs from getting too close. Finally, a whistle sounded. The white man called, "Heel!"

The dogs stopped midstride, retreated to the sandy bank

and milled around their master's legs. The black workmen patted the oxen's flanks and held them steady.

"Who've you got there, girl?" Pa shouted in Afrikaans, and looped the plaited whip over his shoulder.

"The police." Karin scrambled down to the river's edge. Emmanuel and Shabalala followed, giving up on saving their leather shoes from damage. "These are Detectives Cooper and Shabalala from Durban."

Pa frowned at the sight of Shabalala and said in Afrikaans, "They have kaffir detectives now?"

"A handful," Emmanuel replied in the "Taal," as insiders of the true faith called the Afrikaans language. He waited for the man to sneer at the idea of black detectives.

"Good. You need a native to catch a native." Pa extended a gnarled hand. "Sampie Paulus. You've met my daughter Karin."

"I have." Emmanuel shook hands, struck by Sampie's powerful grip and the sandpaper texture of his skin.

"Those are my boys, Johannes and Petros. Brothers. Good with the oxen." Sampie pulled a tobacco pouch from the top pocket of his overalls. "You're here about Amahle."

"Yes. We arrived yesterday morning."

"Make any progress?" Sampie removed two papers from the pouch and tipped a small mound of rough-cut tobacco into the palm of his hand.

"Early days," Emmanuel said. "We know when she disappeared and where she was found. But not much else."

"Here. In the shade." Paulus retired to a damp patch of sand where the remnants of a fire smoldered. The dogs followed. Sampie sank onto his haunches, arms resting on his knees just like a native. "You've been to the Matebula kraal?"

"We met the chief and his number-one son, Mandla." Emmanuel crouched next to Sampie. He ignored the burn in his fatigued calves and Karin, who sat cross-legged and carpeted in dogs. Shabalala stood on the outer edge of the patch of shade and listened.

"Mandla came around the other day." Sampie rolled the cigarette and sealed the papers with a lick. "Asking after Philani Dlamini the gardener at the English farm."

"Did everyone know he was in the area?" If Philani's location was an open secret, the list of suspects in his murder increased.

"Nobody had seen him. Karin and me included." Sampie dug a rusty metal lighter from a back pocket. It took four hits of his thumb against the wheel to produce a flame. "If Mandla was on *my* tracks I'd bury myself good and deep and stay there."

Sampie was right. Philani would not have disclosed his location to a wide circle of people. The killer must have been someone the gardener trusted.

"We're tracking Philani ourselves," Emmanuel lied. "What does he look like?" His gut told him the body in the shelter was the gardener but it would be hours before the corpse was moved and a formal identification arranged. A list of physical attributes to match with the ones he'd jotted down at the crime scene would help give his intuition weight.

"About thirty, thirty-five, give or take a few years. Light-skinned. Small for a Zulu." The blunt-faced farmer pointed to Shabalala with nicotine-stained fingers. "Not like your boy. Now, that's a proper Zulu."

Yes, and all Englishmen were pigeon-chested, with pink skin, and had no idea about Africa. Indians were hardworking but crafty and not to be trusted. Mixed-race coloureds were sly and spiteful and most likely to lead your children into sin. Most South Africans, no matter their skin color, carried a twisted mental illustration of each race group for easy reference.

"Height, weight, hair or eye color?" Emmanuel asked. Sampie's brief description fit the body at the crime scene. Zweigman could use the finer details at the examination.

"He was short. Stocky. Brown eyes . . . I think." Sampie drew in a mouthful of smoke before exhaling through flared nostrils. "What's the gardener got to do with any of it? Mandla gave me a story about Philani owing him money, but that was kak."

"There's a rumor that Philani was involved with Amahle."

Sampie turned to his boys and called out in Zulu, "The Englishman's gardener and the daughter of the great chief. Have you ever heard such a thing?"

The workmen shook their heads in the negative and turned back to tending the oxen. Evidently, the intimate question was embarrassing and any discussion about the dead girl was dangerous.

"In his dreams, maybe." Sampie pinched the end of the hand-rolled cigarette between thumb and forefinger and shoved the butt into a top pocket. A waste-not, want-not man. "Pretty girls do that, hey? Make fellows think stupid things. Dlamini wouldn't be the first."

The Afrikaner farmer stood up and snapped the leather whip in the air, signaling a move back to the homestead. The dogs stretched and yawned, while Karin brushed fur off her pants. Shabalala crouched amid the flurry of activity and watched the river current surge over the rocks.

"See you back at the house, Detective," Karin said, and walked away, the dogs running ahead of her. The workmen steadied the wagon onto two deep tracks cut into the dirt. Even Sampie took up their Zulu work chant as he got behind the cart and pushed.

"Come, Sergeant." Shabalala stood up and headed across the sandy bank in the direction of the departing oxen. "The water is dropping fast. In one hour we will be able to cross the stream to the car."

"*Ja,*" Emmanuel said reluctantly. He was in no hurry to tell Philani's mother that her son was in pieces on a rock ledge.

The churn of wagon wheels and oxen hooves turned the farmyard into mud. Johannes and Petros, Sampie's boys, rolled the full water barrels across the stoep and rested them against the rear wall of the house.

Emmanuel and Shabalala crossed the muck, their shoes and trouser bottoms caked with river sand and now more mud. Smoke from the kitchen fire made a long gray finger against the sky. A male figure sprinted from the stand of pomegranate trees and closed the distance to them in a blink.

"That was quick," Emmanuel said.

Cyrus the runner was back at Covenant, dripping sweat and sucking air into his mouth. His shirt, already shabby and eaten with holes before the run, was now ripped and hanging loose from one shoulder. Cyrus must have cut through thorn-bush to travel the quickest route to Little Flint Farm.

"For you." The runner presented the split stick with a shaky hand. "From the little madam at the English farm."

Emmanuel dug in his pocket and exchanged a handful of coins for the message.

"Thank you, Cyrus. And sorry about the shirt," he said,

and unfolded the note. Six words were written across the page in blue ink: *No answer at the police station.* Ella's signature looped under the reply. He gave the paper to Shabalala.

The Zulu detective read it and handed the note back to Emmanuel. "We are still on our own," he said. A tribe was nothing if all the factions did not pull together in times of trouble. The police force demanded the same kind of allegiance.

"It's just you, me and Zweigman again," Emmanuel said.

"*Yebo,*" Shabalala said. "But we know well how to work that way."

Emmanuel laughed and remembered that, yes, they had worked well together—it was just the trouble they got into on those other cases that bothered him. He wondered if nosy police detectives and Jewish doctors had as many lives as cats.

Karin crossed the yard with a confident stride. "Cyrus brought bad news?" she said. She hooked her thumbs into the belt loop of her dirty jeans and waited.

"No answer at the police station," Emmanuel replied. Removing the body without Bagley's help would be a challenge.

"Pa says your boy can eat lunch with the workers at the kaffir hut." Karin pointed beyond the milking shed to a whitewashed hut with a grass roof, adding to Shabalala, "Come back to the big house when I call, okay?"

Shabalala tipped his hat and walked off.

Emmanuel had the honor of joining the whites-only table in the homestead. Sampie, Karin and Emmanuel ate springbok stew with potatoes in almost complete silence. Occasionally, Sampie grunted requests and Karin obeyed. For dessert she served peeled oranges accompanied by a nip of peach brandy poured into old jam jars. Emmanuel had eaten only half his serving of stew and was about to request second helpings of the brandy when a shout came from the yard.

"What's that?" Sampie jumped up and cocked his head to the right, listening. More shouts and the slap of gum boots on dirt. Karin stood and reached for the rifle in the corner of the kitchen.

The dogs pawed the ground at the back door of the homestead, their unclipped nails digging into the dirt floor. Sampie pushed them out of the way and turned the handle. "Go!" he growled, and the boerboels sprinted into the yard, howling. Father, daughter and Emmanuel followed the pack of dogs outside, Karin slinging the rifle over her shoulder like a seasoned army sniper. The air was cool after the kitchen, the sun past its zenith.

"By the coop," Sampie said. "That's where they are. Go, Karin."

The dogs were already running along the perimeter of the wire fence surrounding the poultry yard. Sampie and Karin closed in. If anyone was still inside the henhouse there'd be no escaping now.

"Thieves," Shabalala said when Emmanuel moved in the direction of the fracas. Workmen scattered among the farm buildings, shouting. The dogs barked. Guinea fowl in the woods raised their own alarm. "Stand and be quiet, Sergeant."

The growls of the boerboels overwhelmed the crow of a rooster and the clucking of chickens. Emmanuel stood in the yard, straining to listen through all the sounds of panic.

"Did you hear?" Shabalala whispered.

"Footsteps," Emmanuel said. The sound was only just discernible. "Where from?"

A string of filthy Afrikaans curses issued from the direction of the chicken coop. Both Karin and Sampie were calling down a plague on the thief, who must have slipped the net.

A thud came from inside the Paulus homestead. Emmanuel and Shabalala ran to the front door left open by the maid, who now huddled against the wall in fear. The house was dark after the sunlight outside. Rusted metal clicked against rusted metal.

"Back door lock," Emmanuel said, and ran the obstacle course of rickety chairs and piles of yellowed newspaper in the passage. Something heavy fell from the top of the family organ and hit the floor. A gasp of breath was heard and then the creak of an opening door.

Emmanuel and Shabalala entered the kitchen together. A slim male figure bolted across the stoep and sprinted for the treeline. Alert to a new front of attack, the boerboels streaked around the corner of the lean-to. The figure melted into the brush, the dogs following him.

"Did you see that?" Emmanuel said after the dogs had disappeared.

"*Yebo,*" Shabalala said. "My eyes saw it, too. A white boy in a school uniform."

10

SAMPIE PAULUS'S FACE dripped sweat and his pale eyes glittered in the dim light. He tapped the bottom of a jam jar on the kitchen table and Karin poured more peach brandy into it. The dogs had come back from the hunt and were now asleep in front of the woodstove.

"It was that Reed bastard," Sampie said. "For sure."

"Of course," Karin agreed. "Who else?"

"From Little Flint?" Emmanuel was still trying to make sense of a white thief in a public school uniform stealing from people living below the poverty line. What did they have that he could possibly want?

"*Ja.*" Sampie downed half the contents of the jar. "He steals from all the farms around here. Been doing it for years, but what does that shithead Bagley do about it? Nothing. Filing a police report is a waste of time. The whole business is a fokken disgrace."

Emmanuel glanced at Karin, who stood back in the shadows and said nothing. Shabalala kept to an unlit corner and also remained silent.

"I met Thomas, Ella and the parents this morning," Emmanuel said. "Who is the boy?"

"The younger son," Karin answered. "The *befokked* one."

"What makes him crazy?" Emmanuel almost felt her shrug in the gloom.

"He's just not right in the head. Never has been."

"Give me an example," Emmanuel said. By some standards he'd be considered "befok" himself.

"Well." The word came out short and exasperated. "He runs away from school every term. He lives in the woods and steals from all the farmers, even from his own people. The shops in town have banned him because he steals from them, too."

"Easter holidays he beat one of the farmhands at Little Flint and the doctor had to come from Roselet," Sampie said. "The constable kept that quiet."

"What's his name?" Emmanuel asked. A disturbed, violent young man at Little Flint could have killed Amahle, he thought.

"Gabriel," Karin said. "And he speaks funny, doesn't he, Pa?"

"Like a skipping gramophone record. All here and there." Sampie swallowed half the remaining brandy and tears welled up when the alcohol hit. "What did he take this time?"

"The honey." Karin was annoyed. "I only got it this morning. Plus the gray and yellow blanket from my bed."

There was a long a pause before Sampie said, "Funny, he normally takes eggs from the chicken coop or sardines from the pantry. Sometimes jam. First time he's ever taken anything that wasn't food."

"Befok. Like I said."

Emmanuel considered the new information. Every family had outcasts: embezzling uncles, aunts pickled in gin, curb-crawling sons or promiscuous daughters. The Reeds weren't special in that regard. "Gabriel might have taken the blanket because he was cold," he said. "The temperature drops at night, especially out on the hillside."

"*Ja,* but not so much in spring," Sampie said. "And he knows how to build a fire. Karin found one of his hideaways last Easter, didn't you, girl? A rock tunnel behind a tree."

Emmanuel heard Karin shift her weight from one foot to the other, the way a boxer might before dodging a blow. "Do you know all the caves in the mountains around the farm, Karin?" he asked.

"Not all," she said defensively. "I don't know where that boy is hiding. His pa and brother normally get one of their Zulus to track him down and then they drive him back to school, crying like a baby."

The Zulu man Thomas Reed had dressed down in the cattle yard might well have been a tracker. "Do you know how long Gabriel's been on the run this time?" Emmanuel asked.

"No idea." Sampie rolled the jam jar between his palms, considering a top-up. "First we know about the little bastard being out in the woods is when he gets into the henhouse or the pantry."

"Today was the first time in a while, then?"

"*Ja.* He must have ditched school two or three days ago. That's how long it takes him to run down the valley and back home." Sampie pushed the jar across the table. "I'll give him his due: he outfoxes my dogs every time."

"The devil knows the darkness, Pa," Karin said, and Sampie nodded in agreement.

Emmanuel drew the threads of the story together. If what Sampie and Karin said was true, then the Reed boy was a habitual runaway and thief sheltered from the consequences of his actions by Constable Bagley's willful blindness. Emmanuel knew how this story could play out. It was easy to go from breaking minor laws to breaking major ones. In fact, if the perpetrator remained unpunished, it was almost inevitable. Some of Emmanuel's childhood friends had graduated from school to running the streets and then to prison before they reached twenty years old. He'd felt the insistent pull of the shadowy, dangerous corners of Sophiatown himself. In one of life's ironies, joining the army had saved him and perhaps ruined him at the same time.

"So, Gabriel could have been in the hills for days without anyone knowing about it," Emmanuel said. Depending on when the boy had absconded from school, he might have been in the area on the night Amahle was murdered.

"That's the Reeds' business, not mine. You'll have to check with them. And while you're there, Sergeant Cooper, ask them when they're going to buy me a new blanket and replace the jar of honey." Sampie pushed back from the table. "We'll check the river level in half an hour, see how we stand."

Karin removed the jam jar from the table while Sampie shuffled out of the kitchen and back to work.

"Have you seen Gabriel in the last few days?" Emmanuel asked Karin. A schoolboy could have made the prints around Amahle's body.

"No." She stared at the alcohol swirling at the bottom of the jar she held in her hand. "Haven't caught sight of him." She made eye contact with Emmanuel and swallowed the brandy in one shot. "I have to get back to work," she said, and walked away.

She was almost through the passage doorway when Emmanuel stopped her. "Wait. Your pa said that Gabriel Reed hit one of the farmworkers at Little Flint Farm."

"*Ja.* The doctor came out from town to fix things up." She rubbed a fingertip along a seam in the mud-brick wall.

"Must have been bad."

"Doctor couldn't come out here when Pa had the flu last winter but she travels to help a kaffir. What do you make of that?"

"I think someone got hurt badly," Emmanuel said. The family had been forced to send for proper medical help instead of using the first-aid box or calling on a local nun with a supply of novocaine. "Do you know what led to the beating?"

A smile curved Karin's mouth and she appeared soft and pliant in the half-light. "I can't say for sure. It might have had something to do with a workman laying a hand on one of the Reeds' special kaffirs . . ."

"Amahle?" Emmanuel asked.

"I don't know. That's English business." She left the kitchen.

"Well, that was either a hint about Amahle being the cause of the problem, or spite," Emmanuel said to Shabalala. "Karin doesn't like the Reeds or the way they treated Amahle when she was alive, that much I do know."

"The kitchen gardener with the broken face must have been the one beaten by the little Reed baas." Shabalala made the connection. "He will never talk. We must ask the constable and the doctor about the fight."

"Bagley is nowhere, so let's ask Dr. Daglish when we get back to Roselet. If the workman's injuries were serious she would have visited Little Flint a few times." Emmanuel swallowed a mouthful of brandy and offered the bottle to Shabalala, who declined. "Daglish knew Amahle after all," he said. "Why would she lie about a thing like that?"

—

The creek had receded and the main road to Roselet was two stepping-stones away. Shabalala cleared the water first and Emmanuel followed. By now, keeping dry didn't matter. They both looked ragged as hobos in stolen suits.

"No Mr. Insurance Policy," Emmanuel said, and crossed the grass verge to the Chevrolet. It was two p.m. and Zweigman's examination of the body was probably finished by now. The results might yield some answers.

"No one has heard of him, Sergeant. He is not a Zulu from the valley."

"We'll ask in town, but it feels like that lead is going nowhere." He fished out the car keys and inserted them in the driver's-side door. The angle was wrong, the keyhole at a lower level than normal. He stepped back to look.

"Little bastard." Emmanuel now knew how Sampie Paulus felt when the Reed boy stole from the homestead and escaped without punishment. "The front tire's been slashed."

"Huh . . ." Shabalala crouched down to examine the damage. "One cut with a small knife. The tire must be changed."

Another delay, Emmanuel thought. It was no wonder he hated the country. Dirt, flies, cow dung and now a thieving schoolboy with a malicious streak and a knife.

"I'll check the spare." He opened the boot, praying the police motor pool was up to standard. It was—this time, at least. He removed the tool bag and lifted the spare from the well. Shabalala unpacked the jack and wrench and set to work. Despite not having the authority to drive a car, at some stage the black detective had learned to change a flat.

11

TOWN WAS QUIET. A wrinkled white woman and her bulldozer of a black maid trundled past two farm trucks parked outside Dawson's General Store. A spindly yellow dog trotted at the side of the road with its nose to the ground.

"Three main stores," Emmanuel said. He'd filled Shabalala in on Amahle and her payday purchases. "The café is Europeans-only, so she didn't go there. That leaves the farm supply depot, the general store and the spaza shops hidden in the backstreets. A couple of hours' work at best."

"I will ask at the spaza shops," Shabalala said. These hidden businesses operating out of back rooms and side windows were the lifeblood of the black community. Spaza shops traded without a license and remained out of sight of the authorities. "Maybe the chief's daughter bought a Fanta or some other small thing."

"Very possible." Emmanuel turned left and into the doctor's driveway.

"Sergeant . . ." Shabalala's fingers gripped the dashboard. "Look out."

Zweigman and Daglish appeared out of nowhere, running full-pelt toward the car like two escapees from a demented physicians' home. Emmanuel slammed on the brakes and the tires kicked gravel into the air. The Chevrolet stopped inches from Zweigman's outstretched hands.

"Quickly." The German doctor was sweating heavily, a raised lump swelling at the center of his forehead. "He's still inside."

"Who?" Emmanuel cleared the driver's seat in seconds. Shabalala was one step ahead of him, surveying the garden and the side path for signs of danger.

"We tried to call the police station from inside the house." Margaret Daglish's cheeks were red, her words tumbling out. "There was no answer, so we ran."

"Tell me what happened," Emmanuel said.

"Shhh . . ." Shabalala raised a finger for quiet. He said, "Footsteps splashing in water."

"The creek," Margaret Daglish guessed. "Thank God for that. He's running back to the valley."

"*Hamba!*" Emmanuel said to Shabalala. "Let's move."

They hit the side path and broke out of the rear of the property in less than thirty seconds. Another thirty seconds brought them to the shallow stream crowded with stones. Across the water and too far in the distance to make a clean identification, a black speck sliced across the veldt at incredible speed.

"Wait." Emmanuel placed a hand on Shabalala's arm before the Zulu detective could jump the stream. "Reckon you can catch up?"

"Yes," Shabalala said, then added, "Eventually."

"Let him go." That was the only option. It would take precious time to close the gap, with no guarantee of capture or an interview at the end. The speck melded into a rock outcrop and disappeared into the landscape. "Let's find out what happened to Daglish and Zweigman."

"A moment, please." Shabalala crouched down at the edge of the stream and examined the faint indentations in the sandbank. Next he doubled back on the path leading to the cellar, stopping every few feet to examine the crushed grass and disturbed soil. Emmanuel held his breath. Shabalala only stopped when he thought he had something valuable.

"It is he," Shabalala said. "The same man who stayed with Amahle on the mountain."

"Dr. Daglish knows who made these prints," Emmanuel said. "We may have a suspect."

The path back to the doctor's house sloped upward but the climb was easy. Answers waited at the top of the rise: a name for the man at the crime scene and a clear direction for the investigation.

A loud thump drew them more quickly along the path. Dr. Daglish stood outside the cellar entrance, while Zweigman slammed a stooped shoulder against the door, trying to force entry.

"We shouldn't have left her." Daglish was distraught. "It was cowardly."

"We had no choice in the matter," Zweigman said, and pounded both fists against the locked door in frustration.

"Let us take a look." Emmanuel stepped closer and examined the door: a solid slab of wood strong enough to keep a maiden safe from dragons. Ironic, given the present circumstances.

"Think we can kick it in?" he asked Shabalala.

"No," came the short answer. "Even together, we are not

strong enough." The lock was solid brass weathered by the elements. Green threads of moss spread across the pitted metal surface.

"Get the crowbar from the boot of the car, Constable."

Shabalala held out his hand for the keys. A perfectly normal interaction, but one that Emmanuel found intensely embarrassing. The keys to the car, the office filing cabinet and station gun locker would never be in Shabalala's pocket . . . Not in this lifetime.

"There's a crowbar in my toolshed," Daglish said, eager to help. "Just here." She rushed across the grass to a rectangular outbuilding and pushed open the rusting door. The sound of soft curses and clanking bottles was followed by a triumphant "Aha!" She emerged with the crowbar and gave it to Shabalala, clearly the strongest of the three men. He hesitated, uncertain how to proceed. Protocol demanded that European officers go first in all things.

"Be my guest," Emmanuel said, and moved aside to give Shabalala access to the lock. Trying to match the Zulu's power-to-weight ratio was a waste of time.

"What do you think he did in there?" Daglish whispered to Zweigman. "Something bad?"

"The bad thing has already happened. The girl is dead," the German doctor replied with cold logic. "No more harm can come to her."

Wisdom gained from war, Emmanuel knew.

"Haaa . . ." Shabalala breathed out and pulled hard on the crowbar. The lock snapped, sending metal and wood fragments into the air. The door creaked open to darkness. A chill emanated from the interior.

"With me, Constable." Emmanuel ducked under the low

eaves and stepped inside. He flicked the light switch. Loose bandages and surgical instruments littered the floor, evidence of a paroxysm of rage or grief. He noticed the disarray in passing. Shabalala fell into step and they moved deeper into the room.

The white sheet covering Amahle was tucked under her shoulders and pulled over her bare legs and feet. Karin Paulus's stolen gray and yellow blanket was neatly rolled up beneath her head.

"Gabriel Reed," Emmanuel said.

—

Zweigman picked up scattered probes and steel scalpels and arranged them next to each other on the side table, systematically reordering his thoughts and his emotions in the process. "It happened fast," he said. "One moment Dr. Daglish and I were alone, finishing up the examination. The next, he was inside shouting and throwing instruments to the floor."

"I didn't think to lock the door," Daglish said quietly.

"Understandable. There was no danger." Zweigman bent to retrieve a wad of cotton wool and tottered sideways. The lump on his forehead was egg-shaped and getting larger.

"Sit down before you fall down." Emmanuel caught Zweigman by the elbow, ready to lead him to a chair.

"No. Thank you." The German doctor patted Emmanuel's hand. Emmanuel let him go. Zweigman continued sifting through the medical debris. "I'm looking for something very specific."

"Of course . . ." Daglish crouched next to Zweigman and joined the search. "I almost forgot."

Each piece of equipment was held up to the electric light

and examined, every inch of floor raked over in detail. Emmanuel and Shabalala moved back and gave the doctors room.

"Aha . . . there you are." Zweigman fell to his knees and leaned close to the floor. "Tweezers and a bowl, please, Doctor."

Daglish handed over the items. It took a moment for Emmanuel to make out the tiny object held in the tweezers' grip, a finely sharpened fragment of white and brown organic material. He had no idea what it was.

"A porcupine quill," Shabalala said, and Daglish smiled.

"That was my guess," she said. "I've found them in the garden and on walks across the river."

"Where did this one come from?" Emmanuel asked. The Zulu women guarding Amahle's body had translucent quills decorating their head coverings, a privilege reserved for married women. Chief Matebula's pouting little wife also had them woven through her hair.

"It was buried deep in the puncture wound on the girl's back. We probed the wound this morning and found nothing. After lunch we decided to try again—for luck," Zweigman said. "The mad schoolboy broke in right after we found it."

"We were laughing," Daglish confessed. "Not because the situation was funny. It's just that we didn't expect to find anything, and there it was—a sharpened quill. It was a surprise."

"The situation must have appeared ghoulish to a child." Zweigman dropped the quill into the metal dish. "Two grown-ups laughing in the presence of a dead body."

"Yes, it might have looked that way to Gabriel. He was furious. Told us to get out of the cellar."

"I declined the offer," Zweigman said with characteristic dryness. "He bounced my head against the wall and said he'd cut us both with a knife, the way we had cut the girl. So we ran."

"Then I called the station and nobody answered," Daglish said. "I didn't want to abandon the cellar and leave the boy with the body but I was afraid. And he'd already hit Dr. Zweigman."

"You did the right thing," Emmanuel assured her, and noted again the white sheet tucked under Amahle's shoulders and the blanket rolled snugly under her head. After vandalizing the room and violently assaulting Zweigman, the boy still took time to care for Amahle. He was a contradiction, aggressive one minute, gentle the next.

Emmanuel had witnessed that paradox a few times at crime scenes, a tender act following a sudden, horrific act of violence. Making the body comfortable with a pillow or a blanket, closing its eyes, pulling down the hem of a dress or arranging the limbs just so allowed the murderer to express love or remorse one last time.

"Is that what killed Amahle?" Emmanuel pointed to the quill fragment lying in the bowl. About two inches in length with a sharp tip, it didn't look capable of harming anyone.

"Not on its own," Zweigman said. "Left in the flesh it might eventually have led to an infection. Or it could just as easily have worked its way to the surface of the skin and been expelled without any real harm being done."

"Constable?" Emmanuel prompted Shabalala for ideas based on intuition and bush skills rather than medical facts.

"The quill did not get so deep by accident," the Zulu detective said. "It was stabbed into the flesh, like a needle."

"Interesting." Zweigman peered at the hollow body of the quill, open at the far end. "Any needle made from a strong enough material can be used to inject medicine into the bloodstream. Or toxins."

"She was poisoned?" Emmanuel said. An internal attack on Amahle's vital organs would explain the lack of broken bones and serious bruises on her body.

"That's an educated guess, Sergeant Cooper," Zweigman said. "A test on the quill tip would confirm the use of poison, but only a full autopsy can provide a definite cause of death."

That was not good news for the investigation or for Amahle's family crying out for her return home. Results from the autopsy and the toxicology test could take weeks, depending on the backlog of cases.

"Any other educated guesses on the cause of death?" Emmanuel could not hide his frustration at the inconclusive result of the examination. Gabriel Reed would be easier to crack in an interview if they had leverage—such as a definitive idea of how Amahle was killed, for a start.

Zweigman placed the specimen dish onto the side table and retrieved a sheaf of papers. He thumbed his glasses higher on his nose and peered at his own chicken-scratch writing. "The victim is a native female aged between sixteen and nineteen. She was in good health at the time of her death, with no evidence of physical abuse. She was well nourished and well groomed. The only visible injuries to the victim were a small bruise on her inner left thigh and a puncture wound on the lumbar vertebrae. A red swelling runs from the wound to the base of the neck. Cause unknown. Estimated time of death between six p.m. Friday night and eight p.m. Saturday." Zweigman stopped reading and set the papers aside. "Much as it grieves you, Detective, neither Dr. Daglish nor I can give you what we do not have. Speculation is not science."

"If you did have to speculate." Emmanuel used a gentler tone: it must sting for a man of Zweigman's stature to admit he'd come up empty. "What would the most likely cause of death be?"

"I've never seen symptoms like these before. Not in Germany and not in South Africa." Zweigman returned to the steel dish, fascinated by the destructive power of such a small object. "If the tip was poisoned and then stabbed into the body, the wound and the swelling along the length of the spine make sense."

The hollow in the quill could hold only half a teaspoon of liquid. "Powerful stuff," Emmanuel said.

"Indeed. No known compound springs to mind," Zweigman said.

"Maybe not to a European mind." Dr. Daglish leaned closer and spoke in a whisper. "The Zulus have witch doctors who use the plants and the animals in the valley for medicine and for magic. The potions are secret."

Emmanuel did not believe in the mystical powers of these traditional healers, who threw animal bones to diagnose and treat ailments. He caught Shabalala's eye. The Zulu policeman was clearly trying to ignore the whispered conversation.

"What do you think? Could a witch doctor mix up a poison strong enough to kill?"

"I cannot say. All *sangoma* are different." Shabalala spoke the word with a mixture of fear and respect. *Sangoma* meant not just a healer but also an individual with the ability to cross from the ordinary world into the supernatural one. *Witch doctor* was a missionary term adopted by Europeans and educated Africans. Shabalala's use of the proper title reminded Emmanuel of a major difference between them. His partner allowed himself to believe in the possibility of magic and spirits, although he'd never admit to it in front of two medical professionals.

Zweigman traced his fingers around the swelling on his forehead. "What treatment do you recommend for my injury, Dr. Daglish? The pain is getting worse."

"A cold compress, two aspirin and a cup of tea. In that order," Daglish said.

"An excellent prescription." Zweigman proceeded to the broken cellar door. "I'm sure Detectives Cooper and Shabalala will be ready for a break in a few minutes."

"Of course." Daglish paused at the door on her way out. "A drink for you both?"

"Tea," Emmanuel said, and wondered if the old Jew really needed aspirin or if he was just giving Shabalala the room to talk freely. Zweigman's ability to read a situation was uncanny—another product of wartime, when the slightest pause in a sentence could mean the difference between going home for dinner or ending up in a cattle car headed east.

"Tea also, thank you," Shabalala said, and the two doctors filed out of the cellar. Footsteps sounded on the stairs leading to the back door of the house.

"It's not a *muti* killing." That much Emmanuel knew from years of living side by side with Zulus, Tswanas and poor whites in the chaos of Sophiatown. *Muti* was the Zulu word for "medicine," but when used by cops it referred almost exclusively to the dark spectrum of traditional medicine, which relied on harvested body parts to increase the strength of spells and to effect cures: a severed hand incorporated into the doorway of a shop to attract customers, a fetus cut from a pregnant woman and buried in a field to increase crop yield, the intestines of a young child eaten to give strength and success. The grim trade continued in the cities and the countryside, nourished by an ancient, unshakable belief in the power of witchcraft.

"Not *muti,*" Shabalala agreed. "The blood and the organs of a young girl are very powerful. Amahle is intact."

"A *sangoma* could be involved in the making of the poison, right?" Emmanuel asked.

"Yes. Every *sangoma* must learn how to heal and how to cause harm. What they do with this knowledge after they finish is for them to decide."

"So any traditional healer would know where to look for naturally occurring poisons, not just the healers who use black magic."

"That is so, but . . ." Shabalala paused, thinking of a simple way to explain the rules governing the use of black *muti.* "If a *sangoma,* a male or a female, opens their medicine bag to bring pain or death to a person, a darkness enters the bag and never leaves. Even if they try to do good, darkness will always follow."

"They're contaminated." Emmanuel understood. A favorite hymn at boarding school boasted, "Surely goodness and mercy shall follow me all the days of my life," but he'd known, even at the age of fifteen, that the opposite was also true. Shadows and blood possessed the same staying power.

"This is why almost all the *sangomas* stand back from black *muti.* It cannot be picked up and then put down again," Shabalala said. "It stays."

"Who would employ a *sangoma* to kill our girl?" Emmanuel asked. "None of the Zulu we've met so far had a motive for killing her."

Shabalala began to reply but clamped his mouth shut instead.

"Spit it out, Constable," Emmanuel said. Hitting the race barrier at every bend and bump in the road was tiring.

Shabalala glanced at Amahle, tucked under the sheet. "There are Europeans who use *sangomas*, but they come at night, creeping in the dark. They are ashamed of what they do, so keep their activities hidden from other white people. This boy, Gabriel, does not hide anything. He stayed through the night to guard the body and now he comes in daylight with his face uncovered to pay tribute."

That was beffoked behavior by English, Afrikaner and black African standards. Openly displayed affection across the color barrier caused intense embarrassment to the community and attracted the attention of the police.

"The boy might be crazy," Emmanuel said. "But breaking into this cellar is a whole other level of insanity. He's put the hangman's noose around his own neck for no reason I can figure."

"It could be that this boy does not think he has done anything wrong."

"True." That opened up the possibility of an unfit-to-stand-trial plea and a long stay in a mental health facility. Family money would buy a single room and daily sessions of basket weaving to classical music. "Let's face it, no one in their right mind kills a girl, stays with the body and then tracks her corpse down to make sure that her head is resting comfortably."

"That is a mystery," Shabalala said.

The chirp of birds brought the sound of spring and wide horizons into the dank cellar. Emmanuel walked through the broken doorway into the open air. Details from the crime scene flashed through his mind: the rolled-up tartan blanket, the scattered wildflowers, the sheltering branches of the fig tree spread like angels' wings over the body. Gabriel's behavior, however odd, was driven by a desire to care for Amahle, even after death.

"A poisoned quill," Emmanuel said, trying to put the use of this elegant weapon into context. Poison was a stealth killer that left no fingerprints, whereas Gabriel did not give a damn about keeping hidden or covering his tracks. "Doesn't exactly match with a crime of passion or a violent argument. Planning was involved."

"Another mystery." Shabalala ducked under the eaves and joined him in contemplation. The two men looked at the mountains rising up across the field. A whistling kettle drowned the swell of classical music playing on a radio in the Daglish kitchen.

"We have to find the Reed boy, and we aren't the only ones looking." Emmanuel described the interaction that had taken place in the cattle yard of Little Flint. "I think big brother Thomas has a Zulu tracker on the trail. If the family finds Gabriel first we can kiss access good-bye. At least until the lawyers and medical experts are lined up in defense."

"Tracking the boy will be easy," Shabalala said. "But he is fast. Catching him will be hard."

"Tell me what we need."

"Food, water, matches, one blanket each. Comfortable clothes and running shoes for you, Sergeant." Gabriel's knowledge of the mountainous terrain and his sheer wiliness gave him the advantage. With the blanket safely delivered to Amahle, he wasn't coming back into town anytime soon. Shabalala knew that and was prepared for an overnight excursion.

"We're going camping."

"Hunting."

"When do we leave?"

"Now. Before the day grows old."

"Right after we've gathered supplies and I've arranged a mortuary van to retrieve the body from the ledge above Covenant Farm," Emmanuel said. "Dawson's should have everything we need."

"Not for me." The Zulu detective pinched a new crease in the crown of his hat. "I have all that I need."

"You're not running up mountains in a suit and those shoes. Not again," Emmanuel said. "Neither am I."

Shabalala's reluctance to spend money was understandable. Expenditure while on the job was reimbursable when accompanied by stamped and dated receipts presented with the final investigation report. Then came weeks of bureaucratic scrutiny to determine if the items purchased were a legitimate expense. The whole process was better avoided.

"Don't worry," Emmanuel said. "Van Niekerk will reimburse me in cash." Working for a police colonel who did not stick to the rules had its perks.

"Then we must go quickly to Dawson's." The sun was lower in the sky now, signaling the rapid unfolding of the afternoon. Every moment put Gabriel deeper into the mountains and farther out of reach.

"Tea, gentlemen." Zweigman descended the stairs with two mugs. Daglish walked a step behind, carrying a tray with a teapot and two more mugs.

"Thanks." Emmanuel accepted the creamy white tea from Zwiegman and smelled the sweet overload of sugar. Lunch at the Paulus farm had left a greasy taste in his mouth. Shabalala's meal would have been even less appealing, he knew: a cob of steamed corn washed down with fermented corn drink or a slab of stale bread slathered in lard. At Little Flint Farm they'd been offered nothing at all. He caught sight of the plate of biscuits on Daglish's tray. Shabalala was already chewing shortbread and gulping tea.

Emmanuel ate two buttery slabs of shortbread and drained his mug. Fuel for the cross-country search.

"That barely touched the sides," Daglish said, and rested the tray on a middle step. "Another tea, Detective Cooper?"

"For both of us, thanks." He held out his mug for a refill and Shabalala did the same. The gap with Gabriel Reed was widening, but they'd never close it on empty stomachs.

"Perhaps we should have killed a cow," Zweigman said with dry humor. "When did you last eat?"

"A few hours ago," Emmanuel said. "But neither of us had much. We were at Covenant Farm—the Paulus place." He turned to Daglish. "They told us you were called to attend an injured workman on Little Flint Farm during the Easter holidays."

"Oh . . ." The doctor held her now-unbandaged wrist close to her chest as if the mention of Little Flint brought pain surging back into the joints.

"I'd like to know what happened. In your own words."

Daglish fidgeted, adjusting the angle of the teapot and fiddling with the silver spoons on the tray, placing them together and then pushing them apart. "I knew that night would come back for me," she murmured softly, the words colored by regret.

"Grab your tea and let's walk, Doctor."

"Yes." Daglish didn't argue. "Let's walk."

12

FIVE MINUTES," EMMANUEL said to Shabalala. He and Daglish set off in a counterclockwise direction taking them through the garden and around to the front of the cottage. Daglish picked a fallen leaf off the path and threw it under an azalea bush.

"The garden boy and the maid have the day off," she explained. "Talk spreads fast in Roselet."

"Did the Reeds phone you personally?" Emmanuel stared out to the hills, his face turned from Daglish like a priest preparing to receive an admission of sin.

"No." She hesitated, then continued. "Constable Bagley came to the house and said there was a medical emergency in the valley. He drove me out to Little Flint."

"Was that usual?"

"I prefer seeing patients here at the cottage. My husband Jim often has the car, so house calls are difficult. He's away a lot."

"Jim" and "difficult" were given equal emphasis. There was no car in the driveway now and hadn't been for the last two days. Maybe Margaret's husband was on the wide-open road, notching up car crashes. "The car was here that night but Constable Bagley insisted on driving me out to the farm. I thought it was odd at the time, but the Reeds are the biggest landholders in the area and the police are the police."

"The farmworker needed your help," Emmanuel said. "You didn't have a choice."

"That's true." Daglish flexed her fingers, releasing tension in the joints. "I wouldn't have refused even if I'd known about the situation at Little Flint." That she was honoring her oath to heal the sick and tend the wounded had not seemed to occur to her till now.

"Go on," Emmanuel said. The doctor was ready to talk and he was here to listen. In this lifting of burdens lay the unspoken beauty of police work. "Tell me what happened after reaching Little Flint."

"Thomas Reed was waiting at the gate. He took us to the servants' quarters at the back of the house. It was so quiet, I remember. Not a sound from the family or the servants in the other huts."

A hushed silence crept into places in the aftermath of violence. The air felt as if it were robbed of sound, leaving a blank in its wake. Emmanuel knew that emptiness well. "The workman's injuries were severe," Daglish continued. "A broken nose and a fractured eye socket. There was a lot of blood. The floor of the hut was covered in it."

Enter the cleanup team, Emmanuel thought cynically. A fresh and growing pool of servant's blood was enough to frighten the richest of landed gentry into action—a family's reputation took generations to repair. "And Gabriel?"

"Two broken fingers, cut knuckles and forehead, bruises

to the arms and chest." Daglish pinched a spent bloom from a rosebush and twirled it between her fingers. "That was about seven months ago. They both pulled through. No major complications."

"Two happy endings," Emmanuel said. "What aren't you telling me, Doctor?"

"It was Bagley, the way he was that night. He stood at my shoulder the entire time, blood soaking through his shoes, waiting for a prognosis on the workman. The moment I said, 'He'll live,' the monologue started." A black hawk glided high in the slate-blue sky above them, hunting. Daglish watched it for a minute. "Bagley told the workman he was lucky that Baas Reed wasn't going to lay assault charges against him or expel his children from the farm school. If he was a good boy and behaved, the job in the yards would be kept for him."

"Generous," Emmanuel said.

"The whole episode was awful. I liked Bagley before that, thought he was a good policeman. The firm-but-fair kind."

Emmanuel recalled Sampie Paulus's bitter accusations that the local station commander acted like he was tucked in the pocket of the Reed family. "Amahle was around that night?" he asked.

"Yes, the girl was in Gabriel's room, sitting on the end of the bed. There's nothing unusual about a servant being in an injured person's bedroom. At least, I didn't think so until I started stitching the cut on Gabriel's head." Daglish began walking again, circumnavigating the cottage. The path began to lead them back to the rear garden and to Zweigman and Shabalala. "The needle set him off. He tried to jump out of bed but she took his hands and talked to him in Zulu. I don't know what she said but it calmed him down and he let me keep working so long as she was there."

They walked on. Emmanuel waited.

"Funny." Daglish frowned at the memory. "Gabriel speaks Zulu fluently. Better than English. The girl, Amahle, even had a nickname for him."

"Remember what it was?" Maybe Mr. Insurance Policy's identity was about to be revealed.

"Nyonyane. I think that was it. She said it over and over, like a chant."

The doctor's pronunciation was off by at least two syllables but close enough to make a guess. "Little bird," Emmanuel said. The name conjured a frail and vulnerable creature in need of protection from predators—not a boy who broke into homes, stole things and pushed an old man's head into a wall. The name was all the more interesting because Zulu nicknames were given only after the true essence of a person was revealed to the name-giver.

A workman at the Fountain of Light School had named Emmanuel Imvubu "the hippo." The name had nothing to do with the animal's size but with its nature. The hippo was considered a "mixed-up creature," unruly and uncontrollable. Emmanuel spent four years living up to the name.

The rear corner of the house drew closer. Daglish stopped talking.

"Holding hands, talking sweet. That's all very lovely," Emmanuel said. "Now tell me the rest."

The doctor's face reddened and she said, "I finished stitching the cut and made Gabriel sit up and take two aspirin, for the pain. He lay down again and pulled the girl onto the bed beside him. They didn't kiss or touch but the whole thing was . . ." She searched for the right word and couldn't find it.

"Intimate," Emmanuel suggested.

"Shocking." Daglish stopped and picked at the petals of an azalea bloom to hide her embarrassment. "I'm no supporter of Prime Minister Malan and his Afrikaner volk, but it was obvious that Gabriel and this girl were used to being in bed together."

Like many of the English, Daglish played hide-and-seek with her own beliefs. The National Party at least said what they believed in: blacks and whites shall not, under pain of imprisonment, mix sweat and bodily fluids. They made no excuses, never blamed anyone else for their beliefs. People like Margaret Daglish couldn't reconcile their discomfort at races mixing with their desire to appear enlightened.

"You despise people like me, don't you?" Daglish kept tearing petals. "The middle-class English who pretend they want the best for Africa and the Africans but shudder at the idea that one of us might be going black."

"*Going black.*" Such a quaint expression. Emmanuel hadn't heard it in years. "Going native" was the more usual way to express the deep-seated colonial dread of reverting to a primitive state. If left unchecked, this pull back to the wild would see white men and women squatting in grass huts, surrounded by naked children gnawing on impala bones.

"You thought Amahle was pregnant," Emmanuel said, suddenly struck. "That's why you didn't want to conduct the examination."

Daglish plucked the last bloom and dusted pollen from her fingers. "The Zulus have a saying, 'When elephants fight it's the grass that suffers.' I wanted to steer clear of the Reed family. Constable Bagley also. It was cowardly, I know."

"But understandable," Emmanuel said. Guilt was unproductive. "Constable Shabalala and I get to leave Roselet after the investigation is over. You don't."

"I'll survive." She began walking slowly to the rear of the house. "It turns out I was wrong about everything. Amahle was still a virgin."

"Zweigman confirmed it?" Virginity didn't rule out a sexual relationship. There were plenty of ways to scratch an itch.

"He did," Daglish said. "Constable Bagley and I were the ones to jump to conclusions that night."

"Hold on." The town doctor's comment got Emmanuel's full attention. "You're saying that Bagley was in Gabriel's room with you?"

"Oh, yes. He stayed close to me during the whole visit." The smile faded. "Making sure I knew I should keep this quiet, no doubt."

"He was in the room the entire time?" He pressed. Bagley's every minute had to be accounted for, otherwise Emmanuel knew the constable would claim to have been elsewhere during Gabriel's medical treatment.

"From beginning to end." Despite the warmth of the day the doctor rubbed her arms. "The expression on his face will stay with me for a long time." Emmanuel lifted an eyebrow to encourage her. "It was disgust mixed with desire. I think he hated Gabriel for being so morally weak but envied him at the same time."

The Roselet station commander was a coward and a liar. That changed everything for Emmanuel. To hell with the police brotherhood, Bagley deserved whatever he had coming to him.

"Maybe I was mistaken . . ." Daglish hesitated before turning the corner of the cottage, anxious that she'd damaged the policeman's reputation.

"I'm sure you read the situation just right," Emmanuel said, and quickened his pace. Constable Bagley was out in the hills with the native constables. That made the locked filing cabinet at the police station fair game.

Shabalala and Zweigman stood in the middle of the garden. They made a striking pair, a towering Zulu and a wizened German Jew, both grinning at an image Zweigman was holding in a black leather wallet. Yet another picture of Dimitri, Emmanuel thought, the adopted genius baby. Shabalala's continued enthusiasm for these pictures mystified Emmanuel.

"Constable," he called to Shabalala. "Time to move."

Shabalala turned, looking startled. Zweigman snapped the wallet shut and stuffed it into a pocket and out of sight. No smiles now, just an uncomfortable silence matched by a visible effort on both their parts to act normal.

"Coming, Sergeant." Shabalala cut across the grass, hat tilted low to shade his eyes.

"Dawson's and then the police station." Emmanuel brushed off the image of his two closest friends huddled over a secret and excluding him. Obviously the picture in Zweigman's wallet was for married men with children only. That was fine; he didn't have to time to coo over family snapshots.

"What are my orders, Sergeant?" The German doctor fiddled the edge of his wallet deeper into his pocket before approaching.

"I'll check with van Niekerk and let you know," Emmanuel said. "The colonel might want you to stay on. Or he might decide to send you home."

"I have every intention of staying on," Zweigman said. "I am the attending physician here at van Niekerk's personal request."

"We'll see," Emmanuel said. Predicting the colonel's mood was an inexact science he'd never mastered. "Shabalala and I will be back soon."

He turned to Margaret, who hovered in the background. "Can you get our German friend more tea and keep him out of trouble till we get back?"

"Tea will be easy," she said. "But after this morning, I can't make any promises about avoiding trouble."

"A promise would be useless in any case," Zweigman said. "Detective Sergeant Cooper and trouble are best friends. They travel, eat and sleep together."

"I thought as much." Daglish smiled and the ghost of the bright young girl she must once have been—determined to rid the world of plague and pestilence—momentarily stirred to life.

Emmanuel and Shabalala started walking to the car.

"Detective Cooper." The town doctor caught up and spoke in a whisper. "There's a spare room at the back of the house. Dr. Zweigman is most welcome to use it."

"We're here on police business. The department will pay for a room at the hotel where I'm staying."

"Yes, about that . . ." Daglish stopped dead, forcing Emmanuel to stop, too. "The hotel doesn't take natives or certain types of Europeans."

That took a second to translate. "No Jews," he said.

"That's right," she replied.

Emmanuel rubbed the back of his neck, thinking. The right to discriminate was enshrined in law and perfectly legal but he took the small, domestic tyranny of South African life as a personal insult. A distinguished surgeon denied a hotel room, a Zulu detective stuck at the rank of constable till death—it was all self-defeating bullshit.

"Offer Zweigman the room," he said. "Tell him that Shabalala and I will be away for the night and you'd rather he spent the evening with a friend instead of strangers. Don't mention the hotel."

"Of course not," Daglish mumbled, and then added in the typically nervous way of the English when confronted with an embarrassing situation, "I'm so sorry about this."

"Not your fault." Emmanuel moved off before Margaret Daglish started in on how most folk in Roselet were good country people, kindhearted and hospitable. Every South African was perfectly reasonable within the boundaries of their own families and their own race group. It was the point of crossover that killed them.

"Grab the crowbar, Shabalala," Emmanuel said when the Chevrolet boot was open. They could shop for supplies later. He needed to burn energy. Now.

"Let's do some damage."

The lock snapped under the force of the crowbar and the last drawer opened. Listed in alphabetical order with dates penciled along the top right corner of each file, Roselet's criminal history was neatly cataloged. Emmanuel threw the crowbar aside. It clanked on the concrete floor.

"Check for the names Reed, Matebula and Paulus. Then

see if Gabriel and Amahle have their own files," he said. "I'll call the colonel while you search."

"Yes, Sergeant." Shabalala was uneasy. Breaking-and-entering was against the law, even for the police.

"Relax." Emmanuel picked up the telephone and dialed the operator. "Bagley's not going to lodge a complaint. Believe me. If he does, I'll toss him into a departmental hearing that will end his career."

Shabalala began flipping through the files. "You have no wish for a peaceful life, Sergeant," he said. "Maybe a wife and some sons and daughters will make you more cautious . . ."

Emmanuel smiled. "I'll take the heat for this little break-and-enter, Shabalala. Your family is safe."

The telephone in Durban was picked up. "What news, Cooper?" The connection was clear, the colonel's Dutch accent clipped and precise.

Emmanuel said, "Another dead body, sir."

"Black or white?"

"A black man, killed in a similar way to the girl." He didn't mention the mutilation of the corpse. The colonel wasn't interested in native rituals and customs, and they'd take too long to explain anyway.

"Any Europeans on the list of suspects?"

"Gabriel Reed. Youngest son of a rich farmer. Biggest farm in the valley. He was at the crime scene and had regular contact with the girl."

"Don't be coy, Cooper," van Niekerk said. "If he was fucking her, then say so."

"They were physically close but she was a virgin at the time of death. Zweigman's examination confirmed it."

"Cause of death?" Van Niekerk was assimilating the facts

and calculating what professional gain he might achieve from the investigation. A European killer added profile to a native murder. The press would swarm the court and the newspapers would splash photos of the accused killer under headlines like "White boy slays black lover." Detectives and their superior officers fought each other for that kind of attention.

"Cause of death still unknown," Emmanuel said.

"What does the old Jew recommend?"

"A full autopsy and a toxicology test. He also wants to accompany the body."

The colonel paused again, weighing up effort expended against personal gain, then said, "The collection of a native girl so far out in the country is unusual, but I'll make an exception. A van will collect the girl's body and the doctor tomorrow morning."

"Thank you," Emmanuel said. "Zweigman will be pleased."

"If this boy is guilty, then detain him. But do it quietly, Cooper. No press. No celebratory drinks with the local constable." Van Niekerk was already planning ahead. "Tell the family that the kid is helping the police investigation, nothing more. Keep the charges under wraps."

"For how long, sir?"

"Till we're ready to announce the arrest."

To a roomful of police brass and to the Dutch and English press, was Emmanuel's guess. Van Niekerk never let an opportunity pass. He was always reaching, ready to grab the golden ring that would bring him closer to the position of police commissioner.

"Will do, Colonel."

The line went dead and Emmanuel turned to Shabalala,

who still looked uneasy with the role of lawbreaker. "What did you find?"

"One file only for the boy." Shabalala placed a brown folder onto Bagley's desk. *GABRIEL* was printed on the top in black ink. No surname. "For the rest there is nothing."

"Find the station occurrence book and check the entries for Saturday morning. See if Amahle is listed as a missing person." Emmanuel was sure Amahle's disappearance had never been recorded, but a log that confirmed that fact would prove Bagley was a liar. He opened the folder and took out a single page with one entry.

"Edmund Crisp. Principal. King's Row College. That must be the school that Gabriel runs away from."

Emmanuel rang through to King's Row and eventually got Edmund Crisp on the line after talking his way past a suspicious receptionist. Calls from the police were clearly not welcome.

"Yes, Gabriel Reed is a student here," Crisp said. "He's on a special excursion at the moment. Camping in the hills as part of our outdoor education program. The participating boys are due back in four days' time."

Emmanuel admired the cunning mix of fact and fiction in the headmaster's story. The best lies always included an element of truth. Gabriel really was camping out in the hills. "I'll call back, then," he said, and hung up. There'd be an auditorium or a science lab at King's Row College with the Reed family name etched onto a brass plaque.

Shabalala slid a hardcover ledger across the desk. "The station occurrence book. It was hidden behind the files in the first drawer. Look and see."

A break-and-enter at Dawson's and the theft of some cows

from Dovecote Farm were written in black pen. Then Amahle's name, misspelled *Amahlay,* dashed off in faint blue ink on the last line.

"Added afterwards," Shabalala noted. "The station commander is a liar."

"And a bad one." The childish subterfuge was ridiculous. It showed complete contempt for the investigative skills of detectives from the Durban branch. "Still regret breaking into the files, Constable?"

A shrug accompanied the reply. "Sometimes it is necessary to steal honey from the bees."

"Or from Sampie Paulus's kitchen." Emmanuel pushed the file and the occurrence book to the very center of Bagley's desk. He left the cabinet drawers yawning on broken rails. Petty stuff but a clear sign to the town constable that he had fooled no one.

Emmanuel picked up the crowbar and tucked it under his arm. "Let's find the kid," he said.

13

THE DYING SUN spread gold light on the hills and illuminated the clusters of white arum lilies growing along the riverbank. Birds flitted through the grass and the wind carried the smell of dirt and wildflowers.

Emmanuel sank to his haunches, aching. Every muscle and tendon in his legs hurt. Two hours of uphill climbs and downhill scrambles, one hundred and twenty minutes of cross-country running and hurdling property fences, and not a glimpse of Gabriel.

"Please, tell me we're close," Emmanuel said when Shabalala knelt down at the river's edge and scooped water into cupped hands.

"Just ahead." The Zulu detective slurped mouthfuls of water and splashed the remainder onto his face and neck. He pointed across the broad field to a forested rise. A slash of red lit the horizon, softening the outline of rocks and branches. "Up there. On the hill."

"How do you figure that?"

"The boy moved fast from one place to the next, hiding his

trail, but he stayed a long time here at the river. Resting." Shabalala stood and stretched. "The day is almost finished and he must find shelter."

"A wooded hill is better than a field." Basic combat strategy. Never stay on the beachhead; run for the dunes and take cover. Always seek the high ground and force the enemy to fight an uphill battle.

"We must do the same, Sergeant."

"Thought so." Emmanuel hoisted up from the sandy bank a compact kit bag containing essential supplies. It took effort. The kit was packed light but fatigue made it heavy.

"Half an hour. Then we will rest for the night."

Half an hour for you, Emmanuel thought. Forty-five minutes for mere mortals. He crossed the river, jumping from one rock to the next, and reached the opposite bank with dry shoes. An overgrown path twisted through the arum lilies.

"Hear that?" Emmanuel slowed. The rhythmic thumping sound was not his frantic heartbeat.

"I hear it." Shabalala fought a tangle of bulrushes to get to the summit, crouched low and peered across the field. "Runners," he said.

Emmanuel scrambled up to the vantage point. Across the green veldt, a group of muscled Zulu men ran three abreast in tight military formation. They held steel spears and cowhide shields and were heading to the river. The red sky and failing light made identification impossible. "They'll be on us in a minute," he said. "Let's take cover till we know who they are."

"Off the path." Shabalala indicated a thick stand of lilies with willowy stems. "Here."

They crept low and fast to the protection of the blind. A narrow gap gave a limited view. The sound of pounding feet and hissed breath drew closer. Grasshoppers and three tiny birds sheltering in the reeds took off from the path. Stones rolled down the decline and bounced into the air.

"*Sheshisa!*" a voice commanded. "Hurry."

The runners ascended, now in single file, cowhide shields held over their heads, spear tips aimed at the ground. Emmanuel could see the first three were Mandla's men, dripping sweat and reeking of body odor. The fourth, with salt-and-pepper hair, struggled to keep up.

The path fell silent again. Emmanuel crouched low and rested. Shabalala did the same. The rest of the Zulu impi was yet to reach the river.

"*Hamba,*" growled the voice, now recognizably Mandla's. "Go."

Three boys with skinny limbs and smooth faces negotiated the way with stumbling enthusiasm, child soldiers eager for battle but unprepared for the weight of shields and spears. Mandla came last, sleek-skinned and confident.

The impi rested by the river's edge and drank from cupped hands. Mandla splashed his face and chest, then looked up to the sunset. He took one gulp of water from the river and retrieved his spear. "Enough," he said. "We have far to go."

The impi regrouped and set off at uniform pace, the oldest member trailing the pack by a body length. Emmanuel stood slowly and watched the squad run off in the direction of Roselet. A dot of electric light winked on the horizon, inconsequential in the gathering darkness.

"What's drawing him to town in the last hours of the day?" he asked.

"There is no way to know." Shabalala was resigned. "And I cannot track Mandla and his men till the morning."

"One thing at a time." Emmanuel lifted the pack again and felt its weight. "We're here to find Gabriel, the one person we know for sure was at the crime scene. Mandla can wait."

"*Yebo,*" Shabalala said. "To the mountain."

They set off into the lengthening shadows, the sky above them now bloodred and charcoal gray. The day closed down. Emmanuel ran now not to find shelter but to escape the sadness that crept into him at nightfall when the dead came to warm their hands at his fire.

—

"Sergeant!" The voice was urgent, the hands on his shoulders broad and strong. "Sergeant Cooper!"

Emmanuel sat upright, fighting for breath. The night air was cold. A flashlight lay on the ground, shining on the pile of leaves he'd scraped together to make a primitive mattress.

"Sergeant," Shabalala said. "Are you unwell?"

"I'm fine," Emmanuel lied. "Really."

He wiped a hand across his cheeks, praying the moisture he felt was sweat rather than tears. Grown men crying out in their sleep, torn by dreams that were not dreams at all but memories of real events, were a daily occurrence at the rehabilitation hospital. They took turns, the injured veterans, in waking each other from the night terrors and repeating the wisdom of the doctors and the nurses and the shrinks; memory fades, the heart and mind heal, life goes on.

"Sorry to wake you," Emmanuel said. His eyes were dry, thank Christ, but he was embarrassed by his display of weakness. "Did I wake up the birds as well?"

"No." Shabalala kept the flashlight low so their faces

remained unseen. "You said a few words, none of them in English or in Zulu."

That left French or German, bastardized phrases of which he'd picked up marching toward Germany. The dream itself was a black space with flickering images and muffled sounds. Remembering details of the dream was key.

"I need to stretch my legs. Try to grab some sleep if you can, Constable." Emmanuel kicked the blanket aside and moved to a stand of trees haloed by moonlight. Repairing the breach in his walls had to be done in private.

"The torch," Shabalala called.

"I'm not going far." Emmanuel slipped between the tree trunks, desperate to escape the intimacy of the situation. He encouraged Shabalala to speak his mind, to ask questions, but not now and not of him. An insomniac ex-soldier might understand the hornets' nest that was his mind, but not a married Zulu man with a loving wife, a home and three healthy children. The kind of stable family man his own mother believed Emmanuel would grow into.

Loose stones shifted under his feet and he arched backward and landed hard on the ground. Lying there, winded, he glimpsed distant stars winking through the tree branches.

"Sergeant?" Shabalala's voice cut through the night.

"Relax, Constable. No broken bones." Emmanuel spoke through a wave of pain flooding each vertebra and drumming against his skull. "I'll call if I need help."

A lengthy pause preceded the reply. "If that is what you say." Zulu code for: *Bullshit. You say one thing but I know the opposite is true. Something in you is definitely broken.* But the color barrier stopped Shabalala from asking more questions and from offering help. Emmanuel was grateful. The glare of the flashlight was the last thing he wanted.

He lay still and accepted the pain, didn't try to fight it. Just like old times. The pressure against his skull built to a deafening roar and the roar found a voice.

"Christ, that old man really fucked with you, didn't he, soldier? Went straight for the jugular with that story about your ma and the wee ghost children. Brutal stuff." The internal snarl belonged to the Scottish sergeant major from basic training, one of the old breed who fought through the wet mud of Flanders Fields and the dusty sands of Palestine and believed soldiering was a calling, a profession, a blessing. His job was to weed out the unworthy and the weak.

"What took you so long?" Emmanuel slipped into the voiceless conversation. Fighting the presence of the Scotsman was useless. God knows he'd tried and failed numerous times. The sergeant major was garrisoned in a dark recess of Emmanuel's mind and unassailable without morphine.

"I've been thinking about the case," the sergeant major said. *"Messing with the town constable—not a smart move on your part, soldier."*

Emmanuel sat up, felt the breeze touch his face and dry the sweat. *"You crawled out of your hole to tell me I've been a bad boy?"*

"No, a stupid one. Granted, the old Jew and the Zulu are hiding something from you, but that was no reason to make a fresh enemy," the sergeant major grunted. *"You've stretched yourself too thin, Cooper. Keeping tabs on Mandla and the town constable plus finding the boy. Herr Hitler made the same mistake, fighting on three fronts."*

The comment about Zweigman and Shabalala disturbed

Emmanuel. *"I opened the station filing cabinet to look for evidence,"* he said. *"It had nothing to do with Zweigman or Shabalala."*

"You crowbarred that fucker because you were scared, boyo."

Emmanuel stood up quickly and brushed the leaves off his back. *"Scared of what, exactly?"*

"The two of them huddled like thieves, whispering secrets in the garden."

"Zweigman was flashing new baby photos. That's what friends do."

"If you say it is so, Cooper." The sergeant major repeated Shabalala's words, deadpan, with all the subtext intact.

In the silence that followed, a small animal scuttled through the underbrush. Obsessing over Zweigman and Shabalala's private picture show would lead to suspicion and paranoia, Emmanuel knew. Combine that with insomnia and his disturbing dreams, and he might as well be back in combat and on the edge of a meltdown.

"Track down Mr. Insurance Policy, Cooper." The voice resumed. *"He's the key to everything."*

"Nobody's ever heard of him. Amahle probably met a man in town on the day she was left behind. He bought her a drink and a bag of sweets and made promises he had no intention of keeping. It's an old story."

"Yeah. Fair enough," the sergeant major said. *"I've got a feeling about it, that's all."*

"You're a detective now?" Emmanuel asked. *"Go back to your Edinburgh slum."*

"You need to get some sleep, Cooper," the Scotsman said. *"We'll talk when you're less of a grumpy bastard. Okay?"*

"Yes, sir." Emmanuel gave a mock salute to the air and then picked his way back to the moonlit campsite. Dawn was still hours away. The sergeant major was right about one thing: he badly needed sleep.

Shabalala lay on his side, facing the opposite direction from Emmanuel's mound of leaves and discarded blanket. Still awake but pretending to be asleep, Shabalala was too polite to ask a second time if the sergeant was well.

The leaf mattress did not make the hard ground much softer and the pain in Emmanuel's back throbbed when he eased under the blanket. He closed his eyes but didn't think he could sleep.

"Remember that village cemetery with stone walls and an avenue of oak trees, Cooper?" the sergeant major whispered inside Emmanuel's head. *"The sun set behind the row of crosses and there was a white marble angel with a lamb cradled in her arms."*

Yes, he remembered. Autumn was closing in, the leaves had begun to turn copper and yellow. Fading light and shadows dappled the walls of the ancient church, now bombed to ruins. Then, from the open window of an apartment building, the soulful swell and dip of a cello floated out over the blackened rooftops and the low-lying fields, the music mending the world.

Emmanuel fell asleep.

Pebbles arranged in the shape of an arrow pointed northeast toward Roselet. A second arrow pointing in the same direction at the base of the hill on which they'd camped repeated the instruction: *Go back.*

"Huh . . ." Shabalala was at once annoyed and impressed by the hand-formed signs. "This one was placed here only one hour ago while we searched the place where he slept." They'd found a nest of leaves scraped into a circle, Gabriel's burrowing ground, where he'd curled up without a fire or a blanket.

"Is he heading back to town or are the arrows telling us to abandon the chase and go home?" Emmanuel stifled a yawn. Dawn had just broken and a flock of black-winged swallows dipped and swooped through the mist that lay over the fields.

"The boy has gone straight, straight." Shabalala pointed directly across the grasslands dotted with sagebrush. "In the footsteps of the impi."

"The boy is following Mandla and his men and he wants us to tag along," Emmanuel said. The arrows weren't a warning but a finger pointing them in the right direction.

"That is what I think, Sergeant."

"Roselet's suddenly the place to be." A runaway schoolboy and a Zulu warrior were running to the little town. "We'd better catch up. We don't want to miss anything."

The stone arrows marked a straight path across the grass meadows. On this journey, Gabriel did not detour or loop back on his tracks as he had the previous day. It took Emmanuel and Shabalala one hour to make the edge of Roselet.

"The boy ended here." Shabalala stopped to examine one last arrow, hastily arranged and with a crooked shaft. "His footsteps go into the water but do not come out the other side."

Across the stream, the whitewashed walls of Dr. Daglish's cottage glistened with dew. The entrance to the cellar was wide open, the timber doors held ajar by a stone.

"Mandla and his men didn't stop on this side of the stream, did they, Shabalala?"

"No. They went on."

Emmanuel leapt the breadth of the water in one bound. He attacked the steep gradient, knowing with each footstep that he was already too late.

The cellar was dank and cold as ever. The white sheet used to cover the body lay on the stone floor. A brown moth circled the naked bulb above the empty gurney.

Amahle was gone.

14

EMMANUEL WALKED THE southern boundary of the yard and met Shabalala in the empty front driveway. It was hopeless. Amahle's body was deep in the mountains by now, carried on a platform of rawhide shields.

"The mortuary van was not here," Shabalala said. "Mandla and his men have taken Amahle back to her mother." Put that way, kidnapping a corpse was a community service provided on behalf of the dead. No white judge or jury would see it that way.

"Daglish?"

"Gone, but not with the impi," Shabalala explained. "She did not leave the house till after the men took the body and crossed the stream."

"Thank Christ for that," Emmanuel said.

The National Party loved an interracial crime with sexual overtones. They would turn it into headline news to ensure that liberal whites and redneck farmers alike got the message: *Your women and children are in danger from savage forces. Only We Can Save You.*

"And Zweigman?"

"Gone with the town doctor." Two shoe tracks led down the gravel drive. "Both running to Greyling Street."

"Let's find them, make sure they're safe."

"This way, Sergeant." Shabalala walked to the road and swung right past the closed café and then Dawson's General Store—already open for trade, a cream-colored cat sleeping on the threshold. Three white farmers in khaki pants and worn cotton shirts stood outside the farm depot, smoking their first cigarettes of the day. They marked the strangers moving through their town, stone glances passing judgment on the black and white men who appeared too close, too intimate for a baas and his servant. Emmanuel walked on. Righteous farmers held power over the boy he once was, not the man he'd become. Let them think what they wanted. The police van was out in front of the station, tires splattered with mud, dead insects smeared across the windscreen and on the grille. Smoke drifted from a side window of the station house and a pyramid of spent butts lay beneath the sill. Voices came from inside.

"The girl was taken by force and it is your job to retrieve her, Constable." That was Zweigman in full steam, his German accent shredding the English language to tatters. He was angry.

"I know my job." That was Bagley, not taking any shit from a foreign stranger. "You've reported a criminal activity and I will take the appropriate action at the appropriate time."

"After your cigarette?" Zweigman snorted. "Or after your afternoon naptime, perhaps?" The doctor would argue the point no matter how many enemies he made.

"Out!" Footsteps slapped the floor, a prelude to action.

"Get out of my station or I will arrest you for disturbing the peace."

Emmanuel stepped through the front door and walked behind the long counter. Margaret Daglish, still in nightdress, gown and slippers, sat in one of the interview chairs, trying to make herself as small as possible. Zweigman and the station commander stood face-to-face, neither backing down.

"Sergeant Cooper." Zweigman was gray with fatigue. He looked as if he'd slept in his clothes. "You saw what happened?"

"Yeah. How long ago?"

"One hour." The German glared at Bagley, who'd returned to the windowsill to finish his Dunhill. "We waited until the men crossed the river and then came here to report the crime. No action so far."

"Unlike you to stay indoors and not try to stop them from taking the body," Emmanuel said. He was aware of Shabalala hovering in the doorway.

"Dr. Zweigman tried to leave the house, but I stopped him." Daglish loosened her hold on the chair arms. "The leader said he'd spear anyone who came into the garden. I believed him."

"Good call." Surrender was the only option for two unarmed physicians pinned down by a Zulu impi. Constable Bagley's foot-dragging was another matter. "Why are you still here, Constable?" Emmanuel asked. "Your native police probably have a good idea where Mandla is headed."

"Got a message for you." Bagley scratched the bristles on his throat. He was haggard, with black smudges under his eyes and nicotine stains on his fingertips. Probably up at dawn, marooned on the back steps again, smoking to forget whatever plagued him.

"Fuck," the sergeant major growled. *"The bastard has something, Cooper."*

Emmanuel waited out the station commander in silence.

"Colonel van Niekerk said to call." Bagley flicked ash out of the window. "It's urgent."

"Don't answer him, Cooper," the sergeant major said. *"Don't even look at him. Just make the call, soldier."*

Emmanuel followed orders and rang through to Durban on a static-free line. The sweet scent of bruised sagebrush crept in through the open window, dampening the smell of burnt tobacco and of leaf litter clinging to his shirt. He turned to face the broken filing cabinet, blocking out Zweigman's anxious expression and the blank imprint of Shabalala's face.

"Colonel," Emmanuel said when the phone was picked up at the other end. A photo portrait of Queen Elizabeth on the far wall smiled down at him, beatific in pearls and a diamond tiara.

"Do you know what it's like being pissed on from a great height by an English general, Cooper?" van Niekerk asked with chilling calm.

"No, sir. I do not."

"It's scalding hot and smells of defeat."

"Sorry to hear that, sir." Emmanuel retrieved his notebook and pen from his pocket, determined to appear calm. "What happened?"

"A call from General Hyland at seven last night, half an hour before my wedding rehearsal dinner. Have you met Hyland?"

"Never, sir."

"He's an old boy from King's Row College. Life member of the Durban Club. Still calls England home. You get the picture, Cooper?"

"I do, sir," Emmanuel said, even though the question was rhetorical. The windowsill creaked under a weight: Bagley settling back to watch the show.

"This fucking Englishman called me to say he'd received a complaint about my boy. That's the phrase he used, Cooper. 'My boy.' Like I was a dumb Boer with an even dumber kaffir working for him." The colonel paused. "Because the complaint was made by Thomas Reed, an old boy of King's Row College and a personal friend of the general's son, he was obliged to take swift action."

"Meaning?" Emmanuel knew the answer to that question, knew it down to the bone.

"You're off the case, Cooper. Effective immediately. General Hyland's replacements will get there in a few hours."

"Is that final?" Emmanuel bent forward, easing the tension from his body, stretching the knots from his neck and shoulders. Ripping the broken drawers clean from the filing cabinet and sending them in Bagley's direction could wait till he was absolutely sure that working the case was out of reach.

"Yes, it is. The general is not open to negotiation or persuasion. The mortuary van you ordered has already been canceled."

That was it. One phone call and he and Shabalala were back on sanitation duty for the Durban Detective Branch. Only now they had to shoulder the added burden of van Niekerk's humiliation.

"Who's being sent out to replace us?" he asked.

"Detective Sergeant Benjamin Ellicott and Detective Constable John Hargrave."

"Bad cop. Worse cop," Emmanuel said. "They'll turn over a rock, find nothing, then drink the local pub dry and leave the next day."

"Not our problem, Cooper. Not anymore." There was a tight pause before the colonel added, "Bullying helpless women and destroying police property. Doesn't sound like you."

"There's no truth in it, Colonel." Not in the fine details. He'd spoken to a fragile white woman in the presence of her daughter and, yes, he'd broken into the police files, but for good reason.

"Pack up and come home, Emmanuel. There'll be other opportunities to break out of police purgatory."

The colonel's use of his first name opened an escape hatch from the situation. He straightened up, fingers tight on the receiver. "Did the general mention Detective Constable Shabalala, sir?"

"No. Just you. *My boy.*" That term, reserved almost exclusively for natives, still rankled. Bowing to an English general reminded van Niekerk that despite his education and blue blood, he'd always be the equivalent of a black in the eyes of some British settlers.

"I've been ordered off the case but not Shabalala." Emmanuel needed official clarification.

"That's technically correct. Why?"

A deep silence permeated the interior of the police station. Everyone, including Bagley, was listening in, trying to determine the direction of the conversation.

"Native detectives aren't allowed to drive police vehicles,

Colonel. If Shabalala is technically still on the case he'll need someone to drive the Chevrolet. Police policy." Emmanuel heard the uncomfortable shuffling of feet on the concrete floor and the sharp intake of Zweigman's breath. He knew he was stepping into uncharted territory and didn't much care about the consequences.

"You as driver," van Niekerk said. "I don't buy it, Cooper. No one else will, either, least of all General Hyland. You can't make it work."

"I'll plead ignorance and wear the consequences of my actions, sir."

"Jesus Christ, you're a hungry beast, Cooper," the colonel said. "First you fuck my girlfriend and then you fuck the case and now you expect me to look the other way while you disobey a direct order from a general. Have I got that right?"

Adrenaline shot through Emmanuel's chest. Van Niekerk knew about Lana . . . of course he knew.

"*Hold steady, soldier.*" The sergeant major gave the order. "*There's only one thing to do when a superior officer has you by the short and curlies. Bend over and smile.*"

"Yes, Colonel," Emmanuel said. "That's correct. With your permission, sir."

Van Niekerk's laugh was soft on the line. "Now, *that's* my boy, always running ahead of the pack."

"Is that a yes, sir?"

The colonel was silent a long while. "You can stay on as official driver for Detective Shabalala of the native police, but undercover operation rules apply."

"I understand." The rules were simple. A positive result in the murder case belonged to the colonel. A bad result belonged to him. If he were caught disobeying an order from a general, van Niekerk would deny all knowledge of his activities; would call him a rogue policeman and a disgrace to the uniform. "You ordered me to leave. I disobeyed the order."

"You have till Friday night, Cooper. I expect to see you, the old Jew and Shabalala at the church on Saturday morning. Clear?"

"We'll be there, Colonel." Emmanuel held on to the heavy plastic receiver long after the line went dead. He kept his back to the room. He needed two minutes to think.

"First order of battle." The sergeant major took control. *"Be nice as a Quaker's wife to Bagley. Extricate Daglish from the room and send her home. Don't say a word to Zweigman or Shabalala till you're well outside the constable's hearing. You're good to go, soldier."*

Emmanuel replaced the receiver and stood up. He turned to the station commander and smiled.

"We'll leave you to it," he said. "Good luck with the rest of the investigation and pass my greetings on to Ellicott and Hargrave. Fine chaps, the both of them."

Bagley flicked his cigarette butt into the yard and frowned. "You're off the case. General's orders."

"That's right." Emmanuel kept smiling. "But I've decided to stay in town for a couple more days. See the sights. Take in the mountain air."

"What sights?" Bagley's face turned red.

An activity from the "things to do while in Roselet" list read out by the hotel receptionist came to Emmanuel's mind. "The bushman paintings at the game shelter pass in Kamberg Reserve," he said. "They're supposed to be the Rosetta stone of rock art. Worth a detour."

"You're disobeying a direct order, Cooper." Bagley

straightened up from the windowsill and tried to assert control.

Christ above, Bagley was a fool. Years of ruling this backwater station had given him a false sense of his own power. "Did you go to King's Row College, Constable?" Emmanuel asked. The station commander was the servant of an elite social institution, not one of its members.

"No." The question threw Bagley. He couldn't figure how where he went to school was relevant to lodging an official complaint.

"In that case you should contact Thomas Reed with the complaint and he'll phone General Hyland on your behalf. I doubt the general would take your call." Emmanuel made for the door and waited for Zweigman and Daglish to follow. "That's how the chain of command works in Roselet, right?"

Shabalala opened the station door for the two doctors and kept it open for Emmanuel. They moved into the yard without speaking. Shabangu, the native policeman, was cleaning up the spent cigarette butts with a metal rake and deposited them in a bucket. He might have heard the entire conversation with Bagley or nothing at all.

"What next, Sergeant Cooper?" Zweigman asked. "I assume, perhaps naïvely, that you have a plan."

"Home and rest for you, Dr. Daglish. We'll walk you back." Emmanuel stuck to the sergeant major's basic instructions. "I'll think up a strategy on the way."

Zweigman lifted an eyebrow but kept quiet. They walked along Greyling Street, cutting across the threshold of Dawson's General Store. The sight of the town doctor flanked by three strange men stopped pedestrian traffic. That she was still in a nightdress and dressing gown added a titillating element to the story. Black and white, Indian and coloured, by late afternoon theories on the doctor's bizarre outing would unite the racial groups in gossip. After supper and with the children safely in bed, the adults would whisper, *And true as I stand here, one of the men was a Zulu big as a sycamore tree, the second was a small foreigner with gold glasses and the third man looked white but walked down the street like a township gangster.* Three men, one woman; they imagined the permutations.

Daglish greeted each stare with a cheery, "Hello. Lovely day." She was worn thin by the time they reached the cottage and fled indoors with a quick wave good-bye.

Emmanuel led Shabalala and Zweigman to the back of the house and found a shade tree to stand under. They were out of sight of the police station and the people on the street. "I've been ordered off the Amahle Matebula murder investigation," he said.

"And yet here we stand," Zweigman said. "Making plans to find her, I imagine."

"I've been removed," Emmanuel stated. "But not Shabalala. He stays on active duty."

"That cannot be right, Sergeant." The Zulu detective was visibly uncomfortable with the direction the conversation was taking. "A native constable cannot lead an investigation. It is against the rules."

"Ellicott and Hargrave will lead the investigation. You'll work parallel to them, taking statements and interviewing suspects. I'll drive." Now that it was said aloud he realized the idea was ridiculous. Colonel van Niekerk was right. He was a hungry beast, never satisfied.

"What are you really saying, Sergeant?" Shabalala studied

the drift of low clouds crowning the hills and avoided eye contact with his superior officer. This was a tricky situation, asking for the plain truth from a white man.

"Technically we're both off the case. But the general who gave the order didn't mention you specifically. That's the loophole. We stay and continue the investigation with van Niekerk's unofficial approval."

"If we fail and are caught?" Shabalala asked. The clouds were moving fast, throwing shadows over the fields and wildflowers.

"The colonel will wash his hands of me and look the other way." The next part was difficult to say. "You're a native policeman. That will keep you safe. If you're questioned by a disciplinary board, pretend ignorance and tell them you had no idea of General Hyland's order."

"Play the stupid native, you mean." Zweigman was offended on Shabalala's behalf. "Confirm everything that the National Party government preaches about lower intelligence and lack of initiative being bred into black people."

Emmanuel said, "That's right."

A tense silence followed. Zweigman fumed while Shabalala dug the tip of his sandshoe into the dirt. Minutes ticked by. Emmanuel said nothing. The sun broke through the clouds and he stepped out of the shade to warm his face. He needed Shabalala and Zweigman. Without them the clandestine investigation was guaranteed to fail.

Shabalala pushed his toe deeper into the soil and said, "If we are caught, I must keep myself small and quiet and say only 'I don't know, ma' baas'?"

"Yes. Can you do it?"

"Easily." Shabalala stepped out of the shade and into the

sun. The chill from the night spent on the mountainside was still in his bones. "The new detectives will not be happy to see us." That was the polite way of asking how they were going to avoid a physical confrontation with Ellicott and Hargrave when they arrived.

"Two black murders out in the sticks. They won't rush." Emmanuel checked his watch. Seven thirty-five a.m. "Earliest they'll get here is this afternoon. Hargrave looks like a beer barrel and Ellicott has the brains of a sardine. If we stay more than five miles from the pub we won't see them at all."

"These men will not find out who killed Amahle and Philani," Shabalala said with bleak acceptance. It was impressive, the many ways that white men found to win a battle. They fought with telephones and people they knew, not with spears and shields.

"Ellicott and Hargrave won't find a thing." Emmanuel snapped a branch of sagebrush and rubbed it between his palms. "That's the point."

"This is to protect the schoolboy Gabriel." Shabalala's tone was one of understanding. A father must fight for his children and a chief for his clan. The English and the Zulus had that in common.

"When Amahle is buried," Emmanuel said, "her secrets will be buried with her."

Shabalala turned to face Greyling Street, which ran all the way to the valley and the foot of the mountains. "We must tell this to the chief and to Mandla," he said.

Zweigman stepped out of the shade. He had his hands thrust deep into his jacket pocket, his fingers curled around an object. The leather wallet, Emmanuel thought, the one with the photographs he was not allowed to see. The images must be powerful. Zweigman clutched the wallet as if it were a lucky charm.

"Colonel van Niekerk will not catch us if we fall." The doctor thumbed his gold-rimmed glasses higher onto the bridge of his nose and addressed the Zulu policeman directly. "Give me one good reason why either of us should join Detective Cooper's unsanctioned campaign."

"Amahle," Shabalala replied.

"Good answer."

15

FROM THE ROCK ledge, Covenant farmhouse looked like a white dot in the landscape. Emmanuel crouched down and motioned to Shabalala to begin his first-ever identification-of-human-remains interview.

"Is that your son Philani Dlamini under the rock shelter?" Shabalala asked a plump Zulu woman dressed in black widow's robes. She sat on her heels, head down, hands folded in her lap.

"Yes, inkosi. It is he. Philani." She was stoic. Squatting below her on the track were three men from her uncle's kraal come to transport the body. "I knew it would be him."

"Why is this?" Shabalala asked.

Philani's mother loosened the strings of a small goatskin pouch tied to her black hide skirt and scooped out the contents: four bright copper coins and a paper note.

"My son came home on Friday night," she said. "I did not tell the great chief the truth because Philani said it must be a secret. He gave me this money to hide and the sky pressed down on my chest. I could not breathe. I knew a bad thing would happen to my son. It was not his payday."

Emmanuel counted the notes and coins. Close to two pounds, the amount that Amahle was paid on Friday, minus a few bob. It might be a coincidence. It might not.

"Perhaps Philani was holding the money for a friend," Shabalala said.

"This money was not given. It was taken." She placed the cash on the rock and wiped her hands on her skirt to clean them. "My son was scared when he came home with this money and told me to keep it hidden. It is cursed."

Robbing the dead. Emmanuel knew soldiers, souvenir collectors, who stripped enemy corpses of boots, guns, knives and even gold teeth. Philani might have been angry enough to kill Amahle for walking home without him, but robbery didn't fit with this kind of crime of passion.

"You say that Philani was scared." Shabalala found a rock and weighted the money down, careful not to touch it.

"*Yebo.* He instructed me to go to the great chief and say that he was missing. Then he said to take the money and go to the kraal of my uncle." She looked over her shoulder at the stand of marula trees blocking the rock shelter from view. "Philani told me he would come to the kraal today."

Emmanuel scrawled down what she'd said. Philani had been hiding, not running away. He made plans for the future. He had no intention of dying alone on a hillside. Three cold nights sleeping on a rock, waiting for what? Hunted men kept on the move. Philani chose a spot, lit night fires and stayed. It didn't make sense.

"Philani was a friend of the great chief's daughter," Shabalala said. "This is what I hear."

"My son was a friend to her, inkosi. That is the truth." The soft words carried a bitterness that she dared not express outright. A widow without the protection of a son did not criticize the daughter of a chief, even if the girl was dead.

"I hear you," Shabalala said. The friendship between Philani and Amahle was one-sided. Philani had been the better friend. "Is there more to say?"

"I am finished."

A bell tolled in the valley, calling the workmen from the fields. Emmanuel checked the grove of trees for movement. They were due at the Covenant homestead fifteen minutes after the bell. He stood and crossed the flat surface of the rock, heading in the direction of the trees. Zweigman emerged from the underbrush in a white gown and gloves loaned by Dr. Daglish. His battered medical bag was tucked under an arm. "It was not easy," he whispered to Emmanuel. "But I found one very interesting thing."

"Save it for the walk back to Covenant. And try not to look so pleased with yourself."

"Yes, of course." Zweigman hunched into the surgical gown and pretended interest in a red flower growing from a crevice. "Finish your business. I will stay here."

The finish of business was short and sad. Philani's mother stayed crouched in her black widow's robes, dwarfed by a canopy of sky. "With your permission," she said, "I will take my son home now."

"With our blessing," Shabalala replied, and they withdrew to the edge of the grove where Zweigman waited. The Zulu men rose from the bush path and crossed the rock with woven grass mats balanced on their shoulders. "For the body," Shabalala explained.

Emmanuel waited until the bearers were well into the woods before hitting the path to Covenant.

"I have news, gentlemen," Zweigman said as they walked down the hill. "It took a while, but I found it." He held out a gloved hand. A fragment of porcupine quill rested in the palm. "It was pierced into the lower lumbar. Same as with the girl."

"Same killer," Emmanuel said. "Got to be."

"To use this weapon you must get near to the person." Shabalala rubbed his chin, thinking. "Either walking close behind them or with your arms around their body."

"Hard for a stranger to achieve. Easy for a friend." That fit with Emmanuel's feeling that Philani had invited the killer into the rock shelter, confident of his own safety. They continued the descent of the mountain at a brisk pace for fifteen minutes. They did not want to miss their escort to Amahle's funeral.

Inside the yard, a caravan had formed. Four workmen clumped together behind Sampie and Karin. Three women, including the undersized housemaid with the failing eyes, took up position behind them. The boerboel pack lay on the stoep, their giant heads resting on their paws and under orders to "stay."

"Detective Cooper," Sampie called a greeting. "Thought you'd changed your mind."

"Got caught up on the hill." Emmanuel joined father and daughter at the head of the procession. Karin nodded hello and fiddled with the cuffs of her ironed going-out shirt. "Sorry to keep you waiting," he said. "We appreciate the invitation to walk with your house."

Sampie grunted and they set off along the trail churned up by wagons. Sunshine hit the gravestones in the family plot and birds sang from the tall grass. Shabalala and Zweigman walked a pace behind Emmanuel.

"It was the gardener on the hill," Karin said. "So, I guessed right."

"You did." Philani's location was more than a lucky guess. The stranger lighting night fires on the property must surely have caught Karin's attention. "His mother is arranging the burial."

"Poor thing. Nobody will turn up at the funeral. They're scared of the chief." Karin unbuttoned her cuffs and rolled up her sleeves, unused to the feeling of starched linen against her skin. "Plus there's all this going on."

Four Zulu women with babies tied to their backs waited for the procession to pass, then tagged along with the other women on the end. Still more people waited by the river crossing.

"How many by the time we get there?" Emmanuel asked.

The Afrikaner woman shrugged. "Fifty or so. The kaffirs from the kraals all around will join along the way."

This massing of people was the reason Emmanuel, Zweigman and Shabalala had stayed away from the Matebula family compound this morning. Amahle's funeral was equivalent to a tornado tearing across the valley; it could not be stopped or delayed. Sampie Paulus's invitation for them to walk to the great chief's home meant they could witness her farewell as well as observe who came to pay their respects.

The group of Zulus at the river crossing swelled the numbers. Sampie Paulus led the way across the water, stepping from one flat stone to the next like an Afrikaner Moses. He waited till the entire group reached the bank and then set off again.

"Ever been to a kaffir funeral before, Detective Cooper?" Karin brushed sand from the hem of her good jeans.

"Town funerals," he said. "Nothing like this."

"Be prepared," Karin said. "It'll be noisy."

The Matebula kraal came into view, nestled in a field of aloes. Wails and screams drifted from the compound and the women in the procession began to wail, too. The men split away and formed their own group. The pounding rhythm of their feet hitting the ground added to the sound.

"See what I mean?" Karin stepped aside to give the Zulu procession right-of-way. "Your kaffir and the other one can stand with us. There's a special area for nonfamily near the burial site."

"Zweigman and Shabalala." Emmanuel said their names, knowing it was pointless. Karin's world was divided into two groups: white people, who mattered, and servants. Jews occupied a messy space between the two clusters.

Sampie cut across the field to the front entrance of the Matebula kraal. Scores of Zulus gathered. Dozens more arrived from the mountain paths, raising trails of dust. The kraal dogs barked amid the excitement.

"We're in the specially marked area," Emmanuel said when Shabalala and Zweigman caught up. "Stick close to Sampie. We weren't formally invited but the Matebulas live on his land."

The group entered the compound and a Zulu man indicated where they should stand. The special enclosure held a sprinkling of whites: two missionary women in ironed black dresses and hats, a red-faced farmer in clean khaki, and Thomas and Ella Reed. Constable Bagley was a no-show.

"Afternoon." Emmanuel tipped his hat to the other guests:

some nodded and smiled in return. Thomas Reed stepped up. His black suit was elegant but his expression was savage. "What are you doing here, Cooper?" He spoke close to Emmanuel's ear, careful to avoid a public scene. "I will have your police ID for this."

"I'm a private citizen attending a private funeral. There's no law against it. Call General Hyland and check."

Shabalala and Zweigman closed ranks behind Emmanuel, one at each shoulder. Reed blinked hard but a natural sense of superiority kicked in. He kept his composure: a tick for a King's Row College education. "You're in trouble, Cooper," he said. "Your friends as well. This time next week the three of you will be queuing up at the labor office looking for factory work."

Emmanuel stared into Reed's eyes, almost curious at the man's stupidity and his sense of entitlement.

"A factory job. That's your idea of hell?" he asked. "Have you ever had to fight for anything in your life? You can't even fight your own battle right here, right now." Reed opened his mouth to speak but Emmanuel's expression silenced him.

Sampie Paulus came over. "Squabble afterwards," he said. "This is not the place. The ceremony has started."

"My apologies for the disturbance." Emmanuel moved to the thorn fence. He regretted reacting to Reed. Fighting at a funeral was something his schoolboy self would have done.

Dozens of Zulu mourners took up the ground between the spectators' enclosure and the grave, which had been dug by the side of Nomusa's hut. Nomusa and her surviving daughter were seated on grass mats in the female mourners' area: distant phantoms in the dust. Bodies pressed in on the great chief's family. The women wailed and threw their hands into the air, the men stamped the ground. More dust rose and it was hard to see. The noise increased.

The great chief emerged from his hut and walked around the inner ring of the kraal. An old man preceded him, a praise singer, who listed the chief's victories, wealth and children. The missionary women moved closer to the fence, engrossed in the native funeral rites. Shabalala craned over the crowd, squinting into the sunlight. "That grave does not look right," he said.

Emmanuel shifted position and found a space between two adolescent boys that allowed a partial view of the freshly dug earth. "Hard to tell," he said. "There's a lot going on."

"The grave is not right, Sergeant," the Zulu detective stated. "It is not right."

The praise singer moved closer, shouting more of the great chief's attributes. Mandla and his impi moved in a sinuous rhythm at the front of a column of fighting-age males.

The mourners parted. A group of men carried a cowhide stretcher bearing Amahle's body to the grave. The women's wailing increased and grew sharp. The hair on the back of Emmanuel's neck stood up. He pressed forward. The body was wrapped in cowhide and bound by plaited grass ropes. Three branches, stripped of bark and wedged into the hide, held the corpse in a grotesque sitting position.

"What's going on?" Emmanuel asked Shabalala.

The women were howling now, their arms thrown up to the sky. Nomusa jumped to her feet but a ring of matrons pulled her back and anchored her to the ground with their weight. Two of the bearers wound lengths of rope around their hands and lowered Amahle's upright body into the grave.

"Bad things are happening, Sergeant. Only those who have

caused great offense in life, criminals and murderers, are buried sitting up. Amahle's spirit will not find rest until she is laid down."

"Eternal punishment?" Emmanuel said. "For failing to deliver the herd of cows her father wanted?"

"I can think of no other reason," Shabalala said.

Male mourners dragged their feet, children ceased fussing and young unmarried girls shielded their faces from the unfolding horror. The only people who appeared unaffected by the body were the great chief and his smug fifth wife, who stood up to get a closer look at Amahle's corpse.

"Old fool," Sampie muttered in Afrikaans, and moved from one clump of white spectators to the next with the same message: "Go now. Leave the kraal."

The missionary women and the Reeds made for the exit. Three Zulu men armed with spears and battle-axes sprinted into the compound, blocking the way out. Emmanuel recognized them. They were members of the impi who'd stood guard over Amahle's body.

"Now there will be war," Shabalala said, and unbuttoned his jacket.

The invading impi rushed the grave and the gathered crowd dispersed in panic. Nomusa broke free of the arms holding her and flew at the great chief, whose praise singer had finally run out of superlatives.

"This is native business," Sampie Paulus shouted over the melee. "We must leave."

Mandla and his men moved to block the attack. Metal spear tips flashed in the sun. A surge of mourners running for the exit knocked an elderly woman to the ground and a child screamed in the crush.

"Stay here," Emmanuel said to Zweigman, and jumped the thorn fence. Shabalala cleared the barrier just after him and landed farther into the chaos. He pulled the old woman to her feet and pushed her clear of the warring men. The warriors pressed in on each other, the Zulu detective caught between the two sides.

The noise was deafening as Emmanuel tried to extricate Shabalala. A fighter of the invading group staggered back, blood pouring from a stab wound to his torso. He fell to the ground. For Emmanuel time simultaneously sped up and slowed down. Everyone's movements took on a dreamlike quality: limbs floated, mouths screamed, weapons sliced through the air. Sounds fragmented. The crash of spears against shields, the hard breath of the impi's efforts and a baby's cry provided a discordant sound track to the fight.

"Fall back, soldier." The Scottish sergeant major gave the command. *"Grab Shabalala and the injured and retreat. Mandla and his men are too strong. You will be crushed."*

Shabalala was trapped against the wall of Nomusa's hut, ducking and weaving to escape the thrust of stabbing spears. A narrow space opened between two fighters. Emmanuel called out, "With me, Samuel!"

The Zulu detective wheeled at the sound of his first name and jumped through the breach and into the clear. Emmanuel looked down and saw blood staining the dirt where the injured man had fallen, but the man was gone.

"Move back." Emmanuel gave the order to the elder who'd first greeted him and Shabalala on the hill path days ago. "Move back while you still have men."

The retreat was chaotic. Mandla and his impi pressed their advantage, the great chief nursed a scratched cheek like a teenage girl in a catfight, and Nomusa was again pinned to the ground by the other wives. Zweigman knelt by the injured man, who was lying near the spectators' enclosure. Emmanuel realized that the doctor must have retrieved the man himself.

Then Mandla's men made another push. A spear flew through the air. A moment later, Shabalala lifted the injured man onto his shoulder and ran. Sampie Paulus stood guard at the mouth of the kraal with the stunned white spectators squeezed behind him. The missionary ladies clung together in fear.

"Go," Sampie said. "Get as far as you can. I'll try to calm the chief."

"Run like the devil's on your arse, soldier," the sergeant major breathed. *"Quick-time to that wooded area yonder."*

Trees meant cover. Cover meant time to rest and regroup and figure out what the hell had just happened. Shouts came from inside the Matebula family compound. Emmanuel gave the order to move fast. The uninjured warriors set off across the field at a lope. Shabalala steadied the wounded fighter to his feet and shouldered his weight on the stumbling run for the grove. Zweigman tagged behind them, pale and covered in blood from the stabbed man's wound.

Brown birds flew up from the grass ahead of the human stampede. Emmanuel glanced over his shoulder, alert to the rising level of danger. Sampie still blocked the center of the entrance, arms spread wide like Christ crucified. Mandla and his impi would have to go through the Afrikaner farmer to leave the kraal.

"Tough old bastard," the sergeant major said with admiration. *"He'll hold them just long enough for you to disappear, Cooper."*

A surge of adrenaline and fear propelled Emmanuel to the safety of the woods. The stand of trees was dense but narrow. Dappled sunshine broke through the canopy and reached the leaf litter and ferns as twilight. Emmanuel wove between the dark trunks, his heartbeat thrumming in his chest and forehead. A few feet into the grove, the land fell away to a deep ravine. Shabalala, Zweigman and the retreating impi stood on the edge gazing down into the chasm.

"*You're shit out of luck, soldier,*" the sergeant major said.

Emmanuel wiped sweat from his eyes and calculated the distance. With a solid run up and superhuman effort, the jump to the other side was possible. Shabalala might make it. The rest of them would end up littered across the floor of the chasm, too far down for help to reach them in the unlikely event they survived the fall.

Emmanuel checked the woods, mentally running through a number of escape scenarios. All ended in death or serious injury. Twigs snapped and leaves crunched in the brush. He unclipped the Webley from its holster.

A bedraggled white boy in a filthy school uniform appeared out of the gloom. Small, with a shock of black hair matted into tendrils, he might have stepped from a sorcerer's catalog of forest spirits. His right eye was pale blue, his left eye dark brown.

"Come," he said.

16

GABRIEL REED, RUNAWAY, habitual thief and number one suspect in the Amahle Matebula murder case, jumped a trickling stream and jogged into the fold of a hill. Bony shoulder blades pressed against the fabric of his gray wool jacket, detailed at the cuffs and lapels with scarlet piping. Matching gray trousers hung loosely from his hips and the hems trailed in the dirt. The King's Row College uniform probably cost more than Emmanuel earned in a month.

Gabriel navigated a hairpin bend in the path and ducked under a tangle of branches. Behind the wooded barrier a wide rock platform jutted out from the mountain, and beyond it, on a higher level, the black mouth of a tunnel could be seen. A distinct four-syllable birdcall echoed in the leaf canopy and Gabriel peered into the overhanging tree branches.

"*Chrysococcyx cupreus,*" he said. "The emerald cuckoo."

"*Strange bedfellow indeed,*" the sergeant major whispered. "*How befok is he, do you reckon?*"

"*Befok enough to know about this place,*" Emmanuel

answered. *"For our purposes that makes him the good kind of crazy."*

"Until you ask him about Amahle," the Scotsman said. *"This is the same boy who went batshit on Zweigman and Daglish. Don't forget it, Cooper."*

He would not. Gabriel was odd in the extreme and unpredictable, but till they were rested and ready to move on, this mountain hideaway was their port in a storm. He'd keep a watch on their host.

Two members of the defeated impi squeezed into the hidden space, tired from the quick climb. The flood of adrenaline released during the fight in the kraal had drained away and they were running on empty. Emmanuel bent the branches back to allow the third member of the attacking group through. The injured fighter made it to the rock without assistance thanks to the painkillers and the thick cotton gauze dressing applied to the flesh wound by Zweigman during a rest stop half an hour ago.

The German doctor ducked off the path with his medical bag held to his chest and his hair looking like exploding gray fireworks. His steps were slow and awkward, which Emmanuel found odd. Even when masquerading as a shopkeeper back in the town of Jacob's Rest Zweigman had moved with purpose.

The doctor shuffled to the rock and slumped down. Bright red drops splattered the ground where he'd walked. Emmanuel went over and examined Zweigman's pale face and dilated pupils. He pulled the medical bag from the doctor's clutched hands. A metallic taste he associated with combat patrols into enemy territory flooded his mouth.

"Lie down," he said to Zweigman. "Gently, now."

Fresh blood soaked the doctor's jacket and shirt and stained his leather medical kit. Emmanuel pushed the clothing aside, copying the actions of the medics who'd worked the battlefields.

A wad of cotton wool was stuffed deep into a cut on the doctor's upper right shoulder. It was a mirror opposite of the old bullet wound on Emmanuel's left shoulder. He remembered the initial feeling after the bullet struck, a dull fist punched into the flesh, and then the real pain had set in, raw and unrelenting. He looked up; the Zulu detective had silently joined him.

"Put pressure on the wound, Shabalala. I'll check the kit."

Emmanuel searched the medical bag for a morphine syrette or a bottle of painkillers. A single pill rattled in the bottom of a glass jar; on its own it was useless for severe pain. No medicinal brandy, either. Even the supplies of bandages and gauze were low. Zweigman had used them on the injured fighter, knowing there'd be nothing left to treat his own injury.

"What the hell did you do that for?" Emmanuel snapped the bag shut in frustration. He curled his hands into fists to stop them from trembling. Other emotions—anger, helplessness and terror at the thought of losing Zweigman—he pushed out of his mind.

"Young man . . ." Zweigman motioned to the injured fighter, then back to himself. "Old man . . ."

—

Gabriel stood at the tunnel entrance, a bedraggled angel backlit by afternoon sunlight. The three members of the impi had now left the rock sanctuary to circle back to their kraal, anxious to defend their homes and families from any revenge attack carried out by the Matebula clan.

"Will he die?" Gabriel's voice was devoid of any emotion other than curiosity. Like a malfunctioning flashlight, the schoolboy swung from intense focus to a diffuse emptiness in which his emotions appeared to have little connection with the outside world.

"Not today," Emmanuel said.

Among the treasure trove of stolen goods stored in the tunnel he and Shabalala had unearthed a feather blanket, a bag of quilting rags and a bottle of peach brandy lifted from Covenant Farm. Zweigman's wound was re-dressed with the fabric remnants, a bed made from the blanket and the pain in his shoulder dulled by the alcohol. It wasn't enough, though. Not by a long way.

Zweigman groaned in pain and Shabalala lifted the covering to check the wound. Blood soaked through the new dressings in the shape of a rose. "Not good," he said.

"I know. The bleeding has to be stemmed and the stab wound stitched." That was a job for a trained medical professional with the right tools. Emmanuel swallowed the dull metallic taste flooding his mouth and scrambled for a plan, any plan to prevent Zweigman from dying on a cold dirt floor miles from his wife and new son. One person could help. "We can't move him in his condition. I'll have to bring Daglish here."

"She will come?"

"I've got to try." There was no other option. If not for this assignment, Zweigman would be safely in the Valley of a Thousand Hills dispensing cod liver oil and basking in the brilliance of his adopted child. The burden of guilt was on Emmanuel.

He walked to the boy, who'd crouched to examine a black

and yellow lizard sunning itself on a rock. Amahle was buried and the investigation stalled. Questioning the boy about the murder had to wait till Zweigman was well.

"*Pseudocordylus melanotus.*" Gabriel whispered. "Drakensberg crag lizard."

The teenage boy had a mania for classification but defied it himself. The term *befok* wasn't specific enough. At fifteen or sixteen years old he was still childlike. His different-colored eyes gave the clearest indication that he was a bizarre mix: fully sane one moment and off the air the next.

"I left my car at the turnoff to Covenant Farm," Emmanuel said to Gabriel. "Can you take me there?"

"Why?"

"My friend is sick. He needs help." Simple phrases, expressed clearly, seemed to be the best way to communicate.

"That man is bad." Gabriel studied the lizard's scales and long tail. "He took off Amahle's clothing and cut her with a knife."

"Dr. Zweigman was conducting an examination of Amahle's body to find out what killed her. He meant no harm."

Gabriel picked at the red piping on the lapels of his jacket with dirty fingers. "He didn't have to hurt her. I could have told him what killed Amahle."

"Can you tell me?" Just one more minute, one more answer to satisfy the craving to know for certain who'd killed the chief's daughter.

"A witch put a spell on her," Gabriel said. "And a wizard."

A whole minute wasted. Time to move on. The mission to secure Daglish had to be completed in daylight and it was already almost four in the afternoon. Gabriel continued to watch the lizard.

"You are right, little baas. A witch used black *muti* to kill the chief's daughter." Shabalala placed Zweigman's folded glasses next to the temporary bed and approached the tunnel mouth. He crouched by the schoolboy's side. "The man in there under the blanket can help find this witch."

"Is he powerful?" Gabriel switched to Zulu and immediately sounded less stilted and formal.

"Oh, yes. He is a healer who uses only good *muti* to heal the sick and fight evil wizards and witches."

Gabriel fixed Shabalala with an intense stare. "He should have used his power to break the spell over Amahle. He should have given her new breath."

"Ahh . . ." Shabalala made a sound of regret. "Only the great, great one is capable of breathing life into someone. We must accept that the ancestors have built a hut for Amahle and that is where she will stay from now on."

"She will never come back to this cave and play?"

"No, little baas. Never."

Gabriel looked away and wiped his nose on the sleeve of his wool jacket. He gripped his knees and pulled them close to his chest. The hard stone surfaces of the tunnel amplified the wet sound of his sobbing. Emmanuel stepped back. Gabriel's guilt or innocence in relation to Amahle's murder was irrelevant. With the talk of wizards and witches and his unnatural intensity, young Reed would be found not fit to stand trial and transported from police lockup in a padded wagon.

Shabalala stayed by Gabriel's side and waited for the tears to stop. He did not speak. Like a river, the boy's grief would find its own course.

The lizard scuttled into the leaves and Gabriel raised his

face to the sky. He sat perfectly still and watched white clouds form against the blue. "*Cumulus mediocris.* Low to middle clouds." The joy had gone out of the naming game. He turned to Shabalala, lost. "Must I help the sick healer?" he asked.

"If you are able, little baas."

"My name is Gabriel. My father and my brother are the bosses."

"And I am Samuel. This other man is called Emmanuel."

It was a smart idea, putting them all on a first-name basis. For good or ill, the odd schoolboy had now become a part of the effort to save Zweigman.

Gabriel stood up and pointed to the valley floor. "Sampie Paulus. The Voortrekker. He lives at Covenant Farm. Three miles due east."

"That's the place," Emmanuel said. "The car is on the main road. Just by the turnoff." The Afrikaner farm was connected to the outside world by an eroded mud track strangled with kaffir weeds and thornbush. Fine for a team of oxen to navigate but not a Chevrolet.

"That's where it was parked yesterday. A matte-black 1951 Chevrolet Fleetline Deluxe." Gabriel jumped from the mouth of the tunnel to the rock ledge below, ready to head off. That he'd slashed the front tire of said Fleetline Deluxe with a knife seemed a detail not worth mentioning.

"Exactly the same place," Emmanuel said. He suddenly remembered the knife, sharp enough to cut hardened rubber. The boy might still be armed. And while he was tired from crying and malleable now, that could change at any time.

Emmanuel jumped down a level and turned to Shabalala standing guard at the tunnel entrance. Words failed him.

Shabalala said, "I will take care of the doctor till you get back. *Hamba kahle*, Sergeant. Go well."

"*Sala kahle*, Constable. Stay well."

Emmanuel followed Gabriel's agile movements through the forest as best he could. The boy paused every few minutes for him to catch up. Just when Emmanuel was sure the same protea bush crowded with yellow butterflies had been circled three times and they had crossed the grove of sycamore trees once before, they stepped onto the main road a foot away from the Chevrolet.

"Can I sit up front?" Gabriel sprinted to the passenger door. "Can I sit in the front seat, Emmanuel?"

"Of course." Emmanuel dug out the car keys. The truth was he hadn't thought about what to do with Gabriel after they got to the Chevrolet. Dragging a thief into a town where he had robbed every shop was not part of the plan. Then he remembered that only Gabriel knew the way back to the rock tunnel and to Zweigman. "Get in," he said, and unlocked the door.

The sun dipped lower. The dirt road cut into the hills and mapped the contours of the valley floor. Gabriel wound down the window and leaned out to smell the air. Emmanuel kept the Chevrolet at sixty, high for the potholed road but he needed to make up time.

He drove with hands tight on the wheel. Gabriel called out the scientific names of plants and animals followed by their common nomenclature. Emmanuel stopped listening and rehearsed his approach to Daglish. The town doctor respected Zweigman's medical knowledge and expertise. That would help. This morning's long walk down Greyling Street in a nightdress and dressing gown would not.

They hit the edge of town and Emmanuel slowed down. At the side of the road, a hefty black woman sold freshly grilled corn from a stand. Two young children hunched in the shade her body cast and played with rusty bottle tops.

Emmanuel shifted down a gear and drew parallel with the first white-owned house, a cottage with the windows shut and the curtains drawn.

"Mrs. Violet Stewart," Gabriel said. "Frightened Mole."

Each consecutive dwelling prompted the same response: the proper names of the inhabitants and then a special nickname assigned by Gabriel. A sprawling residence encircled by box hedges and two topiary elephants standing guard in the front garden belonged to "Mrs. Samantha Eggers. Always Screaming." A buttoned-down Indian man in baggy blue trousers, white shirt and thin bow tie: "Mr. Bijay Gowda. Bus Ticket."

The shops appeared along the dirt road. A white cat jumped a fence and settled into a patch of sun just short of the turnoff to the police station.

"*Felis catus.*" Gabriel rested his chin on the top of the leather seat to get a prolonged look at the pet. "Snowflake."

Naming and cataloging the world seemed to be a way to make sense of it, although Emmanuel had noticed a particular enthusiasm for animals over plants and people. Snowflake held Gabriel's attention for a whole minute. The police station, Dawson's General Store and the café rolled past. Emmanuel turned into Daglish's driveway.

A bronze convertible, low to the ground, with flashing chrome teeth, was parked by the front door. The cream hood and freshly waxed paintwork gleamed in the sunlight. This automobile was a well-loved toy; Jim, Daglish's husband, the most likely owner.

"Nineteen forty-nine Mercury convertible. Mint condition." Gabriel reached for the passenger door handle, ready to leap out and put his filthy handprints across the hood.

"Wait a moment," Emmanuel said, looking for a delaying tactic. "If I can tell you your secret name, will you stay in the car for five minutes?"

"Both names?" the boy asked.

"Yes."

"If you're wrong, can I play in the Mercury?"

"Yes, you may." He hoped to Christ that Daglish's memory wasn't faulty or her Zulu completely mangled.

Gabriel's fingers curled on the door handle, intrigued by the proposition. "Okay," he said. "Guess."

"Gabriel Reed. Nyonyane. Little Bird."

The boy was awed, his blue and brown eyes wide with surprise. "How did you know? It was a secret."

"Luck." Emmanuel pulled the car keys from the ignition. "Don't move. I'll be back in five minutes."

"Grown-ups always say that." The boy sank back against the leather, already bored.

Emmanuel went to the front door and knocked. Swing music blared from inside, a trombone and trumpet fighting for supremacy. The convertible in the driveway and the music spinning on the gramophone made Daglish's house look like a party venue.

The music brought back memories of Paris in the grip of postwar hedonism: the bright white neon signs that shone a false daylight onto the streets and the dim hole-in-the-wall clubs filled with music and girls. He knocked louder to compensate for the Glenn Miller Orchestra.

"Yes?" Daglish's voice was sharp. If there was a party hopping out back, she'd yet to have a drink and loosen up.

"It's Detective Sergeant Cooper. I need your help."

The lock turned and the door opened a crack. Daglish's face appeared in the narrow space. The kick and jive of the music contrasted with the tight set of her jaw and the narrow cast of her eyes. She'd shed the nightdress and dressing gown of this morning for a plain brown dress with three-quarter-length sleeves and a high neckline.

"This isn't a good time." Daglish kept the door closed as much as possible to stop the sound of their conversation from drifting down the hallway. "You'll have to come back later, Detective Cooper."

When Jim had finished throwing his own homecoming party and the gramophone records were back in their paper sleeves—or else the broken pieces swept up from the floor and dumped in the garbage.

"Dr. Zweigman is injured. He needs medical attention urgently." Emmanuel decided to focus on Zweigman, the man in need, and kept Daglish's duty and responsibility for later, if he needed them. "I came straight to you. No one else in Roselet can help."

Daglish slipped out of the house and closed the door with a quiet click. She leaned back and pressed her palms against the wood like Pandora trying to keep a lid on her box of evil. "Where is Dr. Zweigman?" she whispered, even though the heady blast of trumpets was loud enough to drown a baby's wail.

"In the valley, close to Covenant Farm. We'll have to drive to the turnoff and then walk the rest of the way."

"That's miles away. It will take hours to get there and back."

"It will be an overnight trip," Emmanuel said.

"That's impossible." The blood drained out of Daglish's face. "I can't."

"Why not?"

The drawn expression, her simmering panic and the nervous flick of her gaze to the ground: Emmanuel recognized the signs of distress, knew every twitch from long years of reading his own mother's face. While the music played, the world was safe. The moment the horns ended, a grim domestic war would begin.

"Jim is home," Daglish said. "I can't walk out the moment he walks in."

"Because it's your job to be here, waiting for him, whether he's on the road for days at a time or at home for one night," Emmanuel interpreted.

She scraped a fingernail against the door, chipping away at the surface. "You don't know what you're asking of me, Detective Cooper."

"Believe me," he said. "I do." The emotional cycle of the heavy drinker was a lesson Emmanuel's father had taught him by personal example. Two lagers and the world became grand and every joke funny. Four drinks and the tide turned. Six empties and every wrong, every hurt, was unearthed.

"I can get you supplies from the surgery, anything you need, but I can't help beyond that. I'm sorry."

"I need *you*, Dr. Daglish. Not a roll of bandages and a bottle of iodine."

The music stopped abruptly, replaced by the faint clink of ice rattling against glass. Footsteps creaked on the wooden floor.

"Go back to your car and wait there." Daglish spoke quickly. "I'll bring my medical bag as soon as I can."

"Dr. Zweigman won't pull through without your help," Emmanuel said. "And I promise to get you there and back safely."

The footsteps reached the door. Daglish sucked in a breath and held it.

"What are you doing out there, Margaret?" The accent was public school mixed with officers' club.

"Talking to a patient," Daglish said. "Won't be long."

"We've just run out of ice and the bloody maid has disappeared."

"I'll get a bag from Dawson's." She pressed a finger to her mouth to signal for quiet. "Five minutes."

"What you should do is sack the maid. Hauling ice is a kaffir's job, for Christ's sake, and you made a big enough fool of yourself in town this morning."

"Yes, of course. Won't happen again."

A grunt and a rattle of ice cubes in glass preceded Jim's retreat to the lounge room. Emmanuel waited for Daglish to relax her shoulders and breathe normally. He understood the situation. Jim needed ice. If it was supplied in enough quantity to drown a few bottles, then a messy sleep on the couch instead of a fight was a possibility.

"What's he doing here?" Daglish looked over Emmanuel's shoulder and frowned. "Did you bring him to my house, Detective?"

Gabriel was out of the Chevrolet and tracing his dirty fingers across the Mercury convertible's wheel arch. Sliding into the pristine leather seats and honking the horn was the next step.

Exasperated, Emmanuel said to the boy, "We had a deal."

"I waited five minutes." The teenager leaned over the hood and admired the mellow light bouncing off the waxed surface. He looked as though he could stay there till nightfall, nose to the paint.

"Leave, please," Daglish said. "I'll get my medical bag and bring it to you at Dawson's. Then you can help Dr. Zweigman. Cross my heart."

Freedom of choice was fine in theory but a bitch in practice. The spirit of the old soldier who'd hauled him through ghost towns reappeared in Emmanuel.

"*That's the way, soldier. Take the offensive.*" The sergeant major assumed control. "*Zweigman is down, bleeding out on a hillside. The choice here is life or death. The rules of war apply. You will do whatever is necessary to get Daglish into the car.*"

Emmanuel walked to the back of the car and unlocked the boot.

"Is it time to go already?" Gabriel asked. He looked up from the ground, where he'd crouched down to count the spokes on the wheel.

"Yeah," Emmanuel said.

"*The boot's big enough for the job,*" the sergeant major confirmed. "*Make sure the radio is turned up loud on the drive out of town in case she tries to kick her way out. Tying her up will help.*"

Daglish would have to be rendered innocuous and contained, military language for captured and imprisoned.

Emmanuel knew he'd do it easily and without conscience. The sergeant major was right, the rules of war applied.

"Dr. Daglish will pack a special bag and deliver it to us at Dawson's General Store." He walked around to the front of the car, leaving the boot cracked open an inch.

"Mr. David Dawson," Gabriel said. "Cash Only."

"That's him." The one time Emmanuel had been into the store with Shabalala, the surly shopkeeper had shadowed their steps, calculating every purchase on scrap paper and mumbling, "Cash only. No credit. Store policy." Emmanuel had wondered at the time if local whites received similar treatment or if the peculiar behavior was reserved for European visitors and black detectives. Dawson distributed his paranoia fairly across all the race groups.

Emmanuel glanced at Daglish now, calculating her height and weight. She was taller than the average woman and reasonably strong. He'd have to surprise her in order to disable her and load her into the car. "I'll take those supplies now, Doctor. Jim's ice has to wait."

"Of course." She forced a smile. "The supplies are in the cellar."

"Follow close but not too close, Cooper. Give her an item to carry to the boot. That will get her in place."

Gabriel finished counting the silver spokes and stood up, satisfied with his inspection of the car. Daglish stepped back, wary of him. Gabriel smiled and said, "Dr. Margaret Daglish, Play Happy, and Mr. Jim Daglish, Empty Bottles."

"What did you say?" The doctor flinched as if she'd been slapped.

"Dr. Margaret Daglish." He pointed directly at Daglish's solar plexus. "Play Happy."

"Where did you get that name from?" she asked. The dry sound of her swallowing could be heard in the still garden.

Gabriel shrugged and traced the sleek outline of the Mercury convertible from bonnet to boot, unaffected by the doctor's stunned expression.

"Play Happy and Empty Bottles." Daglish repeated the nicknames with a bleak smile. "Clever Gabriel."

"Every tree and rock has a special name." Emmanuel felt like Shabalala defending Baba Kaleni's ability to rip the bandages off the hidden wounds of his own past.

"Not a special name—the right name," Daglish said. "All the time I've spent smiling and pretending to be happy while the maid hides the empty bottles in the back shed. It's pitiful. Even the boy can see that."

Gabriel's unintentional cruelty exposed the rot at the center of Daglish's life. She stood amid the spring green, looking lost. A moment before, the garden was a welcoming place. Now, with her sadness out in the open, it seemed old and artificial—a stage set for an imaginary life. Her eyes welled with tears.

"Patience," the sergeant major said. *"Don't rush things, Cooper. Let her have a wee weep if she needs to. She'll be easier to handle afterwards."*

"We were fabulous ten years ago," Daglish said. "I was the smartest woman in the room and Jim was the best-looking South African Air Force pilot on the base. It was a match made in heaven. That's what it felt like at the time. Then the war ended. Jim found work managing a garage, then supervising a construction site and then running a café: then a dozen more things, none of them lasting more than six months. I kept practicing medicine, earning most of the money. No children. Now look at us. Play Happy and Empty Bottles."

"Going from saving the world to pouring coffee is a hard transition to make," Emmanuel said. Every ex-soldier suffered the stress of returning to civilian life and some never quite got there.

"You feel sorry for him." Daglish wiped away tears.

"I feel sorry for you both," Emmanuel said. Christ, he'd switched soldiering for policing because he needed to create order out of chaos and to uphold some notion of good regardless of the consequences. He'd kept fighting the war long after the war was over. His marriage disintegrated while he chased an ideal.

Vera Lynn's "When the Lights Go On Again" hit the turntable in the cottage.

"This used to be my favorite song," Daglish said. "I couldn't wait for the war to be over. Oh, the life I was going to have!"

"One more minute, laddie. Get yourself together. Saving Zweigman is more important than this lass's domestic drama." The sergeant major liked to remind Emmanuel of mission objectives.

"Well, the war is over, the lights are back on and the boys are back home, but I'm living in the dark." Daglish turned to Emmanuel, her mind set on a new course of action.

"What kind of wound?" she asked with sudden resolve.

"A stab wound to the right shoulder. Deep. Bleeding through the dressing."

"It'll need cleaning and stitching and re-dressing." Daglish interrupted Gabriel's detailed examination of the Mercury's antenna by opening the driver's-side door and motioning to the sleek leather seats. "You can play inside till Detective Cooper and I come back. Promise not to move?"

"Promise." Gabriel slid onto the two-tone leather seat and smoothed his fingers across the steering wheel, delighted.

"That will hold his attention for a while," Daglish said, and took the side path to the basement, her journey accompanied by Vera Lynn's yearning ode to the joys of peacetime. "Tell me what we need, Detective Sergeant."

"Do what the lady says, Cooper," the sergeant major said. *"She's a volunteer, not a conscript, now."*

Emmanuel accepted the unfolding miracle without examining it. The universe, and Vera Lynn, had spoken.

It wasn't Zweigman's time to go.

Not today.

The temptation to speed down the main road and clear town quickly was great but Emmanuel controlled the impulse. He carried irreplaceable cargo. A boot crammed with medical supplies for Zweigman's treatment, food and blankets, Gabriel's encyclopedic mind and Daglish's rediscovered courage.

"Look." Gabriel pointed to the general store. "Cash Only."

A thin white man in a blue-and-white-striped grocer's apron stalked a fat white tourist with a Brownie reflex camera slung around his neck.

"Who's that?" Daglish joined in the game and pointed out a sallow woman wrestling a tiny boy onto the back of a Ford pickup truck packed end to end with ragged children.

"Mrs. Beatrice Carson," Gabriel said. "Baby-a-Year."

Daglish laughed and wound the window down to get air. She was riding high on the crest of freedom, but five hours from now, with nothing but starlight to illuminate her own dark corners, Emmanuel suspected the wave would crash and Daglish would find herself stranded on a hillside with four strangers, wondering how her life had drained away.

Emmanuel slowed at the entrance to the police station and checked the parking lot. Constable Bagley and two white men in baggy blue suits and crunched fedoras stood near a black police Chevrolet: Detective Sergeant Benjamin Ellicott and Detective Constable John Hargrave of the West Street Branch in Durban had arrived.

Gabriel shuffled across the seat to the window to get a better look at the three men in the police station yard. He pushed a fingertip to the glass.

"Constable Desmond Bagley," he said. "Mr. Insurance Policy."

17

TEN MILES OUT of town, with blood still roaring in his ears, Emmanuel loosened his death grip on the steering wheel. He had driven ten miles trying to calm down and suppress the urge to slam on the brakes and shake answers about Mr. Insurance Policy out of Gabriel Reed. But getting to Zweigman was the first priority.

He kept the speedometer at sixty and ignored Daglish's muffled gasps when stones pinged against the undercarriage and red dust coated the windscreen. He checked the rearview mirror and tried to figure out the best way to unlock the knowledge trapped in Gabriel's brain while driving fast down a corrugated road.

"The names you give the trees and animals come from science books. How do people get their names?" he asked.

Gabriel lolled against the warm leather seat, watching light patterns flicker across the interior walls of the car. "The people tell me who they are."

"I see." Emmanuel didn't see at all but saying otherwise might throw the boy out of the conversation. He tried another tack. "Mr. Bijay Gowda is Bus Ticket because he sells bus tickets?"

"Yes."

"Mrs. Beatrice Carson is Baby-a-Year because she gives birth every year?"

"Of course."

"And Constable Desmond Bagley is Mr. Insurance Policy because he sells insurance to the Zulus in the valley?"

"Not all of them," Gabriel said. "Just Amahle."

Daglish caught the drift of the conversation and laced her fingers tightly together. She glanced out the window. Late afternoon sun hit the tops of the marula trees and long shadows fell across the road. It was too late to turn back now.

"Insurance is expensive," Emmanuel said. "I'm sure Constable Bagley was a nice insurance agent who gave Amahle a policy for free."

"No," Gabriel said. "She paid."

A large cowlike antelope grazing the upper reaches of a mountain slope distracted Gabriel's attention. He pressed his nose to the window and fogged the glass with his breath. The thread that held him in the previous conversation broke. "*Taurotragus oryx*. Common eland."

After that, the scientific and common name for a Cape chestnut tree, a wild hare, a yellow butterfly and a spray of purple wildflowers tumbled out of Gabriel like milk from a broken jug. Emmanuel shifted down to third gear and took a wide bend in the road, waiting for an opportunity to reintroduce the topic of Amahle. The turnoff to Covenant Farm was two miles ahead. Gabriel would be out of the car and running barefoot through the hills before the hand brake was up.

"Please don't," Daglish said to Emmanuel. "He's scared.

Naming everything twice makes him feel safe. Let's give him time to calm down."

"All right." That was a fair suggestion. He had enough information to light a fire under the station commander and see which direction he ran in. Gabriel's fact train rolled on, some species cataloged twice in a row and at astonishing speed.

"Do you think the constable killed her?" Daglish whispered.

"Bagley admits to being in the native location on Friday night. He claims he made two arrests. The station occurrence book will verify the story or prove if it's a lie. The native police had to have been there as well." Prying information from the Zulu police was a job for Shabalala. "How far is the location from Little Flint Farm?"

"Ten or so miles."

"Close enough for Bagley to hit both places on the same night." The fine details didn't hold together, though. Putting down a fight on a native reserve, arresting two men and then hiking into the hills to murder a black girl required a combination of luck, impeccable timing and an invisibility cloak: a white policeman on a native pathway would be seen and deferred to and then whispered about in the safety of huts and kraals. Repeating the same feat over the next two days to murder Philani would have required superhuman abilities.

"Bagley's involved with Amahle's murder," Emmanuel said. "But I don't know how. Not yet."

He parked the car close to the Covenant Farm turnoff, unlocked the boot and unpacked the supplies. Blue shadows lengthened over the hills. The sun balanced on the horizon, sinking fast. Emmanuel shouldered the heaviest pack and Gabriel led the way through a group of white pear saplings that glowed in the last light of the day. Prehistoric ferns with fronds like giant green hands reached for the sky.

Bagley slipped out of his mind. The constable was tomorrow's problem. The burnished sky closed over the treetops. He appealed to God, the good fairies and the breath of wind lifting the leaves to keep Zweigman alive till he arrived with Dr. Daglish. You have Amahle and Philani, he reasoned, surely that's enough. Why take an old Jew?

—

The blood-soaked dressings turned to ash in the fire. Twigs and leaves crackled and glowed. Emmanuel threw Zweigman's shirt into the blaze and watched it burn. Shabalala added the doctor's rumpled jacket, stiff with dried blood. Smoke billowed into the night air. The high-pitched yelp of a black-backed jackal calling its mate to a kill broke the quiet night.

Emmanuel found the bottle of homemade peach brandy stolen from Covenant Farm and pulled out the cork. He offered the first hit to Shabalala, who hesitated. Blacks and whites did not drink from the same bottle unless they were park vagrants or insane.

"There'll never be a better time to start drinking," Emmanuel said, and pressed the bottle closer.

Shabalala accepted the brandy and took a mouthful, coughing when the 80 proof alcohol hit his stomach. He handed the bottle back to Emmanuel. They drank in silence and watched the last fibers of Zweigman's jacket vanish in the coals.

"What now, Sergeant?" Shabalala asked.

"We wait," Emmanuel said. And pray and make promises and bargain with the universe: my life for his, my blood to replace the red pool staining the surface of the rock. Zweigman had a wife and son to go home to, people who needed him. Emmanuel had a sister he called on the first Sunday of the month. No promise was sacred enough to tip the scales in Zweigman's favor but Emmanuel knew no other way to fill the black hole inside of him.

"Done for now." Daglish pulled the feather blanket over Zweigman's bare chest and stood up to stretch her cramped muscles. The entire operation, from cleaning the wound to stitching the cut and applying fresh dressings, was completed at ground level and by firelight. "He's lost a lot of blood. It will take a day or two for him to recover enough strength to move."

"Thank you, Doctor," Emmanuel said. He offered three small words in exchange for Zweigman's life. It was all he had.

"I was pushed before I jumped." Daglish moved to the fire and held her hands up to the flames. "Just as well."

Emmanuel looked at Margaret's face in the firelight. It glowed. "I think you like being up here, a witch doctor in the wild," he said.

"Yes, I think I do," Daglish said. "And now I'd like a drink, if you don't mind."

Shabalala cleared his throat and looked to the night sky, mortified by the doctor's request. Respectable white women drank in separate "ladies' bars" with dress codes, tables and chairs. Chugging liquor in the company of cops was usually for whores and bar girls. How far outside the rules was Daglish willing to go?

"It's everybody's bottle tonight," Emmanuel said. "Shabalala and I have already made a head start."

"You can't be half pregnant, Detective." The town doctor held out her hand for the bottle. "And I need a drink. Now."

"Of course," Emmanuel said, and gave Daglish the brandy. No way on earth would Shabalala take another drink from the bottle, and neither would he. Treating a middle-class woman doctor like one of the boys seemed disrespectful.

"*L'chaim.*" Daglish raised the bottle to the fire in a toast. "To life."

She took a deep swallow and then another and tears stung her eyes. Emmanuel wondered how Daglish managed to keep this version of herself so well hidden. And also where she'd learned a Hebrew toast.

"Danny Einfeld. Durban Medical School." She answered his silent query and drained the bottle in one long hit.

The jackal made a series of eerie yelps in the darkness. It was closer now. Shabalala threw a branch onto the fire and sparks floated up to the canopy of stars. Gabriel slept curled up on a bed of stolen clothing with his hands tucked under his head as a pillow. Zweigman breathed deeply, warmed by the flames, peacefully asleep in a pharmaceutical haze from the morphine in his bloodstream. Emmanuel crouched by the fire and felt the weight of worry and guilt lift from his shoulders. He made plans for tomorrow.

18

EARLY MORNING SUN broke the cloud cover and lit the twists and turns of the "Scenic Way" that looped from the hotel to behind the police station. Emmanuel and Shabalala crouched in the grass and waited. Up before dawn and wearing the suits they'd slept in, they looked like gentlemen of the road planning the ambush of a traveling coach. A Zulu man crossed the stream at the edge of the field and walked toward them.

"That's him," Emmanuel said. "Don't ask questions. Look him in the eye. Tell him you know about Bagley and Amahle. He has one, and only one, chance to grow a pair, tell the truth and be a man."

"He will hear me." Shabalala stood up with his arms hanging loosely by his side. Somehow the easy posture was more threatening than if he'd come out with his fists swinging. Shabangu, the Zulu constable, would talk.

"We'll meet under the sycamore tree in ten minutes and then I'll run the same line with Bagley. Hopefully with information from Shabangu to use as a lever." Emmanuel split off in the direction of the station house.

He was confident that Ellicott and Hargrave, the replacements from Durban, would sleep late. Working on that assumption, Emmanuel and Shabalala had an hour to spring the two-part plan before returning to Daglish and the still-sleeping Zweigman.

The smell of coffee and bacon drifted from the back of the commander's house. Emmanuel turned the corner and looked into the empty yard. No sign of Bagley on the stairs. Breakfast must already be on the table. He crossed the raked-dirt square, passed the sycamore tree and peered through the station window. Also empty. He returned to the sycamore, making sure to keep the trunk between his body and Bagley's house.

Eleven minutes later, Shabalala cut across the dirt yard with the stride of prizefighter.

"Tell me," Emmanuel said, wanting just a slice of that glow.

"Shabangu says that Amahle came to the attention of the police twice. First was the day in winter when she was left in town by accident. Constable Bagley was the one to drive her back to Little Flint Farm. The second time was Friday afternoon." Shabalala paused, enjoying the serious weight of the information he'd collected. "She came here and talked to the constable in the station house. Shabangu did not hear what was said but when Amahle left she walked like a queen with the water parting before her."

"Excellent. Ella Reed said something like that, too . . ." Emmanuel grasped for the fragment of conversation and found it. "Amahle came back to the fitting room with change rattling in her pocket and she looked pleased."

"The constable gave Amahle money," Shabalala guessed.

"Let's find out from Bagley himself. Go into the station and sit at the station commander's desk. I'll bring Bagley through in a few minutes."

"But Sergeant . . ." Shabalala knew the rules. White policemen sat at desks in the front office; black policemen, like Victorian-era children, stayed out of sight in a back room until they were called.

"Forget the rules," Emmanuel said. "This whole operation is off the books. We do as we like and live with the consequences. Sit down, fiddle with the pens, make a call if you like."

"I must pretend it is my desk."

"Yes. And don't move from the desk no matter what Bagley says to you." That was insubordination and a punishable offense within the South African Police Force. "If Bagley actually has the guts to report our conversation to the district commandant, I'll tell the commandant you did it on my order."

"Sit, don't move," Shabalala said, warming to the idea but not convinced of its wisdom. White men could take risks that remained impossible even in the dreams of black men and women. The detective sergeant took risks that no sane white man would even contemplate.

"I'll do the rest," Emmanuel said. The old coda, Trust me, was redundant. Faith, loyalty and trust kept them both above the quicksand in this clandestine operation.

Shabalala nodded and made for the front door of the station. A Land Rover packed with farm supplies destined for the valley and a rattling white and blue bus with the name GOD'S GIFT painted on the side headed into town. Shabangu, the Zulu policeman, slipped into the yard and began collecting wind-blown twigs and leaves from the ground before throwing them into a garbage drum. Emmanuel reached the back door of the police residence and knocked twice.

A handle clicked and a plain woman appeared, her fine strawberry-blond hair scraped back in a bun. No more than thirty years old, she wore a green cotton dress that was modest even by nineteenth-century standards. It had long puffed sleeves and a long skirt that came down almost to the floor.

"Can I help you?" Her voice was hesitant and soft.

"I'm here to see the station commander," Emmanuel said. The pity he began to feel for this woman, the same one he'd seen standing by the window and secretly spying on her husband chain-smoking at dawn, had no part in the plan.

"Who should I say is asking for him?"

"Detective Sergeant Cooper. Can you tell him that I'll be waiting for him at the station house?"

"He's in the middle of breakfast." The words came out fast, as if she'd noticed a dangerous crossroads ahead and was steering to avoid a collision.

"He'll see me," Emmanuel said, and then added, "If the commander can't make it to the station, tell him I'm happy to come in and talk with him over breakfast."

Bagley's daughters pressed into the hallway. They stood on tiptoe and tried to see beyond their mother and into the yard.

"Where is your friend?" the elder girl called out. "The black one?"

"Hush, now, and back to breakfast." Mrs. Bagley shooed the girls into a side room and shot Emmanuel a worried glance.

He tipped his hat and walked to the station house. Later

tonight, when the sun was down and the moon high over the mountains, Mrs. Bagley would most likely turn to her husband and ask in a soft voice, *What happened?* Constable Bagley would look her in the face and say, *Nothing important.* He'd lie to her, and not for the first time, Emmanuel was certain.

He ducked inside the low sandstone building and closed the door. The visual punch of a tall, solid Zulu man sitting behind a station commander's desk was stunning and immediate. Shabalala was either a dream come true or a colonial nightmare brought to life, depending on who was looking.

"Suits you," Emmanuel said, and pressed himself flat to the wall behind the door. The first thing Bagley would see was a world in reverse, a black man in the power seat. If that didn't destabilize the Roselet station commander, nothing would.

Hurried steps tracked the width of the yard, growing louder.

"Relax, for God's sake," Emmanuel said. "Write your wife a note on official paper. Tell her how much you enjoy wearing a suit and sitting behind a desk like a fat white man."

Shabalala smiled and lost the stiff posture of a thief caught lifting donations from the church poor box. He pulled a sheet from a drawer and selected a pen from the neat row laid out on the desk. The station door swung open. Bagley stepped in, uniform pressed and black shoes shined, his face like a crumpled paper bag.

"What the hell are you doing, boy?" he asked, shocked by the sight of a black man sitting in his seat, touching his pens and papers.

Shabalala said, "Writing a letter to my wife in Durban."

Bagley moved farther in. "Is this Sergeant Cooper's idea of a joke?"

"Did you really think it was that easy to shake us off your tail, Mr. Insurance Policy?" Emmanuel shut the station door with a hard click and leaned against it. "Make a phone call to a farmer, get a general to breathe fire and have us sent home to bed without our supper?"

Bagley spun a half circle, the telltale vein pulsing on his forehead. "It's official. You are off the case, Cooper. The longer you stay, the worse trouble you're in."

Emmanuel looked over at Shabalala, still seated behind the desk. "Constable Bagley is worried for us. He left a hot bacon and egg breakfast to come over here and personally tell us that we've been naughty boys and that the headmaster—or is that the general?—is going to cane us."

"That was very kind of him, Sergeant," Shabalala said.

"*Ja*, it was." Emmanuel refocused on Bagley. "You don't have to fret about us, Constable, we've been in tougher spots than this. You should be worried for yourself, your family and your police pension."

Bagley's Adam's apple rose and fell. "My pension is none of your business."

The pension was a small but important reward for a lifetime of poorly paid work and formed the foundation of every policeman's retirement fantasy. It was a monthly reminder that the sacrifices made to keep South Africa safe were remembered and rewarded.

"I'm personally not in favor of taking the pension away from a cop who's made one stupid mistake. We're human and we fall as quick as the next man," Emmanuel said. "Amahle was young and pretty. Easy to see how it happened."

"Nothing happened." Bagley pressed his palm against the pulse point on his forehead. "You've got the wrong idea."

"So you lied about knowing Amahle because . . . ?" Emmanuel left the sentence unfinished.

"I knew it would look bad. Me knowing a dead black girl."

"Bullshit." Emmanuel went on the attack. "You gave her a lift to Little Flint Farm, pulled over at the side of the road and fucked her in the back of the van. That's why you lied about knowing her."

Zweigman's autopsy proved that couldn't be true but the accusation sent Bagley reeling back two steps. He bumped against the station counter, sweating. "That's not what happened. I swear."

Emmanuel dismissed Bagley with a look and said, "Pick up the phone, Shabalala. Have the operator put through a call to the vice squad in Durban. Tell them we have a tip-off for them. A high-profile case involving a married policeman and a dead girl."

"No." Bagley held out his hands, as if trying to stop time. "Wait. Please."

"I'm not waiting to hear more of your kak. Tell your story to the vice squad when they get here."

The station commander placed a hand to his chest. "On the lives of my children I will tell you the truth. Just put down the phone and let me speak."

Emmanuel signaled to Shabalala to replace the receiver on the hook. "Okay, let's talk."

"Just you and me." Bagley looked to the concrete floor. "I can't say it in front of a kaffir."

"You mean Detective Constable Shabalala?"

Bagley cleared his throat and said, "Yes. Detective Constable Shabalala."

Life at the top of the race ladder meant a long fall from

grace when the earth shifted. Bad behavior was expected of those on the lower rungs. A white man or woman given to bouts of violence or sexual misadventure let the whole European race down; they made nonsense of the moral superiority of whites.

Shabalala pushed away from the desk and stood up. "I will take a walk."

"Not too far," Emmanuel said, and moved from the doorway. The clock on the wall read 7:35. "Come back in ten minutes."

"*Yebo,* Sergeant."

Bagley and Shabalala avoided eye contact as the Zulu detective left the room and began walking across the yard.

"Sit." Emmanuel threw his hat onto the counter, ready to start. The tick of the clock was loud in the silence.

"Mind if I stand by the window and have a smoke?" Bagley asked.

"Fine." Emmanuel stayed close to the constable in case he was desperate enough to jump out of the window and make a run for it.

"I know what you're thinking." Bagley pulled a packet of Dunhills from his jacket and removed a cigarette. "Dirty white policeman. Poor, frightened black girl. You're wrong. The situation with Amahle was the opposite of that."

"Dirty black girl and poor, frightened policeman?" Emmanuel didn't blunt his sarcasm. He didn't have time to listen to excuses. A simple what-happened-when story would do. "She was left in town by accident, you drove her back to Little Flint Farm. Then what?"

"See, there's your first mistake, Cooper." Bagley lit up, drew deep and blew smoke from his nostrils. "She didn't get left. She was hiding behind the general store, waiting for God's Gift to come through. The farm manager held off driving back to Little Flint for fifteen minutes, got pissed off and then made tracks without her."

God's Gift was the bus Emmanuel had just seen cruise Greyling Street into town. Amahle was not lost or left behind on that day, she was on the run.

"Any idea where she was going?"

"Pietermaritzburg," Bagley said. "Then on to Durban. I found the ticket in her pocket after Reed called and said to find her and bring her back to the farm." Bagley smoked. The memory of being dispatched to hunt down a servant girl as a priority still irked him.

Emmanuel raised the window higher to get some fresh air.

"Two buses. All the way to Durban. That's a big move for a Zulu girl from the sticks," Emmanuel said. He thought of the number of times he'd run away from the Fountain of Light Boarding School and failed to get to the city.

"That's your next mistake, see. That girl wasn't a usual kind of native. She had two pounds and a map of Natal in her pocket and she wasn't afraid of the journey or of me."

"No luggage?"

"Not that I saw."

That surprised Emmanuel. The lipstick, toothbrush and nail polish scattered across the ground by Chief Matebula belonged to a girl with the desire to use them, even if it was in the distant future. Leaving without a suitcase or her box of luxuries made no sense.

"*Ja?*" He prompted Bagley to continue. Loose threads could be tied up later.

"Constable Shabangu walked her to the edge of town and I picked her up from there."

"Why walk out so far when the station is closer?"

Bagley flicked ash into the yard. It took a minute for him to invent an answer as to why Amahle was diverted from the station to the outskirts of town. "I thought it would be better to keep the runaway thing under wraps. For the Reeds' sake."

"That is unmitigated shit in a can, Cooper," the sergeant major said. *"Slam this fucker up against the wall and tell him to stop wasting your time. He was planning to diddle the girl and he covered his tracks from the start."*

"Doing your bit to quell trouble with the natives . . ." Emmanuel flicked Bagley's cigarette from his fingers. It flew out the window and fell to the ground, where it lay smoldering. He pressed a finger to the constable's chest to get his attention. "You're a bad liar and a coward. Let's start again. I'll tell you the real reason you sent Amahle to the crossroads and then you finish the story without mentioning your good intentions. All right?"

Bagley nodded and looked away. He had no choice but to listen.

"You wanted to fuck Amahle and you were afraid it would show if your wife saw the two of you together. You sent her outside of town to protect yourself. It had nothing do with the Reeds. Now it's your turn, and make it quick."

Bagley kept his face turned away. "She got into the van. We drove. Not one word from her all the way to the turnoff to the valley. I admit I was thinking about it, what it would be like to touch her, but I swear that was it. Only thinking."

There was a biblical quote about adultery beginning first in the minds of men but the exact words escaped Emmanuel.

"She started it. She reached over and put her hand on my thigh and then moved it higher to unbutton my trousers." Bagley swallowed deep and focused outside the window. "I pulled over and parked. She finished what she started."

"Hand or mouth?" Emmanuel asked. Levels of intimacy mattered.

"Both," Bagley said. "But I swear to God I didn't touch her. I kept my hands on the wheel the whole time."

"Well, that made it okay, then. Bet you didn't make a sound at the end, either."

Mottled red spots appeared on Bagley's neck and cheeks. Oh, he'd made sounds, all right, probably frightened the birds out of the trees and the rabbits out of their warrens. Bagley believed that hanging on to the wheel exempted him from admitting his involvement in the activity and, by extension, his enjoyment.

"Afterwards"—Bagley flipped the cigarette pack back and forth in his pocket—"she buttoned my fly and sat back like nothing had happened. Not a word or a sly look. It was like she was somewhere else. I drove to Little Flint and dropped her off but I knew that one day I'd have to pay."

"Did you offer Amahle money?"

"Of course not." Bagley was offended by the suggestion. "That's prostitution."

Emmanuel smiled to stop himself from laughing at Bagley's ridiculous, prudish response. He said, "The moral high ground is expensive real estate, Constable. You can't afford land there."

Outside, Shabangu, the Zulu constable, raked the yard. Across the field, Shabalala's figure could be seen heading back to the station house. Time was flying.

"Amahle paid a visit to the station on Friday," Emmanuel said. "A few hours before she disappeared."

"There's no connection between the two." Bagley's face pinched with fear and the words poured out. "I spent four months worrying myself sick about being found out, being arrested, losing my job, my wife, my family. When Amahle finally walked through the door that day it was a relief. Five pounds to buy peace of mind . . . I was happy to pay it and have the business over."

Five pounds took a bite out of a police constable's wages, especially one with a wife and two young girls to support.

"Until the money ran out and she came back for more," Emmanuel said. "Blackmail is a long-term business."

"She wasn't interested in a few pounds here and there. Not that one. Leaving Roselet was the goal. She said five pounds would keep her away for a long, long time, and I believed her."

Five pounds plus two pounds in pay put seven pounds in Amahle's pocket by late Friday afternoon: a huge amount of cash for a servant girl. If the money left on the rock by Philani's mother was the remainder of Amahle's wages, where was the five pounds?

"You're lying about the payoff," Emmanuel said. Gamblers at the track and sugar barons kept wallets with a lot of cash; country constables rattled loose change in their pockets. "Amahle died with nothing on her. Not a cent."

"Then someone must have stolen it," Bagley said. "She left here with the money. On my honor."

"That's not much to go on, Constable. Where did you get the five pounds from?"

The clock ticked. The silence lengthened. Bagley wiped the back of his hand across his mouth. He looked out of the window. His daughters practiced turning cartwheels in the yard, the long strands of their brightly colored hair trailing across the newly raked dirt, their milky limbs akimbo.

"You have a wife and children, Sergeant Cooper?" the constable asked.

"Neither," Emmanuel said, not liking the drift of the conversation. The sanctity of family gave the guilty a dozen excuses for breaking the law, none of which he was interested in hearing. "How's that relevant to the five pounds?"

"Because I'd beg, borrow and steal to protect my wife and girls. A single man can't know that feeling."

"True, but a single man might have been prudent enough to refuse a French polish from a black teenager. Now tell me where you got the money from, Constable."

Bagley waved to his desk without shifting focus from his daughters, who were now stalking Shabalala across the width of the yard. "The petty cash box. I got it from there."

"You didn't beg or borrow—you stole it," Emmanuel said. Money in the petty cash box was for the purchase of paper, pencils, tea, sugar and other everyday items. Dipping into it was something of a police tradition. A handful of fake receipts covered the loss: easy money if the theft remained undetected but a disaster if it was discovered. Bagley risked his job to pay off Amahle. The alternative was worse: a sexual dalliance with a black juvenile, no matter how brief, meant the loss of his job, his reputation and his family if it was made public.

"I did it for my girls and my wife," Bagley said, and turned to Emmanuel. "For them. You understand?"

"Admit you did it for yourself and maybe I'll overlook where the money came from. Spoon-feed me more of the my-family-comes-first crap and I will pick up that phone and call in the theft. Your choice, Constable."

Bagley pushed a hand through his hair and breathed out. "If my wife knew I let a native touch me, even just a hug, that would be the end for us. I don't want to be alone. That's why I took the money."

"Good." Emmanuel was ready to move on to the next area of questioning. "You were at the native location on Friday night, not far from Little Flint."

"*Ja*, I was."

"It was an easy trip to make between the two places, especially for a man in a car and five pounds to retrieve from a wild black girl."

"Look . . ." Bagley rushed to his desk and opened the top drawer. He fumbled for the station occurrence book, found it and flipped the pages to Friday. "Five forty-five, a fight reported in the location. Seven-fifteen, two men charged with grievous bodily harm and brought to the cells. I had dinner straight after. Ask the police boys about the location. They were with me every minute. My wife sat up in bed reading a book and came into the lounge after nine to say good night."

Bagley closed the log. He had a solid alibi and three reliable witnesses for the evening of Amahle's murder. He didn't kill her.

"Why didn't you write her name in the records straightaway and at least pretend to look for her?" Emmanuel was still puzzled by that.

"God's Gift leaves the bus depot at one-fifteen on Saturday afternoons. I hoped Amahle was on it. I prayed she was on her way to Pietermaritzburg and then to Durban."

That was the first truly honest thing Bagley had said without being prompted or threatened. Emmanuel glanced out of the window to locate Shabalala.

Bagley's daughters stood directly in the Zulu detective's path with their hands on their hips. A white man might brush them aside and keep walking. A black man had to figure out the polite way to shake them off without causing offense. Emmanuel leaned closer to the open window and listened in.

"What are you?" the younger girl demanded.

"I'm a man," Shabalala said.

The sisters frowned, copper heads simultaneously tilting to the right as they weighed up Shabalala's claim.

"A special kind of man?" the older girl asked.

"No. Just a man."

"You look different and you dress different from the normal kaffirs." She examined Shabalala from head to toe, secure in her right to do so. "Where do you get your clothes from . . . a white person's store?"

"I did not buy these clothes from a store," Shabalala said. "A friend made them for me."

"A girlfriend?" the younger girl piped in, sensing an opportunity to dig deeper into forbidden territory.

"No," Shabalala replied with a faint smile. "The woman who cut and sewed these clothes is named Lilliana Zweigman and she is just a friend."

"Our ma makes our dresses and our bloomers but nothing nice like you have." The older girl plucked at the neckline of the brown cotton shift hanging on her frame like a potato sack. Biting her lip, she threw a nervous glance at the back door of the house and quickly took hold of Shabalala's hand. She turned it palm up and pressed her own hand into it, comparing them for size.

"Shivers," she breathed. "Come see, Dolly."

The younger girl gaped at the sight of her sister's small fist tucked in Shabalala's palm like a fragile egg in a nest.

"Move over, Rosie," she begged. "Give me a turn."

Shabalala held out his other hand, a magician producing an ace of diamonds out of the air.

"Look," said Dolly. "The inside of his hand is almost the same color as ours."

Soon enough, Dolly and Rosie would not, on pain of death, approach a strange black man or allow any intimate contact across the color bar. In South Africa, this comparison of hands was strictly for children only.

"Brilliant," Dolly said when Shabalala slowly closed his fingers around each tiny fist and made them disappear altogether. "Not even Pa can do that."

"Girls!" a strident female voice called from the back door of the station commander's house. "Come in now. Quick."

Shabalala released his hold and politely stepped back from the girls. He pushed his hands into his pockets and looked away to Greyling Street, absenting himself from the yard.

"But Ma . . ." Rosie said. "We're not finished yet."

"*Ja,*" Dolly added. "Give us another minute."

"Come inside now!" Mrs. Bagley held the door open for her daughters, who moved with insolent slowness toward the house. They glanced at Shabalala once more from the stoep.

"Bye-bye, mister," said Rosie.

"Good-bye," said Shabalala. The girls slipped inside.

Emmanuel turned from the window ready to give the you-didn't-see-us-and-we-didn't-see-you warning to the town constable. Bagley stood by the side of his desk looking pale and nauseated. His daughters' interaction with Shabalala had raised a sweat on his brow.

"Relax," Emmanuel said. "Curiosity is not against the law."

"Not till they're a few years older." Bagley shut the occurrence book and slid it into the drawer. "Then that kind of curiosity most certainly will be."

19

EMMANUEL GRABBED HIS hat and got ready to strike out into the main street with Shabalala. The station door opened. Detective Sergeant Benjamin Ellicott and Detective Constable John Hargrave, in baggy black suits and bright ties, filled up the frame.

"Sergeant Cooper," Ellicott said. "You look like shit and smell like a campfire."

Standing at just five-foot-six and weighing under eleven stone, Ellicott compensated for his compact frame with testosterone. He outclassed heavier opponents in the boxing ring at the police gymnasium and had the respect of the other detectives, who admired the speed with which he produced confessions.

Hargrave was the older of the two by six years but a junior partner in both rank and intellect. The detective department record for drinking twenty whiskey shots in three minutes was his by a comfortable margin and it showed.

Emmanuel leaned against the counter, careful not to rush his exit. "I drove out to the Kamberg to see the cave paintings and got lost on the way back to the car. Had to spend the night on a hill. Nearly froze my arse off."

"Was Cooper bothering you with questions pertaining to the investigation, Constable?" Ellicott walked into the room and plonked himself down in the station commander's chair.

"No, sir," Bagley said. "Cooper came to say good-bye."

"You're supposed to be back at West Street on General Hyland's orders." Ellicott stretched his legs out and linked his hands behind his head. "Why are you still here in the middle of my investigation?"

"I've seen the paintings and now I'm on my way back to Durban." Emmanuel stepped around the end of the counter and edged past Hargrave.

"Cave painting." Ellicott's disdain was clear. "I swear to Christ that you, that Dutch colonel and the Zulu are queer for each other."

Emmanuel said nothing and reached for the door handle.

"Hold up, Cooper," Ellicott said. "I'm not done."

Hargrave stepped closer to Emmanuel and waited for the order to grab a collar or twist an arm. His breath smelled of coffee and peppermint candy, both meant to disguise traces of alcohol. It didn't work. The smell of stale beer and sour-mash whiskey emanated from the pores of his skin.

"*Ja?*" Emmanuel glanced at Ellicott, who was relaxing behind the station commander's desk as though it were his own. Constable Bagley made do with the window ledge.

"You're one of the newer kind of detectives who makes lists of facts but doesn't trust his gut instinct. Am I right?"

Emmanuel shrugged. Without the possibility of a fistfight Ellicott's attention would soon drift.

"Just wondering if you have any pointers for me and Hargrave on how to hold a suspect's hand and talk sweet."

"You've been on the force longer than me, Sergeant." Emmanuel gave Ellicott what he wanted: an acknowledgment of his superior experience. "There's nothing I can tell you about being a cop that you don't already know."

"That's right, Cooper." Ellicott loosened his tie, preparing for a long day at the desk as per General Hyland's orders. "Now fuck off back to West Street."

"Glad to." He escaped to the yard. Shabalala stood at the end of the police station driveway, waiting. Two black boys drifted by, slowing their pace to cast sideways glances at the black man dressed like a white baas.

"Sergeant . . ." Shabalala nodded a greeting that asked: *How bad was it?*

"Just the usual crap," Emmanuel said. "Nothing worth repeating. And you?"

"They said I must go back to Durban. But not with such nice words."

"And we will go back. Right after we're finished. There's something we need to check in town. I'll fill you in on Bagley's story while we walk."

Emmanuel turned left on Greyling. A yard after the café, a narrow path circled behind the shops. It had been worn by the traffic of servants' feet using the nonwhite entrances of the whites-only buildings. A kitchen boy sat on a wooden crate at the rear of the café peeling a sack of potatoes with a paring knife. The clank of cutlery came from the interior as the staff laid tables for the lunch special of roast lamb and mash.

Dawson's General Store was next. Attached to the back of

the business was a small house with a raised porch overlooking a scrappy yard and a chicken coop.

"Around here." Emmanuel crossed to the raised porch and crouched down. The space below the deck was deep enough to conceal a child playing a game of hide-and-seek. "Check behind the stumps and on the ground for any uneven surface where a hole might have been dug and then covered."

Shabalala worked from the opposite end, folded to half his height, crab-crawling around the edge of the porch. Chickens clucked and pecked for worms. Emmanuel reached below the wood deck and pulled out a heavy canvas bag. Seeing it was filled with dried corn, he shoved it back into place.

"Sergeant. Over here." Shabalala hoisted a small black suitcase from deep under the porch. Spiderwebs and silvered snail trails covered the body and the leather handles.

"That's it." Emmanuel blew sand from the lock and snapped open the lid. Amahle's new life was packed inside. Four dresses, a sweater and a pair of black shoes with red trim. "She was planning to come back for it."

Bagley was right about Amahle being somewhere else after she'd finished satisfying his silent craving. In her mind she was here: the black suitcase grasped in her hands, bus wheels churning red dust into the air and then, just at sunset, the hazy outline of a city strung with electric lights growing up around her like a dream made of noise, traffic and possibilities.

"No more," Shabalala said.

"No more," Emmanuel agreed, thinking of Amahle's unfulfilled scheme. How meticulous she'd been, even down to buying herself a travel insurance policy with a quick blow job on the roadside to ensure that next time Bagley was sent to track her down and bring her back to Little Flint Farm she wouldn't be so powerless. He lifted each layer of clothing individually and checked for the five-pound payout.

"Not a penny," he said, and shut the case. "If Amahle was planning to leave town, I can think of a place she might have spent the money Bagley gave her . . ."

Carrying the suitcase, Shabalala followed Emmanuel along the grass path, which hooked back onto the main street a few yards ahead. A black girl drew near with a chubby white baby tied to her back and another towheaded child toddling alongside her. She stepped aside at Emmanuel's approach and lowered her head to avoid the sin of making eye contact with a European man. The baby boy pressed fat fingers into the girl's neck and rolled a pinch of skin between his thumb and forefinger, enjoying the silky feeling.

The National Party split the population into groups based entirely on skin color but Amahle Matebula and this meek Zulu girl with a half smile on her mouth had nothing in common *but* color. Amahle, the beautiful one, could detect male weakness and possessed the audacity to dream of a future bathed in bright, saturated colors.

Bijay Gowda, Mr. Bus Ticket, sat on a high stool behind the plate-glass window of a booth with the words TICKET MASTER stamped across the top in flaking green paint. In his late forties, with thinning white hair, small black eyes and a prominent nose, Gowda resembled a human secretary bird nesting between the shallow counter in front of him and an open cabinet behind. The cabinet was crammed with scraps of paper, bundles of pens and pencils and stacks of old newspapers rolled up and tied with string.

He worked a wooden toothpick into a gap between his canine and incisor teeth and watched Emmanuel and Shabalala approach the booth. "Gentlemen," he said, and tucked the pick into his shirt pocket. "Where to? Johannesburg, the city of gold? Pietermaritzburg, home of the largest brick building in the Southern Hemisphere? Or Durban, city of golden beaches?"

"No tickets today. But we need to ask you a few questions." Emmanuel peered through a smudged circle left on the glass by a previous buyer. Given their situation, it was best to act like the police but without the formal introductions. "Friday afternoon you sold a ticket to a young Zulu girl, white dress, good-looking. Remember her?"

"Yes, of course," Bijay said. "One-way ticket to Durban."

"Paid for how?"

"Most definitely in cash." Bijay sat higher on the stool. "Credit and promissory notes are not accepted. Goods and services in lieu of money are not accepted. All tickets must be paid for and stamped at time of purchase."

Mr. Bus Ticket took the rules of his job seriously; a pencil stub, a booklet of tickets, an ink pad and a stamp were the tools he used to keep South Africa moving.

"Using a one- or a five-pound note?" Emmanuel asked.

"A one-pound note." Bijay was confident. "Most definitely."

"You have a good memory, to recall a single payment made five days ago."

"Roselet is not the Durban bus station, sir. We sell a limited number of tickets and most natives who come here buy what they need using coins, not notes." Bijay fiddled with the red bow tie clipped at the throat of his white shirt, accidentally pulling it loose in the process. "And it is as you say . . . the girl was pleasing to look at."

"Anything else?" There could be more. Mr. Bus Ticket reclipped the tie but his skinny fingers continued to twiddle the red bow from side to side.

"She asked me if the ticket was refundable in case she missed the bus. I said we do not give refunds but that in her case I would." Bijay gave up on straightening the tie and placed both hands on the counter. Ink from the ticket stamp had stained his fingertips and nails dark blue.

"Why the special treatment?" Amahle might have purchased extra insurance using the same payment method as for Bagley. The thought was depressing.

"I recognized the girl from before. When Constable Bagley found her and took her away before the bus came." Bijay tapped his thumb against the counter. "I had a daughter, same age, also bright and pretty. With God now for eleven years. It was because of her that I offered the refund. This Saturday or the next there are always seats on the bus."

"The ticket was issued for this coming Saturday, not last Saturday," Emmanuel clarified.

"That is correct," Bijay said. "The ticket is still valid for travel."

"Philani did not have the five pounds or the ticket," Shabalala said quietly.

Emmanuel moved away from the ticket booth. Bijay resumed working the pick between his teeth but leaned closer to the glass to catch any part of the conversation he could.

"Philani was scared and running on Friday night,"

Emmanuel said. "If he had the five pounds he would have given it to his mother to hide."

Shabalala set the suitcase down and pulled at an earlobe, thinking. "The person who killed Amahle and Philani has the five pounds and the ticket."

"That would be my guess. But waiting for Saturday afternoon to see who turns up at the bus depot with a one-way ticket to Durban and a five-pound note in their pocket isn't practical. General Hyland will have sent in the dogs by then and we have to be at the St. Thomas Anglican Church at ten a.m. for van Niekerk's wedding. If we don't show up, he'll make our lives hell," Emmanuel said, and realized with surprise that he actually wanted to see the colonel get married.

He knew van Niekerk's true nature, the cunning and secretive life he lived away from the garden parties and the lounges of decent society. Despite that ambitious, hidden life, Emmanuel admired this public declaration of unity van Niekerk was about to make. At least the colonel was striving to build a family and a home, the very things Emmanuel had promised his mother he would find for himself.

"We cannot wait till Saturday, Sergeant, so we must ask questions of the one who was there with Amahle on the night she died." Shabalala retrieved the suitcase and tucked it under his arm, ready to move.

Emmanuel thought back to the crime scene and imagined it at night. He saw Gabriel holding a branch, standing guard over Amahle's body as it lay on the ground under the stars.

"Let's get back to the valley," Emmanuel said. "Gabriel was gone when we woke up this morning but he's bound to turn up again sometime."

—

The tangled green bush that screened the tunnel from the path was trampled flat, the branches snapped clean off and thrown on the ground. Emmanuel ducked inside. The roar of blood in his head was disorienting and the outline of the trees and plants pulsed and shook with each breath. He and Shabalala had run all the way from the Chevrolet up to the tunnel. It cut ten minutes off the journey but left a burning fatigue in every muscle.

He straightened up and looked to the tunnel opening. Mandla Matebula stood on the rock ledge with a stabbing spear in one hand and a small shield balanced in the other. He was alone and at ease in the dappled sunlight breaking the tree canopy. The keloid scars crisscrossed the dark skin on his chest and shoulders with silver.

"Like the calm after a storm," the sergeant major whispered. *"I don't blame you for being intimidated, Cooper, but don't let it show, for Christ's sake."*

Two more Zulu men, members of Mandla's impi, appeared from fixed positions in the brush and blocked the exit.

"This man is either very stupid or very brave to have come here," Shabalala said. "Even the son of a chief knows that if you touch one white person you declare war on them all."

"Mandla's no fool," Emmanuel said. "He's just showing up our weakness, having some fun at our expense."

"Let us walk, Sergeant." Shabalala moved to the tunnel with unhurried steps. "Strength must meet strength."

Emmanuel followed, copying Shabalala's confident stride. Every footfall on the rock surface sounded louder than the last. Mandla remained fixed in place, not concerned or frightened by the approach of two policemen. He simply waited.

"Check the doctors, Cooper. They could be lying in the tunnel with their guts all over the floor," the sergeant major said. *"After all, you did get involved in a clan fight and defended the men who attacked the Matebula kraal. Maybe Sampie Paulus was right. Maybe you should have left well enough alone."*

"Dr. Daglish," Emmanuel called out. "Are you okay?"

"Yes." A stone bounced from the tunnel entrance and Margaret peered over the ledge. "No broken bones, Detective, just scared."

"Zweigman?"

"Resting." Daglish's brown cotton dress was rumpled and her blunt-cut bob frizzing at the ends, but she looked fine otherwise. "Gabriel's still out in the woods."

"We'll be up in a minute," Emmanuel said. The doctor flashed Mandla a quick look and mouthed the instruction *Be careful* before ducking into the tunnel.

Underestimating the speed and strength of a powerful Zulu with a battle-scarred body was not a mistake Emmanuel would make, but he was grateful for the warning all the same. He turned his attention to the rock ledge, unsure how to defuse the situation.

Shabalala shot him a look that said, *Stop. Let me go first.* He stepped within range of Mandla's spear. "Have you come to wash your spear in our blood, son of the great chief?" he asked. "Or is there another purpose to your visit?"

"My spear has already been washed. Many years ago," Mandla said, an admission to wounding and perhaps even killing a person in the past. "Washing" one's spear in human blood made a man a man during Shaka Zulu's military reign over a hundred years before. Mandla laid his weapon and shield down on the ground and crouched with his elbows balanced on the top of his knees.

"I come with news," he said.

"If you wish to speak, I am listening," Shabalala replied with grace, and squatted down to begin the conversation.

"I will talk with the boss, not the servant boy." Mandla looked beyond Shabalala's shoulder to Emmanuel, who stepped back to signal his distance from the interview.

"In this matter," Shabalala said, "I am the boss."

Mandla digested that information with a frown, weighing up the possibility that a black policeman had real authority. True or not, there was nothing to be gained from walking away. "I led you to the gardener but you have not found the one who killed him or my sister Amahle."

"We are still looking," Shabalala said.

"Looking must turn to finding. The great chief has called for a powerful *sangoma* to sniff out the witches he believes are responsible for the deaths." Mandla spoke without emotion. "I have heard him say that Amahle's mother and her little sister have evil spirits in them that must be found and cast out."

"Do you believe this is true?" Shabalala asked.

Mandla treated the question with disdain. "Nomusa is a scared woman. The little sister is a child. There are no evil spirits or wizards, only liars and greedy men. Such as my father, the great chief."

Emmanuel inched closer at the mention of Amahle's little sister. "If the *sangoma* believes there's an evil spirit in the girl . . . ?"

"She will be cast out of the kraal with her mother. No clan

will give them shelter. They will live like ghosts out on the veldt, drifting and hungry." Mandla rubbed a scar on his shoulder, an old injury healed but not forgotten. "The chief's fifth wife will make sure of this."

The fifth wife, who'd stood up in the middle of the funeral to get a clear view of Amahle's body being lowered into the short grave.

"My heart is heavy with this news," Shabalala said. "But there is no law against a *sangoma* working a spell unless a person is harmed. We can stop the ceremony if we are there, but once we are gone the chief will proceed with his plan." The harm to Nomusa and her daughter would come after the spell—when they were declared witches and banished.

"That is why you must find the person who killed Amahle and Philani before sunset tomorrow. That is when the *sangoma* will come to the kraal and pass judgment." Mandla stood up and collected his weapons. "The great chief cannot act against the word of the police once they have named the murderer."

Mandla jumped from the rock and landed with animal grace. His men moved aside to allow him access to the mountain path. They disappeared into the bush, three African men in a European century. Their ancient regiments of the eagle, the lion and the buffalo were long gone, along with their dominion over the land itself.

Emmanuel walked over to Shabalala. "What was that really about?" he asked.

"Two things, Sergeant. With his good heart Mandla wants vengeance for Amahle. With his bad heart he wants to expose the great chief as a fool who must be removed and replaced."

"He's planning a coup."

"Planting the seeds," Shabalala said. "The chief did wrong when he buried Amahle upright. If he is proved incorrect about Nomusa and the little sister being the witches responsible for the murders, then he will be further weakened. That is when Mandla will come for him, not openly with a spear, but behind doors with poison or a blanket pressed onto the face."

"And everyone lives happily ever after?"

"No." Shabalala looked away, embarrassed. "The great chief's wives and children will be split up and given to other chiefs or to men who can afford to keep them."

"It's the devil or the deep blue sea," Emmanuel said. "If the chief lives, Nomusa and her daughter will be outcasts. If he dies, they'll be given away to strangers like cattle."

"This is the way of things, Sergeant."

Married off young, a wife, then a mother and finally a widow without a home to shelter her children: Amahle had looked ahead, seen her own future and said no.

"I vote for giving Nomusa and her daughter the chance to start again, even if it's in the house of strangers." Emmanuel moved to the tunnel entrance, mentally flipping through the pages of his notebook, searching for a vital piece of information that might have been overlooked. "We have a day and a half to crack this case, Constable Shabalala."

20

EMMANUEL LOOPED BACK on one of three straggly approach paths leading to the shelter where Philani Dlamini's body had been found. The clearest track, a well-trodden seam of dirt winding up from Covenant Farm to the crest of the hill and down again to the English enclave of Little Flint Farm, gave up nothing of value. Shabalala and Emmanuel wasted two hours walking up, down and along zigzagging lines that disappeared into the bush.

Emmanuel then climbed onto the rock ledge. Shabalala was already there, sitting under the shade of a yellowwood tree. He shook his head to say that he, too, had found nothing on his search.

"The thunderstorm washed the mountain clean," he said.

Emmanuel stood in the shade. It was just after noon and the sun was high overhead. More frustration and wasted hours lay before them. "Someone besides the killer must have known Philani was here. He hid in the shelter for at least two days. He lit a fire, for God's sake!"

Interviews with the inhabitants of Covenant Farm had

come up empty. The Zulu workers claimed to have seen nothing and therefore had nothing to say to the police.

"The housemaid and the laborers are scared that the great chief will say they were to blame for Amahle's and Philani's deaths if they talk," Shabalala said. "For them, it is best to keep quiet."

"Forget the servants," Emmanuel said. "What about Karin? She must hunt in these mountains every two or three days to keep meat on the table. There's no way she didn't know Philani was up here, no matter what she says."

But Karin had been insistent that she, like the servants, saw nothing out of the ordinary in the days leading up to the discovery of the body. Certified bullshit as far as Emmanuel was concerned, but he couldn't prove otherwise.

"There is still the schoolboy," Shabalala said.

"If he ever comes back to the tunnel." Up before dawn and running through the mountains: it was easier to store water in your pocket than to hold on to Gabriel. No one had seen him since the night before. "We can't rely on him for anything."

"Perhaps we missed something at the place where Amahle's body was found."

"I don't think the killer left evidence at either crime scene," Emmanuel said. He was certain now that the murders weren't crimes of passion but were planned and coldly executed. "Searching the area again won't do any good."

A series of long whistles and the crack of a whip rose up to them from the foot of the hill. Sampie Paulus and his oxen were on the move. A thin wisp of smoke drifted from the chimney of Covenant homestead: another meal of stewed springbok on the stove for dinner and then again for lunch tomorrow. The mere thought of it made Emmanuel's mouth feel greasy. He crossed to the edge of the rock, which provided a clear view of the main path that connected the Afrikaner farm to the English one.

"Let's give Sampie five minutes to leave the yards and we'll head back down. I'm going to have another talk with Karin."

"The Dutch woman is hard like a stone in the river," Shabalala said. "She will not break."

"I know it," Emmanuel said. "But we've run out of people to question and leads to follow. We might as well chip away at the granite block, right?"

"If you say so, Sergeant."

Sampie's whistles grew faint and the bellowing of the oxen faded. Shabalala moved to Emmanuel's side and they stood for a minute, hat brims tilted, jackets buttoned up, and brushed the grass and leaves off their suits.

They jumped off the ledge together and landed on the mossy ground. The path was five yards ahead, cutting through stands of marula and stinkwood trees. Movement flashed between the trunks: someone was climbing up the hill from Covenant Farm.

"Wait," Emmanuel said to Shabalala. "Bare feet or boots?"

"Boots."

"Only two people at Covenant with boots, and one of them is driving a team of oxen in the other direction."

"The Dutch woman was also waiting for her father to leave."

Karin might be hunting or on her way to repair a fence. Emmanuel crouched down and Shabalala sank beside him, staying motionless, as if stalking prey.

The crunch of boots on dirt grew closer. Then Karin moved by at a clip with her .22 rifle slung across her shoulder.

She radiated a focused energy. Within ten seconds she was gone.

"Hunting," Emmanuel said, but kept hidden. "There was something about her, though . . ."

"The white flower." Shabalala pointed to his left ear. "Here."

"That's it." The bloom had looked snow-bright against the jet-black of Karin's hair. That a tough Afrikaner female in khaki pants and workboots would choose such a fragile ornament was intriguing. Emmanuel stood up. "Let her get ahead," he said. "Then we'll follow."

Shabalala walked to the path and examined the soil, memorizing the grid pattern left by the boots and the inward turn of the worn right heel.

"When you are ready," he said. "The Dutch woman is moving fast and it is better to keep close to her but out of sight."

"On your lead, Constable."

Shabalala set off and Emmanuel followed. Karin kept to the track until it spilled over the mountain and dropped to the valley floor and they could see the far-off buildings of Little Flint Farm. At that point, she split away and detoured into thick bush, which turned into a green passageway of overhanging trees that blocked the sun. Shabalala crept ahead and looked down the channel that tapered off to an archway made of windswept branches. The air was cool under the trees. "Behind the branches," he said. "I will wait here, Sergeant."

"Why?"

Emmanuel understood the answer before Shabalala could open his mouth. A moan came from the concealed area and then the sound of urgent breathing, growing quicker. Shabalala looked like he might turn and make a dash back to the sunlit path. Alone or with another policeman, the Zulu detective was not prepared to witness Karin's private business.

"Close your eyes and ears and stay put," Emmanuel said. "I'll see what's going on."

He edged closer, careful not to step on twigs and rustling leaves. The moans deepened, two voices working in concert but at different pitches.

Emmanuel pressed forward. Karin's rifle rested against a tree trunk like an umbrella left to dry on a porch. Shafts of sunshine breaking through the canopy lit the dim snuggery, surrounded on all sides by forest. Two figures, partially clothed, straddled a smooth rock platform. Karin, her pants unbuckled and hooked around her knees, ground her hips between a pair of smooth brown legs with white underwear dangling from a foot.

"Are you my girl?" Karin grasped a loop of brunette hair with her lean fingers and held it tight like a leash.

"*Ja . . .*" Ella Reed dug her heels into Karin's backside, the skirt of her green dress pushed up around her waist. "Your girl. I promise."

Karin pressed Ella against the rock, controlling the rhythm of their coupling and drawing broken sobs from the Englishwoman's mouth.

"*Just when the job turns to shit and you're ready to walk away, God sends you a little present . . .*" The Scottish sergeant major's laugh was filthy. "*I paid good money to see a pussy grind in Naples but you get it for free, Cooper. You lucky bastard.*"

Emmanuel stepped aside, embarrassed at the sharpness of his desire to lap up every detail of the sexual encounter.

"Give me a peek, Cooper. Go on, just one quick one before they finish. I'm asking you nice."

Emmanuel stayed put. Watching Ella and Karin through to the end would place him at a disadvantage when he questioned them: his guilt and his pleasure would show.

"They'll be too scared to say a word to you, soldier," the sergeant major fumed. *"Now get back there, Cooper, or I swear I will rip your fucking lungs out and use them as bagpipes."*

"Too late," Emmanuel said.

The groans inside the natural amphitheater peaked and then ebbed to soft exhalations of breath. The love bite on Ella's inner thigh must have happened during one of their more leisurely encounters, he figured.

He reached for the rifle left against the tree trunk and slid it behind a bush. After a short interval, to allow time for pulling on panties and rebuttoning trousers, he turned back to the enclosed space.

Karin held Ella's glowing face between her hands. "Tomorrow?" she asked.

"The day after." Ella pressed a kiss against the Afrikaner woman's rough palm. "My mother has one of her quacks coming to the house. This one uses magnets to draw out bad humors and cure migraine headaches and asthma."

"I'm no doctor," Emmanuel said from the entrance to the secret place, "but your lungs sound just fine to me, Ella. Must be the fresh air and exercise."

Karin stepped in front of Ella to protect her. She glanced at the spot where she'd left the rifle. When she didn't see it, she looked Emmanuel over and weighed her strength against his.

"You'll get the .22 back after the two of you answer some questions," Emmanuel said, adding to Karin, "Even if you get through me, Constable Shabalala is waiting outside and he will pin you like a butterfly."

Ella stood up straight, with her brunette hair teased out and the neckline of her dress askew, but her sense of social superiority appeared intact.

"My brother said you were off the case. You have no right to question us, Detective Cooper."

"Oh, I'm not here as a policeman." Emmanuel knew the frosty accent was meant to put him in his place. "I'm just a private citizen shocked at witnessing an English and an Afrikaner woman having sex in public."

"What do you want, Cooper?" Karin became pragmatic. She understood how a snare worked. The harder you kicked, the tighter the wires pulled.

"Tell me about Philani," Emmanuel said. "You knew he was hiding in the shelter."

Karin and Ella exchanged looks, both searching for the least damaging solution to their dilemma. Talk to the policeman, or appear in the local court on immorality charges?

"Not for the whole time," Karin said. "I first saw him on Saturday night just before sunset collecting firewood near the shelter. He hid but I knew he was there."

"The second time?"

"Sunday evening on my way home. It was dark and he had a fire going. He wasn't too bright for a fugitive. I walked by and . . ." Karin hesitated and Ella stroked her arm with soft fingers. They'd obviously talked about the Philani situation before this. "A Zulu woman was with him. She was in the shelter, so I didn't see her very well except for the brown buckskin with shiny beads on her shoulders. I heard her voice."

"Old, young, fat, skinny?" Emmanuel asked.

"Young but not a girl. Confident-sounding."

"Saying what exactly?"

"Something about personally talking to Chief Matebula," Karin said. "I didn't stop to listen."

"You should have told me this two days ago," Emmanuel said. General Hyland would not have bothered to pick up the phone and kill the investigation if he'd known, or even suspected, that Amahle's murder was a black-on-black crime.

"I told Pa I was going to check traps on Sugar Hill on Friday, which is way in the other direction from here," Karin said. "Sunday I said I was going to the river to pray at sunset and wouldn't be home till after dark. If I'd told him about seeing Philani, Pa would have known I was lying about where I'd gone."

And the deeper truth, that she was sparking an Englishwoman on a rock bed in the woods, was unspeakable. Emmanuel personally knew the consequences of being caught and then judged a sinner. He didn't wish it on anyone.

Karin checked the position of the sun overhead. Each minute took her away from work that needed doing on the farm and buck that she had to hunt across the hills. Ella was a luxurious time-waster. "Can I go now?" she asked. "Pa's expecting me back home."

"Can you remember any other details about this woman?"

"No." Karin straightened her belt buckle and checked that her shirt buttons were fastened. The white flower had fallen from her hair and lay crushed on the ground. "Confident, like I said. Not one of those Zulu women who don't speak without getting a man's permission first."

Karin's observation fit with some of what Emmanuel had figured. The person who'd murdered Amahle and Philani got near enough to pierce them with a small, specialized weapon. This murderer killed with confidence and skill.

"You can go," he said to Karin. "If you double back here with your .22, Constable Shabalala will hear you and bring you down long before you get anywhere close. He's half Shangaan, so don't even try it."

In the pantheon of South African race groups, every tribe had a special talent. Zulus had a gift for fighting and fine beadwork, the Pondo were cunning with money and the Shangaan had a freakish ability to track animals across any terrain.

Karin reached out a hand to Ella and said, "Come."

"Not yet," Emmanuel said. "I have a couple of questions for you, Ella."

Karin hesitated, reluctant to leave her lover in their hideout with a man. If the situation were reversed, however, Emmanuel knew Ella would skip home without questioning Karin's loyalty. No relationship was ever truly equal.

"Day after tomorrow, then." Karin threaded her fingers through Ella's hair and kissed her on the mouth. She threw Emmanuel a hard look to reinforce that she, Karin Paulus, was boss of this English miss.

Emmanuel retrieved the rifle and pulled back the bolt, ejecting the bullet from the breach before unclipping the magazine and removing the bullets. He returned the rifle to Karin. Karin disappeared into the lacework of trees and did not look back.

"You called the murder in to the police in Durban, didn't you?" he said, and turned to Ella, who now sat on the smooth rock with her legs crossed. No other white woman in the valley had a motive for making the call and access to a telephone.

"Constable Bagley is one of my brother's white kaffirs," Ella said. "He'd have taken a couple of statements and closed the case. I wanted a proper investigation."

"Ahh . . ." Emmanuel let his disbelief show. "Calling in outside help had nothing to do with getting your big brother into hot water and watching him get burned?"

"Thomas has everything his own way. It's bad for his character."

"And he keeps pushing the marriage angle, which you're, understandably, not so keen on."

Ella shrugged. "One day, maybe, but not right now."

Emmanuel suspected that Ella understood the preordained trajectory of her relationship with Karin. Girls from posh English families did not set up house with Afrikaner tomboys. They moved to grand homes with rich husbands and, if they felt the need, satisfied their desires as Ella did now—in secret and without promises.

"How did you find out about Amahle?" he asked.

"I went to the lake for a cigarette after dinner on Saturday night. Gabriel was in the boathouse babbling on about needing a pillow to help Amahle sleep on the hill." Ella slid off the stone platform and straightened her skirt. "I got enough out of him to guess she was badly hurt or dead."

"You called the police knowing Gabriel would be implicated in whatever happened to Amahle?" The call to Durban was more than spite at an older brother's power; it was lobbing a hand grenade into the family living room.

"It was risky," she admitted. "But there's no way Gabriel could have hurt her. He was her baby."

"Amahle was like a mother to him?" Emmanuel asked.

"She was more like a sister," Ella said. "A big sister who

didn't care if he made a fool of himself in town or on family trips to the beach."

"Dr. Daglish and Constable Bagley thought there was more to the relationship than that," Emmanuel said.

"I don't think it went that far. All the native men in the valley were after Amahle but she let Gabriel get close because he didn't want her that way. They made their own little world together."

"The other housemaids must have thought their relationship was strange. I bet they didn't like the extra pay Amahle received from your mother, either."

"None of the house servants liked Amahle," Ella said. "Not really. She was different from them. She always wanted more and usually got it from my mother. The other maids stayed out of her way."

Emmanuel ran a mental inventory of the Zulu housemaids at Little Flint Farm: the older, nervous woman who'd waited on the porch to greet them and the shy laundry maid with a basket balanced atop her head. Neither looked "confident" but both of them knew Amahle and Philani well enough to get close without arousing suspicion. Shabalala had talked to the inside maids and the gardeners. He might have more details to add to the new information.

"And you?" Emmanuel asked.

"It worked out for me. Amahle got the run of the house. I got to take long walks in the hills instead of sitting indoors and sewing things for my glory box." Ella was matter-of-fact. "I made sure to slip her a lipstick or a toothbrush once in a while just in case she'd read my diary and figured out about me and Karin."

That was where the luxury items in the cardboard box at

the kraal came from: they were bribes from the little madam to buy a servant's silence.

"You didn't like Amahle, either," Emmanuel said.

"Not at all, but she was clever, I'll give her that. You couldn't tell what she really loved and what she hated. She changed to suit whoever she was with. It was a good trick. I never learned it." Ella picked up the crushed white flower and rolled it between her palms to mark them with its scent.

"Keeping your true self hidden from others isn't a trick," Emmanuel said. "It's a sacrifice."

Dutiful daughter, perfect servant, runaway and manipulator of sexual desire, Amahle was all these things. On dark country nights lit only by the moon and stars, what version of herself did she take to bed? "You can go." Emmanuel stepped aside. "If you stay away too long your mother and brother will be suspicious."

"They already are." Ella paused under the arch of branches, looked at him and said, "You're wrong about me, Detective Cooper. I do love her."

The thoughts he'd had on the longevity of Karin and Ella's relationship had shown on his face as clearly as if he'd spoken them aloud.

"Loving someone and loving to fuck them are two different things." Emmanuel heard the cynicism in his voice. "Karin is a sport and a pastime. If your brother or your mother ever found out about her . . . what then?"

Ella shrugged but broke off eye contact.

"You'll tell them that she forced you against your will. Then you'll cry and they'll believe you because the truth would be too hard to face. Good-bye, Karin. Hello, Stephen or Andrew or Harry, or whatever your future husband will be called. Now tell me what I've said isn't true."

He had lived every chapter of the wrong love story as a teenager at the Fountain of Light Boarding School and knew there'd be no happy ending to Ella's, just the taste of blood in her mouth after being discovered and the mark of her lover still on her skin—long after Karin was gone. Worse than physical pain was the shame and self-loathing on the face of the one who'd come to you at nightfall and promised it was forever.

"You make it sound so mercenary." Ella paled. "I don't make the rules."

"Or the laws," Emmanuel said, and immediately regretted it. If he was guilty of breaking any law it was the one that said, *Look but don't touch. Think but don't act.*

"You wouldn't tell . . ."

"You're right," he said. "I wouldn't."

His own hypocrisy was breathtaking. After being caught with Maria, the predikant's daughter, and brutally punished for the sin of fornication, he'd chased pleasure everywhere and found it. Love, he left alone. He'd given only a fraction of himself to Angela during their brief marriage and never let her get close enough to touch the darkness inside him. The old man, Baba Kaleni, saw the easy paths he'd taken and the opportunities for deep connection that he'd let pass. He was a passenger in life, a stowaway carrying only the baggage left to him by the war.

"I shouldn't have said what I did." Emmanuel walked out to the avenue of trees. "I apologize."

Ella nodded and they trod back through the leaves to the path. Shabalala waited at the point where Emmanuel had left him. He caught sight of Ella and responded by doing what every well-mannered black African did when confronted with the shocking behavior of white people—he studied his toes.

"Good luck with the rest of the investigation, Detective Cooper." Ella similarly ignored the Zulu detective. "I hope you find that woman."

"You mean it?" Emmanuel was skeptical.

"Outside of her mother and sister, Gabriel was the only person that Amahle really loved. My brother will miss her." She moved to the tumbledown path connecting the mountain to Little Flint Farm, taking her time getting there.

"The Dutch woman and the Englishwoman?" Shabalala whispered the question to Emmanuel as Ella slipped out of view.

"*Ja,*" he replied. "It's exactly what you think."

"This is allowed if they are both European?"

"No, it most certainly is not." Emmanuel laughed. Whites were given more freedom than blacks in almost every aspect of life, so it was no surprise that Shabalala needed clarification. "They're like the rest of us, breaking the rules when no one is looking."

The two men moved from tree shade to the sunlit mountain path. The green valley and the whitewashed buildings of Little Flint Farm spread out below. Emmanuel sat down on a fallen tree trunk and passed on the information about the Zulu woman in Philani's rock shelter. "Run me through each of the Reeds' housemaids," he said.

"There are three." Shabalala perched on the log with his notebook flipped to the relevant page. "Betty Zuma is forty-three years old. A widow with two grown sons, both in Johannesburg. She was the one to greet us on the porch. She lives in the servants' quarters behind the big house and stays on the farm every day except Sunday. Friday night she served the family dinner and then cleaned afterwards."

"That strikes her from the list," Emmanuel said. "She was working when Amahle was killed."

"Right, Sergeant. She is not the one." Shabalala flicked to a new page. "The next maid is Lindiwe Mabuza, eighteen years old and still unmarried. On Friday she stayed late at the farm because Amahle left early and the big missus said the tablecloths for breakfast and lunch must be ironed."

Emmanuel could almost hear Lindiwe's sullen tone as she recalled the hours of Friday night ticking away in the company of a coal-heated iron and a bucket of starch.

"Also working," Shabalala said, and found the next interview. "Number three is Mercy Mhaule, twenty years old, unmarried but happy to be a second or third wife if necessary. She works only on Monday, Wednesday and Friday till four in the afternoon."

"Describe her," Emmanuel said. The age was right and Mercy had left before Amahle on the night she was killed.

"She is twenty years old . . ." Shabalala faltered and then said, "Full of life."

"What are you really saying, Constable?" The Zulu detective was holding back, too embarrassed to continue. "I promise not to tell."

"Smooth skin, fat lips and big brown eyes like a doe."

"Pretty," Emmanuel said. He'd missed seeing Mercy himself but the rise of heat in Shabalala's face told him all he needed to know.

"*Yebo.*" Shabalala shoved the notebook away.

"But not the daughter of a chief pulling higher wages than

anyone else. Amahle was also the big madam's pet, and the boy, Gabriel, was hers." Emmanuel checked his watch. A young, pretty, jealous housemaid could be the perfect rival for Amahle. "Mercy knocks off in three hours. I think we should keep a watch on Little Flint Farm and grab her on her way home."

Shabalala stood up and straightened his jacket, ill at ease. Emmanuel waited for him to speak. If the Zulu detective could not share a confidence here on an isolated mountain with the two of them neck-deep in a barely legal investigation, he never would.

"She was so pleasing . . ." Shabalala blew air out through his teeth. "Maybe I did not look at this woman properly and did not ask the right questions."

"Welcome to the Detective Branch," Emmanuel said. "You've passed two big milestones. The first was throwing up at the crime scene, and now you regret not seeing beyond the surface of things and asking harder questions."

"You're not angry?"

"No," Emmanuel said. He stood up to make eye contact. "I had no idea a Zulu woman could be a suspect till we caught Karin Paulus with her khakis down. That was thirty minutes ago. We learn as we go."

"And then we learn more," Shabalala said.

"In theory, yes." Emmanuel started down to the valley. "Mercy might be a dead end but we have to talk to her and see what we find out."

The dirt path twisted through rock fields and under marula trees. Despite what he'd said to Shabalala, Emmanuel had a good feeling about Mercy Mhaule, the pretty maid living in Amahle's shadow.

21

THE DYING SUN set fire to the sky. Birds roosted for the night and a warm breeze stirred the sagebrush and the yellowwood trees. Emmanuel sat cross-legged, bathed in the light of day's end. The indestructible beauty of the world amazed him. A full moon rising above the battlefield, peach blossoms falling on a freshly filled grave, blades of grass emerging from the cracked pavement of a razed town, and mankind toiling like ants across the surface. War or peace, the earth did not care.

"Did we win, Sergeant Cooper?" Zweigman asked. He was propped against the wall of the tunnel, scratching his arms and legs, a common side effect of the morphine in his bloodstream.

"Try not to speak." Daglish tucked the ends of the blanket around Zweigman's shoulders. "You need to rest."

Drugged up and stitched up, the German doctor still refused to take orders. He waved Daglish away and said, "Tell me the news."

Emmanuel got up and walked over to Zweigman. He leaned in close to stop the injured doctor from moving. A full night and day of drug-induced sleep had made Zweigman stronger but he was not completely out of danger yet.

"We did not win and the news is not good," Emmanuel said. "Our main suspect, a maid at Little Flint Farm, has alibis for the times of both murders. She's in the clear and our interview list has nobody on it."

Mercy Mhaule left work on Friday and made a quick round of all the kraals with unmarried good-looking males either resident or temporarily away digging the mines in Jo'burg. She treated her unmarried status as a disease to be cured by the end of the year. She'd even detoured to the Matebula kraal on the advice of a friend who said the great chief might be on the prowl for a new wife. On Sunday, she attended a morning church service, had lunch with her cousins and then attended a late prayer meeting before bed. Mercy had a dozen witnesses for both nights and no marriage proposals.

"Shabalala . . ." Zweigman scratched his bristled chin and neck, drifting in and out of the present. "I saw him. Now he's gone."

"Shabalala's checking a trapline that he set this morning." Emmanuel glanced at the fading red light in the sky. "He'll be back soon."

"And Lilliana and Dimitri are well?"

The thought of how close Zwiegman's wife and son had come to losing their husband and father raised the hair on the back of Emmanuel's neck. "Yes," he said. "They're both fine."

"Lilliana worries too much. Davida is strong. She will adjust to her new life. Her mother will help. So will we."

"Davida?" Emmanuel asked. The Zweigmans had taken Davida into their home and sheltered her in the backwater town of Jacob's Rest. The German couple and their surrogate mixed-race daughter remained close, though Zweigman rarely mentioned her name in Emmanuel's company.

"Shh . . . she needs sleep," Zweigman said.

"Is she sick?" Emmanuel leaned closer and tried to get Zweigman's attention. He wanted to know that Davida was happy and that his own reckless actions with her had not ruined her chances for love and peace.

"Okay, so fucking the girl was a wee bit naughty," the sergeant major said. *"But it was one night, over a year ago, Cooper. She's probably forgotten about it by now. Or is that what you're worried about . . . being a footnote?"*

Emmanuel shrugged. He wasn't sure why the memory of Davida refused to fade.

"I should have learned to play guitar," Zweigman mumbled, and scratched an earlobe. "Instead I learned the accordion. My mother said it would make me popular at parties . . ."

"Rest," said Emmanuel. The German was floating in time and space and morphine. "I have to help Dr. Daglish build a fire."

"Good woman. If I was ten years younger and the man I used to be . . . but those days are gone . . ." Zweigman slipped under the blanket and yawned. "One summer holiday Lilliana and the children ran barefoot across the grass and tried to catch fireflies with a net. I saw the moon in the lake."

Zweigman drifted off to sleep and Emmanuel left the cave to forage for dry wood. He'd dream of Davida Ellis tonight and relive the memory of her running across the veldt in a white nightdress, out of his life forever. Where was she now?

The sun set and the evening star ascended. Red color faded to charcoal on the horizon and then the black night closed around them. This time tomorrow the future of Amahle's mother and her baby sister would be decided by the *sangoma.* While beautiful in spring, this landscape turned harsh and cold in the wintertime. Snow fell on the mountains and food became difficult to find. How long could mother and daughter survive, outcast and alone, before they joined Amahle in the village of the ancestors?

—

A hand crept under the edge of the brocade curtain Emmanuel used as a blanket and moved to his gun holster. He lay still and waited for dreams and reality to separate. The hand reached the brass clip and tugged at the leather. No dream. This was real. Emmanuel reached out and grabbed a bony wrist. He sat up and gripped the thief's wrist tight. Gabriel struggled to break free, sweating heavily in the waning firelight. The King's Row College uniform had deteriorated further and dirt streaked his face.

"What are you doing?" Emmanuel whispered. Zweigman, Daglish and Shabalala were asleep around the night fire, wrapped in sheets and curtains from Gabriel's trove of stolen treasure.

"I'm taking your gun," Gabriel said.

"What for?" Emmanuel let go of the schoolboy and checked his watch. Quarter past four, just before dawn.

"To kill the Red Queen. She's roasting a baby in the coals."

The army hospital in England where Emmanuel recuperated after he'd been shot during the war housed lunatics with homicidal urges, living corpses balled up in corners and night ghosts that prowled the wards, trying to find their way home. The experience taught Emmanuel respect for the strength of the mind to manufacture its own reality. He could hear it in Gabriel's voice: the Red Queen was real.

"Tell me about the Red Queen," he said.

"She's down there." Gabriel pointed to the darkened forest. "I looked all day and then I found her."

"Why do you want to kill her?" Emmanuel applied gentle logic, trying to find the core of the boy's fantasy world.

"She's the one who made Amahle fall asleep on the mountain." Gabriel rocked back and forth, agitated by the memory. "She used bad magic but if I kill her she can find Amahle and bring her back from the other side."

Emmanuel kicked free of the curtain and reached for his shoes. When the cupboard was bare, the most far-fetched ideas opened up as possibilities. The movement brought Shabalala shuffling across the rock and into the dawn world of witches and red queens.

"Sergeant?" The Zulu detective's greeting was also a request for information.

"I found her," Gabriel said. "The woman who cast a spell on Amahle. Emmanuel won't let me have his gun. Do you have one?"

"No." Shabalala leaned closer to the feral schoolboy and whispered, "What is this woman's name?"

"The Red Queen," Gabriel said.

Emmanuel exchanged a glance with Shabalala and got a small shrug in return. Evil witch, Red Queen or silver unicorn, there were no other leads to follow.

"Take us to this woman," Shabalala said to the boy. "Emmanuel will bring his gun in case she tries to cast a spell."

Gabriel stood up and buttoned his jacket, the way he must have when lining up for daily inspection at the college. "We must move fast," he said after looking at the Webley still in its holster. "Before she flies away."

Emmanuel shoved his feet into shoes and Shabalala did the same. Gabriel jumped down from the mouth of the tunnel to the lower level and sprinted into the forest. They followed him, guided through trees and thick ferns by the sound of his footsteps. Pale blue dawn lit the path.

Keeping up with Gabriel and Shabalala demanded all Emmanuel's concentration and he lost track of time and direction. The woods thinned and they cut across a stony field dotted with aloes. A spark of red pricked the darkness.

Gabriel slowed. "Her fire," he said.

They moved from the field and through a sparse grove of marula trees. Smoke from the fire carried the scent of charred flesh and burning herbs. Emmanuel closed down his emotional reactions. Whatever lay in the coals could not be changed, only accepted and then buried.

"Slowly . . ." Shabalala cautioned. "Or she will hear."

"Quickly," the boy replied. "Or she'll disappear."

A mourning dove flew from the trees at their approach and the sound of its wings beating the air acted like a warning siren. Roosting birds twittered and called in alarm. Emmanuel glimpsed a human figure rising from the fireside.

"That's her," Gabriel called out. "The Red Queen."

The figure swung away from the flames and melted into the trees with quick steps. Shabalala broke into a run. Flashes of a tan color appeared between the tall trunks. Emmanuel split to the right, moving parallel to Shabalala in case the fleeing figure cut back toward them.

The blinks of tan disappeared and Emmanuel stopped to try to get his bearings. The pounding of footsteps faded somewhere in the distance and then disappeared into the sound of birds. He turned full circle, disoriented. Light glowed between reedy trunks and he headed in the direction of the light, dreading what he'd find in the coals.

Gabriel Reed hunched close to the fire, fascinated by the charred object thrown into its heart. He shifted position when Emmanuel came closer but kept his eyes on the blaze. "That's the baby," he said.

The organs of a child were deemed the most powerful for casting black *muti* spells, and those of a fetus even more so. Smoke stung Emmanuel's eyes and the radiant heat of the fire burned hot against his skin. He stopped on the edge of the sandy area, unable to move closer. The smoke and flames mirrored the dream in which he stumbled through burning cinders searching for something he could not see, and the presence of a dead child sharpened the fear. Somewhere in the rubble of his nightmare, hidden in the ash clouds, there was a woman and a child wrapped in cotton. He knew that now.

"One step at a time, soldier," the sergeant major said. *"There's no way here but forwards. Complete the mission."*

Emmanuel walked across the sand and looked directly into the smoldering core. Charred black flesh split to reveal ivory-colored ribs and a row of teeth. Emmanuel leaned closer. The set of the molars didn't seem right.

"Find me a long stick, Gabriel. Let's get a better look."

The boy jumped up and foraged in the underbrush before returning with two young branches stripped of their leaves. Fascination with the charred body had clearly overwhelmed any desire to find and kill the Red Queen.

He gave Emmanuel a branch and they scraped the remains

out of the fire and onto the sand. A spine, ribs and hollowed eye sockets confirmed the mass had once been a living being. Emmanuel crouched down and worked the tip of the stick along the jawline, which was long and slender and definitely not human.

"A small animal," he said. "Could be anything. A puppy or a newborn impala."

"A baby," Gabriel insisted.

"Yes," Emmanuel agreed. "But not a human one. Shabalala might know what it is."

The sky lightened and individual plants and rocks became visible. Worrying about Shabalala hadn't occurred to Emmanuel until that moment. The Zulu detective was fast and strong, but what if this black *muti* actually worked and he was chasing an opponent with dark powers?

"Crap times twenty." The sergeant major spat the words. *"Keep yourself busy, for Christ's sake, Cooper. Shabalala will be back directly."*

Emmanuel took the advice. He walked around the fire, widening the circle on every rotation, looking for evidence of the woman's identity. Gabriel followed, carefully fitting his bare feet into the tracks left by Emmanuel's shoes.

A silver bead nestling in the curve of a brown leaf glistened like a dewdrop. Emmanuel picked it up and placed it in the palm of his hand.

"Look." Gabriel crouched near a rock. "Another one and another one."

Silver beads had scattered across the ground and rolled into dirt hollows. Karin Paulus had said something about beads the day before. Emmanuel picked up a dozen of them and put them in his jacket pocket.

"They belong to the witch," Gabriel said. "She has them on her shoulders and her back."

That was it. Karin said the woman in the rock shelter with Philani wore tan buckskin decorated with shiny beads around her shoulders. A shawl of some kind.

"Describe the witch to me," Emmanuel said.

"Black skin, wearing a red crown." A police sketch artist would struggle with that physical description.

"Is she tall or short?"

"She's full." Gabriel continued picking silver from the dirt, taking delight in each individual bead. "But she's hungry."

"She's fat." Emmanuel took a stab at the answer. He'd spent long English winter evenings playing charades with his in-laws in their stuffy living room decorated with porcelain Siamese cats. He hated guessing games.

"No." Gabriel pocketed his haul. "She's full, not fat."

"All right." Emmanuel tried another approach. "Everyone has two names. The one that people call them and the special one that you make up. Right?"

"*Ja.*"

"What's the Red Queen's other name?"

Gabriel frowned. "I don't know what it is, Emmanuel. We've never been introduced."

"But you'd recognize her if you saw her again?"

"Of course."

Not that it mattered a great deal. An unbalanced schoolboy was not ideal witness material. His word would have to be backed up by real evidence or, better yet, a signed confession from the woman.

Gabriel swiveled at the sound of running steps thundering toward them. Emmanuel unclipped his holster. It could be

Shabalala, or the woman returning to collect her black *muti* object.

The Zulu detective broke out of the trees and stopped by the fire to catch his breath. His face was slick with sweat, and two days of rock tunnel living showed in the wrinkled suit and dirty trouser cuffs. The three of them here at the fire could join a soup kitchen line for vagrants and not attract attention.

"She hid and I lost her." Shabalala mopped sweat with a handkerchief. "When the daylight came I found her trail and followed her across the field to Chief Matebula's kraal. There is a loose branch in the fence. That is how she got back inside."

"She probably loosened it herself," Emmanuel said, and wondered how many young, "confident-sounding" women lived in the Zulu family compound. "Karin heard the woman in the shelter talking to Philani about Chief Matebula. Plus Gabriel and I found these . . ." He scooped the beads from his pocket and held them out for Shabalala to see. "Karin said the woman's shoulders were covered with brown buckskin and beads."

"Her shoulders were covered?" The Zulu policeman fixed Emmanuel with a sharp look.

"Yes."

"You should have told me this, Sergeant." Shabalala worked the handkerchief across his brow but not fast enough to hide the expression of irritation on his face. He was pissed off. "It was important."

"I forgot to mention it," Emmanuel said. Where was his mind at the time . . . on the case or reliving Karin and Ella's grind? "My apologies."

Shabalala looked away, embarrassed at showing his emotions. He said, "It is all right. We learn as we go."

Having his words repeated back to him made Emmanuel laugh. "That's right, Constable, we do. Now tell me why a shawl is so important."

"Married women cover their shoulders and heads. Single women do not."

"Staking out Little Flint Farm and talking to Mercy was a waste of time." They had lost a whole afternoon sitting in the bush for nothing.

"Maybe not." Shabalala stared into the dying flames, thinking. "Mercy went to the Matebula kraal on Friday evening because her friend heard the chief was looking for a new bride."

"That's right," Emmanuel said.

"How was the great chief going to pay for this new wife?"

"You're the Zulu expert, Shabalala. You tell me."

"With cattle. Many cattle, if he wished to purchase a pretty young girl."

"And the chief likes pretty things," Emmanuel said. Each of the five women gathered in the wives' area at Amahle's funeral was attractive, with sleek skin and curves. Wife number one, Mandla's mother, and Nomusa were outstanding beauties.

"Five wives, many children to feed and a kraal to keep." Shabalala thought out loud. "There was one certain way for the great chief to obtain cattle to fund his desire for a sixth wife."

"Amahle," Emmanuel said, and the connections clicked into place. "He needed Amahle's bride-price to buy another wife for himself."

"I think that was why the chief was angry and buried his own daughter so disgracefully. He was a child denied sugar."

Emmanuel moved closer to the fire. The glowing red coals released a bittersweet odor. He reviewed the investigation. Every motive for the murder, from robbery to lust and jealousy, had been examined and none of them could be supported.

"Amahle was killed to stop the chief from marrying again." That complex motive would not have occurred to Emmanuel in a lifetime of reworking the case. "Which of the wives would go that far?"

"The one who has the most to lose," Shabalala said. "The one with no children to support her in old age and no friends among the other wives."

Emmanuel remembered the fifth wife standing up to view Amahle's corpse while the other women screamed in anguish. Another detail came back to him: the high ocher tower of her hair woven with beads and fibers to make a stiff red crown. Gabriel's uncanny gift for names hadn't yielded a supernatural metaphor after all—the fifth wife *was* the Red Queen.

"I can't imagine that being married to Matebula is a life worth killing for," Emmanuel said.

"The starving fight over scraps. The youngest wife has nothing without the chief's favor. No children, no money, no allies."

A thought hit Emmanuel. "She didn't know Amahle was planning to ditch the marriage and run."

"*Yebo.*" Shabalala let out a deep breath. "If only she had waited one more week . . ."

One more week and Amahle, the beautiful one, would have flown away. Seven bright spring days made the difference between a disgraced grave and a dream made real.

If only.

"Don't start down that road, Cooper. Those two little words

will fuck with you every time," the sergeant major said. *"If only your father was slower with the knife and your mother quicker to run, if only Hitler had become a painter instead of a politician, if only your marriage had worked out and you weren't a single man, all alone, sorting through the murders of strangers. That shit will drive you mad, soldier. All you have is now."*

Again, Emmanuel listened to the sergeant major. The present moment possessed enough challenges to stave off melancholy. For knowing the identity of the murderer and proving it in court were two separate tasks. He worked over what they knew so far.

"Karin won't admit to seeing Philani and a woman in the rock shelter on Sunday night. She's not going to destroy her life just to bring a Zulu woman to court," Emmanuel said. "Her testimony is out."

Shabalala cast a quick look at Gabriel, who was still rummaging in the dirt for silver beads.

"Same deal," Emmanuel said. "He's white but that won't help our case. He's too odd. Besides, his brother will never let him testify, and I can't blame him."

A boy with a fragile grasp on how to behave and no clue whatsoever about physical appearance could not be put on the stand in a criminal court.

"That leaves us no witnesses." Shabalala looked into his hat. "The fifth wife will go free."

"Unless she confesses to the murder, that's probably what will happen," Emmanuel said. This was the third and most difficult initiation rite into the brotherhood of detectives: watching an investigation shrivel up and die for lack of evidence.

Gabriel pocketed his haul of silver beads and returned to

the burnt carcass. He squatted in the sand to inspect the charred skeleton and the brittle tendons holding the mass together. "What is it, Shabalala?" he asked. "Emmanuel says it's not a baby."

It was full daylight now, the sun well above the tip of the hills and shining bright. Shabalala rested on his haunches next to Gabriel and examined the remains, happy for the distraction from the unraveling murder case. "It is a baby," he said. "But a baby bushbuck."

"Oh." Gabriel found the long stick used for removing the body from the fire and pushed the end into an eye socket. "Why did the witch kill it and burn it in a fire? It was still so small."

"Huh . . ." Shabalala contemplated the scene, the red coals and the bittersweet funk rising with the smoke. "You have asked a very good question. Let me see if the answer is in the fire."

He used the second long stick to lift and sift through the ashes and dying flames. The deeper the branch pushed, the more intense the smell. Emmanuel craned over Shabalala's shoulder and cupped a palm over his mouth to block the odor.

"What is it?"

"Herbs, I think, but more than one kind. There is a mix of sweet, bitter and sour that I cannot remember smelling together." He sat back, bemused. "It is confusing."

"A *muti* ritual," Emmanuel said. The secluded spot and the burnt carcass disturbed him. The smoke and image of the phantom woman and child in the fire seemed taken from his own recurring dream.

"It is *muti*," Shabalala confirmed. "For what purpose, I do not know."

"Could be for good luck." Emmanuel moved back to breathe fresh air. "To make sure the *sangoma* throws Nomusa and her daughter out of the kraal tonight."

Shabalala stood up and turned to Emmanuel. His face wore the cunning expression of a hunter who'd just figured out how to trap an elusive prey. "I know how to get her, Sergeant," he said.

THE LOOSE BRANCH in the perimeter fence gave way and Emmanuel, Shabalala and Gabriel slipped into the Matebula kraal. All attempts to shake the boy had failed and the detectives now accepted that he was stuck to them for the duration of the operation. They inched along the grass wall of a hut lit by late afternoon sun and made their way to the rear of the compound and the great chief's hut. The common areas of the kraal were deserted and shadows lengthened across the cattle byre.

"They are gathered behind the chief's hut, in the meeting area," Shabalala said. "That is where the *sangoma* will throw the bones to find the witches who brought bad luck to the family."

They crept past the row of wives' huts and Emmanuel paused and turned to Gabriel.

"Stay quiet and stay with us. Don't call out to the Red Queen or try to hurt her. Understand?"

"*Ja.* Okay." The boy was sullen but compliant. Running the hills and staying up through the previous night to stalk the witch had drained his energy. When Gabriel eventually crashed, he'd crash hard.

A rumble came from up ahead and Emmanuel moved more quickly. The ceremony was starting. They followed the path to the back of the great hut and hid at the end of the fence, finding gaps through which to view the ceremony. The inhabitants of the kraal, fifteen or so men, women and children, knelt in a semicircle at the foot of the umdoni tree planted in the middle of the dirt area.

The great chief, draped in animal skins, bright printed cloth and beads, sat on a carved stool. His wives knelt to his right with their heads bowed. Mandla stood in the back of the men's section with a member of his impi on either side of him.

"Great chief." A gaunt man crouched on a dried impala skin, his shoulder-length hair smeared with red ocher and grease and fashioned into long tendrils. A cluster of bead containers and goat horns hung from strips of hide around his neck and shoulders. "What ails you?"

"There are evil spirits in this kraal," Matebula said, and the crowd hushed. "My daughter Amahle is dead and her bride-price will never be paid. My limbs are heavy and there is a weight on my chest. I cannot sleep at night. A witch and her accomplice have cast a spell over this family and they must be removed."

"I will call on the ancestors for guidance," the *sangoma* said, and a drumbeat sounded across the yard.

Emmanuel moved sideways to get a better look. A sturdy female *sangoma* with ocher-dyed hair adorned with white beads beat a rhythm from a large cowhide drum.

"Begin . . ." Matebula said. "Find these witches."

The male *sangoma* stood up and stamped his feet to the

pounding of the drum. Dried seedpods attached to his ankles rattled and he sucked noisy breath in and out of his mouth. The drumbeat increased and the *sangoma* danced till sweat drenched his skin and dust rose from his bare feet. He jerked and swayed as if possessed.

"The ancestral spirits are entering his body," Shabalala whispered as explanation. "Soon they will speak through him."

Emmanuel rejected the notion of the living dead but could not forget Baba Kaleni's charged hands resurrecting the memory of his mother and the promise he'd made her. And what were the ghosts of the soldiers and civilians who inhabited his dreams but the dead come back to life as well?

The *sangoma* slowed and a glazed expression entered his eyes.

"The ancestors are here," Shabalala said.

The fifth wife peeked up, anticipating the identification of the evil witches. The rest of the Matebula family held their breath and waited for the spirits to speak.

"The Red Queen," Gabriel whispered, glimpsing the fifth wife. "That's her, Emmanuel. Get her."

"We will get her, but not now," Emmanuel said. "We have to wait for the right moment. Be patient."

The answer did not please Gabriel but he stopped whispering and put his eye back to a break in the fence. The *sangoma* knelt on the impala skin and shook a small medicine bag back and forth before spilling its contents. Bones, stones, coins and shells spilled across the hide. He examined them, reading the signs. Minutes passed without a word from the ancestors. He stood up and circled the bones, frowning.

"Speak," the great chief demanded, impatient even in the face of a holy ceremony.

The *sangoma* said, "There is only one evil spirit in this kraal, great chief. She alone brought calamity to your door."

The fifth wife's head jerked up but she remained kneeling in the shade of the umdoni tree with stiff shoulders.

"You are sure?" Chief Matebula pursed his lips, dissatisfied with the information.

"The ancestors have said it is so, great one. And the ancestors do not lie."

"Then show me," Matebula said. "Sniff out this witch."

The *sangoma* picked up a cow-tail whisk and walked to the female section of the crowd. An unmarried girl in the front row cowered in his shadow and began to cry. Amahle's little sister sat with her back straight and her eyes focused on the beams of light hitting the perimeter fence. The *sangoma*'s whisk trailed across the crown of her head and brushed against her cheeks. The other females shifted away, afraid of being singled out for blame.

"That's not the witch." Gabriel was distressed by the girl's fear and the sound of crying.

The *sangoma* turned from Amahle's sister and approached the chief's wives. He flicked the black whisk above the head of wife number one. Mandla leaned forward, ready to act if the whisk stopped above his mother. The *sangoma* moved on to wife number two and then to Nomusa, who hunched her shoulders and shut her eyes. The whisk brushed her face, trailed across the next wife and came to rest on the head of wife number five.

"Here is the witch who has brought evil to this kraal, great chief. This is she."

"He's good." Gabriel was impressed. "He found the Red Queen."

The fifth wife hit the *sangoma*'s hand away and spun to face Matebula. "It is not true, my husband. The ancestors are mistaken."

The comment brought cries of disbelief from the crowd and appeared to shock even the great chief. He stood up, flustered. "Tell me how she did these things right under my nose."

"With black magic spells and a poisoned quill, which she stabbed into your daughter's spine," the *sangoma* said. "Philani Dlamini was also killed this way. It is in the bones."

"The bones lie." The fifth wife rose from her knees and pushed the *sangoma* in the chest. He staggered back but she kept advancing. "You lie. We will call another diviner to tell the truth. My hands are clean."

Emmanuel exchanged a glance with Shabalala. Now was the time for the *sangoma* to apply extra pressure.

"Your hands are soiled," the *sangoma* said, but his voice lacked the conviction needed to push the fifth wife into retreat.

"I did not put one finger on Amahle or Philani, my husband." This was said directly to the great chief. "The true witch has cast a spell over the *sangoma*. She has that power."

Emmanuel felt the foundations of their plan erode. Neither he nor Shabalala had given the youngest wife enough credit for her sheer determination in executing her strategy.

"I am clean," she announced to the gathered clan. "I have done no harm."

"She's a liar . . . a liar . . . a liar . . ." Gabriel muttered the chant under his breath and sprinted from behind the cover of the fence. He flew across the meeting area, his dirty jacket flapping open like a torn parachute.

"Don't, Sergeant." Shabalala grabbed Emmanuel's arm before he could sprint after Gabriel. "Let the ancestors complete their work."

"And what connection do they have to the boy?" Emmanuel said. The situation was out of control and it looked like they'd limp back to Durban with nothing.

"Look." Shabalala pointed to the meeting area.

Gabriel ran through the crowd, women and children scattering in his path. He stopped inches from the fifth wife and pinned her with a glare from his different-colored eyes. "You are the Red Queen." Gabriel leaned closer. "You put Amahle to sleep. You burned a baby in the fire. I saw you with my eyes."

The fifth wife flinched and stepped back. The rest of the family leaned forward, mesmerized by the white boy. He was already known among the Zulus in the valley to be touched by the ancestors. They watched him roam the hills by day and night, talking to the trees and the animals.

"Husband . . . I beg you not to listen to this child." The youngest wife's tone was pleading. She kept her face turned from Gabriel.

"Great chief." The *sangoma* rallied. "The ancestors brought their message through the bones and now through this white boy who is suffering from *ukuthwasa.*"

Emmanuel looked to Shabalala for help.

"When a *sangoma* is called by the ancestors to become a healer he or she suffers from an illness. Back pain, headaches and sometimes"—Shabalala tapped a finger to the center of his forehead—"a disturbance of the mind. This is *ukuthwasa.*"

"That's what Gabriel has?"

"*Yebo.*"

Chief Matebula leapt over the impala skin and marched past his kneeling wives. The black mark of his shadow crossed over each woman in turn before hitting the empty spot where the fifth wife had been.

"You took my daughter from me," he said. "You robbed me of her bride-price and Chief Mashanini of a bride. How do you answer to this?"

"I did none of these things, my husband."

Gabriel circled around and stopped in her line of sight. He looked her in the eye. "Tell the truth and shame the devil. You are the witch who took Amahle away."

The fifth wife looked away from Gabriel's intense stare and said to the chief, "Amahle was going away from here . . . from all of us. The marriage was never to be. She hated this kraal and this family."

"Lies." Matebula dismissed the words with a flick of his hand. "The marriage was agreed on and Amahle was happy to do her duty to me, her father."

"Look." The fifth wife pulled a piece of paper from the waistband of her black skirt and held it up. She was flustered by Gabriel's unsettling presence and the chief's growing anger. "A bus ticket. Amahle lied to you, husband. She had no plans to stay and marry. Her eyes were on Durban. She was a bad daughter."

Nomusa rose from the line of kneeling wives. "If this bus ticket belonged to Amahle, how does it come to be in your hands?"

"I found it on the veldt."

"My daughter was careful. She did not drop a stitch when sewing or lose a grain of millet from a calabash." Nomusa focused on the fifth wife. "That is not Amahle's ticket. It is yours. You are the one planning to run from this kraal and from your husband, the great chief."

"Is this so?" That one of his wives would contemplate leaving offended Matebula.

"No." The fifth wife's voice was strident. "The ticket was in Amahle's pocket. She was the one to buy it."

Nomusa fixed the younger woman with a withering stare. "My daughter would not let you look through her pockets unless she was dead."

Angry shouts went up from the inhabitants of the kraal and the fifth wife ran for the exit. Mandla and his impi broke from the men's section and moved to stop her retreat, and Emmanuel and Shabalala moved out to block her escape path.

Gabriel was fast and got to the fleeing woman first. He grabbed her around the waist and pulled her to the ground. Black and white limbs flailed in the dirt and a cloud of dust rose into the air. The Matebula family jumped to their feet, shouting and pushing to get a look at the witch and the white boy.

"I have her," Gabriel shouted. "I have her."

Emmanuel moved closer and saw the quick dart of a porcupine quill being aimed at Gabriel's arm. He grabbed the fifth wife's wrist and pulled it away from the boy. Shabalala held her down. She kicked and punched the air, screaming.

"Watch out for more quills," Emmanuel warned the Zulu detective, and knelt to examine Gabriel's sleeve. A small barb was stuck in the fabric of the King's Row College uniform. The tip of the quill was stained red.

"Are you hurt?" Emmanuel asked. "Did you feel a prick on your arm?"

"No." Gabriel reached for the quill and Emmanuel grasped his hand. The red on the tip was not blood.

"Don't touch," Emmanuel said. "It's poison."

The quill was a perfect piece of evidence. It matched the two found stabbed into Amahle and Philani. He pulled it free, wrapped it in his handkerchief and placed it in his jacket pocket.

"Here." Mandla held the bus ticket out between thumb and forefinger. "For your white man's courts."

"Thanks."

"We will escort you from the kraal to the main road. The fifth wife must be taken to the police station in town. She is not safe in the valley."

"If you gave the word, she would be," Emmanuel said.

Mandla grinned and walked off to collect his impi. He was in the ascendancy, the position of great chief not far away.

"Sergeant," Shabalala called. "We must race to beat the sunset."

Emmanuel pulled Gabriel to his feet. The Matebula family was now divided into four smaller groups, with each of the remaining wives clutching their daughters and sons. Nomusa held the little sister close in her arms and whispered into her ear. Amahle's killer was found but the wounds in the hearts of those who loved her would never heal.

Gabriel looked at Emmanuel. He was bedraggled and vulnerable. "I know I wasn't supposed to run but I couldn't stop," he said. "I'm sorry."

"You did well," Emmanuel said. "You did very well. I'm proud of you for being so brave."

"Now will you kill her, Emmanuel? She must die."

"That's not my job or yours. She'll go to prison for a very long time. That might be enough."

"Good." Gabriel was satisfied. He watched a dragonfly hover in the air, waiting for it to land. Emmanuel thought that perhaps the Zulus were right and that Gabriel was tuned in to the voices from another world.

Emmanuel crossed to Shabalala, who held the fifth wife by the arm. Her red crown had been crushed in the dirt and the decorative porcupine quills removed and heaped on the ground. None of them had the telltale reddish tint.

"Why Philani?" Emmanuel asked. By all accounts the gardener was harmless.

"He found the great chief's daughter on the path, just after she passed over to the ancestors." The fifth wife brushed dust off her clothing, still proud of her appearance. "I came out of my hiding place and called him a murderer. He was scared and threw himself on my mercy, saying that he was innocent of the crime. I said that I believed him, but the great chief would not. 'Go into hiding,' I said. 'And I will plead your fate with my husband.' I gave him money to prove my promise of help was sincere. He did as I asked."

"Give me the five pounds you took from Amahle," Emmanuel said to her.

She flashed her big brown eyes and smiled. "I have no money, ma' baas. I'm sorry, ma' baas."

"I can put my hand down your top to search or Detective Constable Shabalala can. Which of us do you prefer?" Emmanuel called her bluff. Forcibly removing evidence from her person would render the search illegal, but she didn't know that.

The fifth wife pulled a five-pound note from the neckline

of her buckskin top and surrendered it with a coy look. The pretty ingenue was part of her personality and would remain so until the doors of the police van closed and the locks snapped shut. Only then would the consequences of her actions become real to her.

"Start out for the main road. Mandla and the impi will go with you," Emmanuel said to Shabalala, and pocketed the five pounds. "Take Gabriel along. I'll catch up."

"This money . . ." Shabalala hesitated and said, "It is not clean."

"It's a piece of cotton fiber," Emmanuel said. "Nomusa doesn't know where the money came from and Bagley won't ask for it back. Giving it away will wash it clean."

"You believe this?"

"Yes," Emmanuel said. "I do."

"Then I thank you for making it so, Sergeant." Shabalala escorted the fifth wife away. The Matebula clan watched them depart with resentment. Some white man in a far-off city would pass judgment and mete out punishment in their private family matter.

Mandla and his men closed in behind Shabalala, leaving the great chief isolated under the branches of the umdoni tree. Emmanuel crouched by Nomusa's side, careful to keep a respectful distance from a married woman.

"You knew the name of the guilty one before the *sangoma* started," she said. The fear of being found a witch and the shock of discovering Amahle's killer in the family kraal had drained Nomusa's energy and etched worry lines on her face.

"There was no proof," Emmanuel said. "We needed a confession before making an arrest. I'm sorry to have put you both through the ceremony."

"It is done." She pulled her surviving daughter closer. "Now maybe the great chief will bury Amahle with honor instead of shame."

"Mandla has promised to talk to the chief and make this so."

"Mandla also knew?" She was surprised and glanced up to check the expression on Emmanuel's face and judge the truth of his answer.

"Yes," he said. "The *sangoma* was also part of the plan. He was reluctant but Detective Constable Shabalala persuaded him."

"How?" she asked.

"Shabalala is a great listener," Emmanuel said. With great patience, some conversation and an ear for detail, the Zulu detective had found out that the *sangoma*'s eldest son was moving to Durban to study. The thought of his child adrift in the city and prey to thieves and *tsotsis* gave the *sangoma* sleepless nights. Shabalala offered an introduction to the minister of his church, the name of a good boardinghouse for the boy to stay in and a pickup from the bus station on his arrival in Durban. A deal was struck. The plan to expose the fifth wife was almost entirely Shabalala's doing. Emmanuel simply rode the wave.

"All has been revealed," Nomusa said. "Yet my heart is not glad."

"In time." There was no salve for the wounds inflicted on a family by murder. He slipped the five-pound note between his fingers and said, "I wish you well."

He took hold of the little sister's hand and pretended to shake it. Touching a married woman, especially in the presence of her husband, was forbidden. Small fingers gripped the money and removed it. Emmanuel stood to leave. The little sister tucked the note into the waist of her beaded skirt and gave him a quick look of thanks. Emmanuel thought how much she resembled Amahle and wondered if there was a bus seat on God's Gift in her future, too.

"Go well, Inkosi Cooper." Nomusa got to her feet and made the traditional farewell. The sounds of women pounding millet and of children running to draw water from the river had started again. Daily life resumed. Maybe one day it would drown out her grief, or most of it, Emmanuel hoped.

"Stay well, mother and daughter," he said, and walked to the mountain path. He left them to mend and repair. He hoped they would.

He remembered that his sister, Olivia, was due a phone call soon, a monthly exchange of hellos that reminded him that he was not alone in the world after all.

Roselet glowed in the last light of day. The streetlamps came on. Ellicott and Hargrave slumped in fold-out chairs placed under the sycamore tree and drank sundowner beers. Smoke poured from a perforated drum with an iron grill placed across the top and the wood fire inside the drum crackled. Bagley dropped a curled length of traditional farmer's sausage onto the heated metal grid and pricked the skin with a long fork. Fat leaked from the boerewors and dripped onto the hot coals.

"Cheers." Ellicott raised his beer in salute. "An all-kaffir affair won't pull the press but General Hyland is very pleased with the result."

"Unfortunately, the names Cooper and Shabalala didn't come up in the conversation," Hargrave said.

Shabalala kept a stony face. Emmanuel shrugged. He expected nothing in return for handing the fifth wife over to the two detectives or for allowing Hargrave and Ellicott to sign the case docket. That was the price for running an unsanctioned investigation.

"In case the boys at West Street might ask . . . what was the reason for the murders?" Ellicott was already mentally back in Durban, sinking pints with the other detectives and talking bullshit about the difficulties of the case.

Emmanuel kept it simple. "Amahle was killed to stop her father from using her bride-price to obtain wife number six. Motive: jealousy. The second victim, Philani Dlamini, was unlucky. He discovered Amahle's body on the path and panicked. The woman who *actually* killed her convinced him to go into hiding while she cleared his name. She gave him some of the money she'd stolen from Amahle's pocket to prove her sincerity. Two days later she killed Philani, too. Motive: the dead don't talk."

"Kaffirs. Can't understand them. Never will." Hargrave drank more beer and contemplated the drifting colors on the horizon. Bagley tended the grill in silence.

"If you boys are hungry you can stay and grab a bite," Ellicott said.

"We'd like to, but we have somewhere we've got to be." An evening of boerewors, beer and bathroom humor didn't appeal to Emmanuel.

He wanted to get back to Margaret Daglish's cottage, where she and Zweigman waited for him and Shabalala. Ella Reed had dropped them off there earlier in the afternoon. From the cottage, she'd taken Gabriel with her back to Little Flint Farm to spend the night before returning him to school.

If he didn't make a run for it again, that is. Emmanuel suspected Daglish's husband, Jim, had hit the road again. If not, Daglish would most likely kick him out. She wasn't the same woman who had turned away a detective with a dead body in need of an autopsy a few days ago.

Ellicott drained his beer and opened another. He took a sip and said, "You're all right for a queer, Cooper. You too, Shabalala."

"Good night, Detective Sergeant. Safe trip back." Emmanuel cut across the yard to the Chevrolet. Shabalala followed with a frown.

"He insults us and yet you smile," the Zulu detective said. "What does this mean?"

"It means that we just made friends. Hargrave and Ellicott will return to Durban tomorrow and tell the other detectives that we're okay." Emmanuel opened the car door and drummed his fingers on the dusty hood. "We're out of the dogbox and back in the kitchen, Shabalala."

EPILOGUE

EMMANUEL WOKE AT midnight with a pounding head and heart. He remembered the dream, down to the fragments of broken glass shining on the asphalt road leading into the French village outside Caen.

The platoon marched under a weathered stone archway into a narrow street. An old woman threw white daisies from her window and the platoon stopped to pick them up and thread them into the buttonholes of their uniforms.

They moved toward the town square. Black smoke poured from a building with broken windows and a tattered flag with a Nazi insignia hanging from one of the front columns. Papers littered the footpath. Overturned desks and file cabinets burned. Ash fell like rain.

The enemy was gone, slashing and burning in retreat. A Welsh private chanced the flames and pulled down the red and black flag. He stuffed it into his pack, grinning.

They moved out. The scattered papers littering the street might be important, but combat platoons traveled light. Rear-echelon troops sifted and filed.

Emmanuel scouted a narrow alley off the main street. It

seemed that all light died once he entered it and it felt cold and damp.

A barefoot woman stumbled out of the darkness. Her head was shaved and she wore a torn silk slip, the two badges of a German collaborator. Her eyes had lost all hope. An older woman who looked to be her mother walked behind her carrying a baby wrapped in a blue cotton shawl. Emmanuel pressed against the wall and let them pass. The mother nodded a silent thank-you and they disappeared into the cold darkness of the alley. The three of them, the mother, the daughter and the baby, were marooned by the shifting tides of war.

Now Emmanuel got out of bed and splashed water from the kitchen tap on his face. The real incident lasted less than a minute, eight years ago and a world away. He searched for a reason why fragments of this memory disturbed his dreams for weeks yet only became clear tonight, a day after he and Shabalala had returned to Durban from Roselet.

He remembered Davida Ellis with her hair cropped short and her elegant mother sitting at the kitchen table mourning the loss of her innocence. Zweigman had mentioned them both in the stone tunnel while the morphine pumped through his blood. He said Davida was strong and she'd adjust to her new life with help.

"She's at Zweigman's clinic," Emmanuel said out loud.

He knew also the hidden contents of Zweigman's wallet. The *muti* fire contained the secret and the dream confirmed it.

He pulled on clothes and rushed into the tropical night. The Chevrolet started right up and the headlights illuminated the wide street and the redbrick houses. He drove to the main road connecting Durban and Pietermaritzburg.

The smooth asphalt turned into an uneven macadam strip winding into the hills. The road would take him all the way to Zweigman's clinic, to Davida—and their child, his and hers. The rearview mirror reflected the city lights behind him. Ahead, just as Baba Kaleni had predicted by the river, the stars shone bright enough to light his way.

BLESSED ARE THE DEAD

MALLA NUNN

READING GROUP GUIDE

INTRODUCTION

When Amahle, the beautiful teenage daughter of a Zulu chief, is found murdered in the remote foothills of the Drakensberg Mountains, Detective Sergeant Emmanuel Cooper is called to investigate. Sensing that something terrible has happened, Emmanuel must navigate the various circles of Amahle's complex world—interviewing everyone from her English aristocrat employers at Little Flint Farm, who favored her over their other servants, to her misogynist father, who was planning to marry her in exchange for a herd of cows, to the local police and medical offices that seem reluctant to offer any help whatsoever.

In a community fraught with racism, sexism, and an ever-changing balance of power, finding Amahle's killer may prove impossible—or even deadly.

QUESTIONS AND TOPICS FOR DISCUSSION

1. How does Emmanuel's military background help him with his detective work? How does his background provide an advantage that other detectives might not have?

2. How does the author evoke the atmosphere of apartheid-era South Africa through her descriptions of characters and place? Did you feel you had a good sense of this time period after finishing the novel?

3. Due to segregation laws, Emmanuel and Shabalala must check into different hotels on their first night on the case. "Shabalala did not complain. . . . How many words and thoughts were sealed in the Zulu policeman's mouth because all that was required in the presence of a majority of whites was a 'Yes, ma' baas,' 'No, ma' baas' and a 'Thank you, ma' baas'?" (page 73). How does Shabalala reconcile his forced submissiveness with the pursuit of justice inherent in his job?

4. When Emmanuel interviews Ella Reed, she scoffs at Amahle's seemingly unrealistic dreams: "She wanted a house. A car. A business in one of the black townships. Like she could ever have those things" (page 96). Emmanuel replies that this was "empty talk" and reflects that "[t]hat was what most dreams came to, his own included. . . . They were vanished wishes, long gone" (page 97). Discuss the theme of unfulfilled dreams in the novel and how it applies to each character. How might "a life unlived" mean different things for different people in 1950s South Africa?

5. How did you react to the parts of the narrative where Emmanuel hears his former Scottish sergeant major's voice in his head? Was this an effective technique in gaining additional insight into Emmanuel's character?

6. Did you notice any hints or signs that foreshadowed the identity of Amahle's killer? If so, what were they? Were you ultimately surprised by the killer's identity?

7. After finishing, does this novel's title, *Blessed Are the Dead,* have a new meaning? What are some instances of literal and figurative "blessings of the dead" in this novel?

8. Discuss the role of women in the novel. In your response, consider Dr. Daglish's relationship with her husband, Lana's decision to stay with van Niekerk, Ella and Karin's relationship, and Amahle's means of getting what she wants. Are these women victims of their societies? Or do

some of them make choices based on fear or desire for comfort?

9. How are Emmanuel, Shabalala, and Dr. Zweigman able to have such close friendships despite their differences? How do they connect with one another in ways that are universal and completely unrelated to race, religion, or class?

10. Discuss Gabriel Reed. Do you think he is actually insane, as so many around him believe? Might his affliction be called something else in present-day society? How is he in some ways one of the few characters who always speak the truth?

11. Emmanuel reflects on Dr. Daglish's attitude toward race relations: "Like many of the English, Daglish played hide-and-seek with her own beliefs. The National Party at least said what they believed in: blacks and whites shall not, under pain of imprisonment, mix sweat and bodily fluids. They made no excuses, never blamed anyone else for their beliefs. People like Margaret Daglish couldn't reconcile their discomfort at races mixing with their desire to appear enlightened" (page 162). Discuss this paragraph. Does Daglish's behavior remind you of anything you have read or heard about in the news? In your own personal experience? How can hidden prejudices sometimes be more harmful than overt prejudices?

12. Although the South African community in this novel is heavily segregated, it's also quite diverse. While the vari-

ous groups of people may not mix heavily, they do live side by side. For example, Amahle was the daughter of a chief, yet she had no power within her family; at the Reed family farm she was a servant, yet she received special treatment compared to her coworkers. What did you think about this? What does this say about the nature of race and class in general?

13. Discuss Emmanuel's dream at the end of the novel and his decision to visit Davida Ellis. How does this twist shed new light on Emmanuel's character? What does Emmanuel's decision say about the nature of dreams, both literal and figurative? How does this contradict Emmanuel's earlier feelings about dreams?

14. Have you read the other books in Malla Nunn's series? If so, how does this one compare? How has Emmanuel evolved a character?

15. How familiar are you with South African history? Did reading *Blessed Are the Dead* spark an interest in you to learn more?

ENHANCE YOUR BOOK CLUB

1. To learn more about South African history through fiction, consider reading *Skinner's Drift,* by Lisa Fugard; *Cry, the Beloved Country,* by Alan Paton; or works by J. M. Coetzee, Nadine Gordimer, or Bryce Courtenay for your next book club pick. For a nonfiction title about South African history, consider *A History of South Africa,* by Leonard Thompson; Nelson Mandela's autobiography, *Long Walk to Freedom*; or *Kaffir Boy: An Autobiography—The True Story of a Black Youth's Coming of Age in Apartheid South Africa,* by Mark Mathabane.

2. In the spirit of the diverse cultures depicted in *Blessed Are the Dead*, ask each book club member to investigate a different type of cuisine. Each member can prepare a dish or snack and present what they've learned to the rest of the group at your next meeting. To get started on finding recipes, visit allrecipes.com/recipes/world-cuisine.

3. Amahle was a member of the Zulu tribe. Have each member of your group learn how to say one conversational phrase in Zulu. Learn more about the Zulu language and how to pronounce key words at wikitravel.org/en/Zulu_phrasebook.

Also by MALLA NUNN

Award-winning screenwriter Malla Nunn delivers a stunning and darkly romantic crime novel set in 1950s apartheid South Africa, featuring Detective Emmanuel Cooper—a man caught up in a time and place where racial tensions and the raw hunger for power make life very dangerous indeed.

ALA Reading List Award Winner | Edgar Allan Poe Best Novel Award Nominee | Davitt Award Winner, Best Adult Crime Novel

ATRIA BOOKS
A Division of Simon & Schuster
A CBS COMPANY